Praise for Rebecca Raisin

'I absolutely fell in love with thi[s]
written by a booklover for booklo[ver]
fabulous – if I could give it mor[e]
Jaimie Admans, author of *The Bee[___ ___ ___] Grove*

'I enjoyed it so much! . . .
This summer's go-to for every bookworm.'
Jane Linfoot, author of *The Little Cornish Kitchen*

'The perfect romantic comedy for bookworms
and library lovers everywhere!'
Annie Lyons, author of
Eudora Honeysett Is Quite Well, Thank You

'I absolutely did not want this book to end . . .
If you love books and libraries and stories about people
starting over, you will love *Elodie's Library of Second Chances*.'
The French Village Diaries

'A gorgeous love letter to libraries . . . There is
something so magical about a Rebecca Raisin book;
they always have this incredible ability to fill your heart
with so much happiness and joy.'
Romance by the Book

REBECCA RAISIN writes heartwarming romance from her home in sunny Perth, Australia. Her heroines tend to be on the quirky side and her books are usually set in exotic locations so her readers can armchair travel any day of the week. The only downfall about writing about gorgeous heroes who have brains as well

as brawn, is falling in love with them – just as well they're fictional. Rebecca aims to write characters you can see yourself being friends with. People with big hearts who care about relationships and believe in true, once-in-a-lifetime love. Her bestselling novel *Rosie's Travelling Tea Shop* has been optioned for film with MRC studios and Frolic Media.

Also by Rebecca Raisin

Christmas at the Gingerbread Café
Chocolate Dreams at the Gingerbread Café
The Bookshop on the Corner
Christmas Wedding at the Gingerbread Café
Secrets at Maple Syrup Farm
The Little Bookshop on the Seine
The Little Antique Shop under the Eiffel Tower
The Little Perfume Shop off the Champs-Élysées
Celebrations and Confetti at Cedarwood Lodge
Brides and Bouquets at Cedarwood Lodge
Midnight and Mistletoe at Cedarwood Lodge
Rosie's Travelling Tea Shop
Aria's Travelling Book Shop
Escape to Honeysuckle Hall
Flora's Travelling Christmas Shop
Elodie's Library of Second Chances

The Little Venice Bookshop

REBECCA RAISIN

ONE PLACE. MANY STORIES

HQ
An imprint of HarperCollins*Publishers* Ltd
1 London Bridge Street
London SE1 9GF

www.harpercollins.co.uk

HarperCollins*Publishers*
Macken House, 39/40 Mayor Street Upper,
Dublin 1 D01 C9W8
Ireland

This paperback edition 2023

1
First published in Great Britain by
HQ, an imprint of HarperCollins*Publishers* Ltd 2023

ISBN (UK): 9780008559366
ISBN (US): 9780008619800

Printed and bound in the U.S.A. by Lake Book Manufacturing, LLC

This one is for you, Jules Percival. We're so lucky to have your bright light in our lives. Keep shining.

Prologue

Ten years ago

In the distance, the rocky mountains of Missoula sit sombrely under an expanse of sky so big it feels like we're the only ones left in the world. On the velvety grass, I lie back on my elbows as Mom loops daisies together like the ultimate flower child.

'It's time for you to fly free, baby girl.'

She *always* knows.

'How . . . ?'

Mom gives me a slow smile. 'You don't think a mother recognises when her own child has itchy feet? Wanderlust can be a curse as much as it can be a cure. But I have to let you go – as hard as it'll be. I expect phone calls every week.'

'At *least* every week, Mom.'

She's silent for a beat as she toys with the daisies. When she looks back at me, the smile has faded. 'Luna, I want you to make me a promise . . . *Never* run away from hard things. Face your problems head on, OK? Running away never solves anything.'

'OK . . . Mom, I promise.' It's not like Mom to talk so seriously. Is it that me leaving is inevitable and she's coming to terms with that? Is she worried I'll be all alone as I travel? I've tried to settle here, but the excitement of being *still* has worn off. It's ingrained in me, to keep roaming, keep searching. Staying put feels like pressing pause. 'But . . .'

'No buts. If I've taught you anything, it's that you've got to follow your heart. There's a big wide world out there that needs exploring. When the darkness comes, you'll find the light.'

Darkness? Is she referring to our aborted trip to Venice just recently? We'd returned to Missoula in a rush, our jaunt cut short with no explanation. Mom had been different there, silent. More contained, holding herself tight as though her secrets might spill out. I didn't understand it; I still don't. But she won't be questioned about it. That's Mom. Open one minute, closed off the next. Still, she loves me fiercely and is always on my side – like a lioness protecting her cub.

'It's just that it's always been us,' I say. 'Who will I be without you?' We've travelled the globe my entire life, until Mom announced in Venice a few months ago she was settling in Missoula. For good. Would she miss roaming? Miss waking up under a different patch of sky? Miss me? Twenty-three years, it's been us together against the world.

'You'll be *you*, Luna. A worldly, smart, strong, independent woman who knows her mind and wears her heart on her sleeve. You might find yourself oceans away but there's an invisible thread that connects our hearts and souls, so that distance will never come between us.'

Mom knows I've been killing time here, wanting to escape but not having the courage to tell her. 'It'll be so strange without you.' Will I enjoy the thrill of a new place if I'm alone?

'It might be strange in the beginning, but you'll find other roamers and you'll never look back.'

'Like you did.'

'Just like I did, baby girl. Like *we* did.' She places the daisy chain on my head like a crown. I look to the mountains once more. They've been here for millennia and they'll be here when I get back. Just like Mom will be. It's time to leave the nest.

Chapter 1

Ten years later

On Ko Pha Ngan island the full moon sinks into the horizon where the sky meets the sea. Soon it will be nautical twilight. Glittery stars shine in the deep dark, helping old Thai sailors navigate their way home.

Usually, I love this predawn time, watching the inky black blanket above dissolve into purple and lilac hues, swirling like the brushstrokes of a watercolour painting. Time slows, as if the earth is taking a deep breath, renewing itself for the coming day, a new sunrise, a fresh start.

But it's hard to absorb the beauty of the slipping sky with the noise, the crowds. The press of bodies: one rhythmic mass. Even the sand vibrates to the pulse of the music. Waves rolling in to the shore shimmy to the beat. What did I expect though? A row of mellow yogis doing the lotus pose?

Hat Rin beach is full of glow-in-the-dark body-painted revellers who dance like no one is watching. The vibe is electric, as if everyone has been hypnotised by the full moon. There's an energy about them, as if their batteries have been fully charged. Partygoers skip through ropes that are aflame. Buckets of beer are carried up and down the shore by wobbly-legged people.

Sharp bursts of laughter carry over the sound of the music as I search faces for my friend Gigi, who I lost an hour ago among the crowds.

A few minutes later, I come to the far end of the beach. It's like stepping through a portal into another world. Gone are the ravers moving as one to trance tracks. Here Bob Marley drifts lazily into the atmosphere, along with the sweet, earthy smell of smoke from bonfires and hand-rolled cigarettes. Dreadlocks abound and everyone wears neon tie-dye, their face-paint sparkling under a black light. Merrymakers huddle in groups, playing instruments, or gazing soulfully at one another. Some chatter away, putting the world to rights. *Vegetarianism is the only way, man. The only way we'll survive as a planet.* And the gentle rebuttal: *Veganism, man. That's the only way!*

I spot Gigi, sitting in a circle, strumming a ukulele as she only half-listens to a British guy lecture her about women's rights. I cast my eyes at the sky once more; has anyone noticed the moon is gone? Soon it will be sunrise, and already the air thickens with humidity.

'Here she is!' Gigi drops the ukulele, jumps up and leads me away from the group. 'If I hear one more guy claim he's a feminist just to get in my pants, I'm going to scream. Did you see that guy and his *Down with the Patriarchy* tee? Like, as if!'

'Let's get out of here. The vibe is off.' There's a subtle shift in the energy, as if it's a warning to call it a night.

Gigi turns to me. 'It is off. Let's head back to the bungalow, and you can tell me all about how you found yourself growing up in a commune in the Thai jungle.'

I've been promising to tell Gigi about my childhood for ages, and it's not as though I don't trust her, it's that people often associate communes with cults, and I don't like having to defend myself to those who lack the grace to listen. But I can't keep putting her off, and I know Gigi isn't like most people.

'Come on, Luna, you promised!'

4

'OK. Strap yourself in.' We link arms and trudge along the soft sand. 'The communes were a place of belonging.' I make a poor attempt at mimicking a documentary narrator because I've told this story so many times it's become rote. 'A non-judgemental, supportive environment where women pitched in together to raise their babies the way *they* wanted, and not the way they were *told* to do.'

'I can picture it already.' There's a wistful note in her voice.

I go way back to stories my mom told me. 'They started in the Sixties when to be an unmarried mother was considered a sin in most Western cultures. But they were just as important for women like my mother who came later.'

'Can you even imagine?' Gigi says. 'Like of all the things to worry about, being an unmarried mother was top of the list. Crazy.'

'Exactly! Why should having a baby out of wedlock change the course of their lives? This was miles before my mom's time but, even when I was born, women still didn't have total autonomy. We still don't.'

It blows my mind when I think about those revolutionary women and how brave they were to go against the grain.

The recollections come thick and fast. 'Mom's home life wasn't good, so she left as soon as she could and travelled alone for years before she stumbled on the Thai commune when she was pregnant with me.'

'Kismet?'

'It really feels like it, right? It was a joy growing up here surrounded by so many other kids. The Thai people took us under their wing, understanding what the women were about while westerners clearly did not.'

Even though I was young, I recall the looks when we went into town for supplies. The side-eye stares from westerners not part of the communes. I remember Mom and her friends being whispered about wherever we went. *How dare these vagabonds live with no rules, no moral compass, and traipse around barefoot!*

Those earth mothers let the judgement slide off their suntanned skin. They had each other. We were a family. Still are to this day, even though we're scattered across the world like so many dandelion seeds.

'We left Thailand when I was about four or five and didn't stop moving until my mom settled in Montana ten years ago. It's still unreal to think of her staying in one place. But, she's happy living on a big stretch of land with other off-grid enthusiasts.'

Gigi shakes her head as if in awe. 'Your mom is the ultimate free spirit. I can't wait to meet her one day. She knew back in the Nineties that she wouldn't follow society's expectations of what a woman's life should look like. She *chose* to live outside the lines, to find what mattered to her. I'm sure it wasn't easy, but it was worth it. Those women who came before paved the way.'

I knew Gigi would understand. My life started here, in Thailand. In a small commune run by women, for women. They say it takes a village to raise a child and that's what I had. A whole village of like-minded women who looked out for one another and their offspring. Until the next adventure beckoned on the balmy breeze, and with babes strapped to their chests they followed their hearts and kept roaming. The communes are long since gone. Those beautiful barefoot women with a baby on a breast are now elsewhere. They were ahead of their time with their wildness, their sense of adventure . . .

'Now Mom's only battle is beating cancer. But she's got her apothecary for that, and she's winning. Every day she gets that little bit stronger.' A year ago, she gave me the news of her diagnosis. Mom told me not to cut my travels short and rush home. It was under control. While Mom might be the best healer there is, she doesn't like being the coddled patient. Still, she's my everything, so rush home I did. I stayed for a few weeks and saw with my very own eyes that she was getting the best care and the prognosis was good.

'I'm so glad she's winning, Luna. The world *needs* Ruby – no two ways about it.'

Gigi adores my mom, even though they've never met except on video calls. 'Sure does.'

We lapse into silence for a moment.

Gigi leans her head on my shoulder as we walk. 'I'm sorry the full moon party was such a bust. Tonight was supposed to be all about you! We were supposed to appeal to the moon gods and offer up a sacrifice, a human one if need be, maybe the guy wearing the *Down with the Patriarchy* tee would've sufficed, so you'd get the answers you need.'

Gigi's only half joking. We came to the full moon party because of my past. Gigi insists something magical will happen because I was named Luna, in ode to this place. I was supposed to be open to some sign, some flashing light showing me the way. Giving me some answers. It wasn't quite the chilled-out peace party I'd been expecting though, from my mom's descriptions of it back in the day.

It could be folklore – so much is where my mom is concerned – but, the story goes, Mom celebrated here one magical night back in 1990. This was before it was the spectacle it is these days. Back then it was a small beach party, the sandy shore full of hippies dancing under the moonlight.

I envision my mom back then, with her long dirty-blonde hair, bikini top and denim cut-offs, swaying to the music. That night she said she fell in love with a guy who had a lyrical voice and a sensual smile. When she awoke at dawn the next day, he was gone, and she thought she dreamed the whole experience. Until a couple of months later when she found out she was pregnant with me. Her full moon baby, Luna.

I've always wondered about the man who fathered me. I know I'm like him physically: dark hair, dark eyes, olive skin. The way Mom described my birth was so magical that I grew up believing I was a gift from the universe sent when she needed me most.

Besides, I always told myself I didn't *need* a father. I had all the moms a kid could want – but the truth is, I've always felt like a puzzle with one piece missing.

7

A wave of homesickness crashes over me. That invisible thread that binds mother to daughter can only stretch so far in this big wide world. I haven't seen her since that hurried visit home, although we talk on the phone at least once a week and send funny cat memes and sunset pictures almost every day.

It's a sign. I need to stay for a bit in her tiny off-grid home, in the chilled-out bohemian enclave that suits her artistic temperament. A modern-day commune of sorts. A great big patch of land, filled with her friends, living peacefully. But I know she'll hate me hovering over her. Hate that I've cut my Thailand trip short on her account. But sometimes you just have to go with your instinct. And my instinct tells me it's time to go back.

It'll be bittersweet to leave Thailand so soon – the place my life began. A tropical paradise where the only definite is that the sun will rise and set. I suppose it was inevitable that I'd return here. And probably will time and again. There are still so many unanswered questions.

While my mom and I are close, she's a vault at times. Why did we leave the commune here? The romantic in me wonders if she stayed for as long as she could, hoping the man who made her a mother would return. On that subject, she only has brief details.

Over time, my imagination has run wild. Would I recognise my father if I stumbled upon him? Do we share the same smile, the same mannerisms?

The sensible part of me knows he's not here. Knows I won't brush shoulders with a man in the street and recognise my features on his. He was a tourist – the chances are less than slim – but what if he's been searching for her too?

Wishful thinking is my specialty.

This is why I roam. Searching for that elusive utopia. Wanting answers I'll never find. Looking for a backpacker from more than thirty-three years ago who remains nameless. Faceless. Mom says it was meant to be. A divine birth.

So, I wander, trying to find my place in the world. It's why I stick to busy cities. I can get lost in the crowd. Be invisible among so many faces while I look for his.

Gigi and I are up again by mid-morning to head to the beach to sunbake away the lethargy after the full moon party. I throw a couple of books into my tote, along with a tube of sun cream and sarongs.

It doesn't take long for Gigi to assume the position: hands up, mouth agape, asleep. While she softly snores beside me, I people-watch as I flip the pages of an epic love story. Romance novels give me life. Who doesn't love love? I want my own fairy tale.

But it's hard to be in a long-term relationship, living the way I do. So far, it hasn't worked out. Maybe I'm too wild, too flighty. But I believe in soulmates. It's written in the stars, in tarot and numerology too. Hope blows stronger on the breeze some days.

While I wait for Mr. Right, I delight in reading about swoony fictional entanglements. Billionaires. Brainiacs. Bad boys. Men from the wrong side of the tracks. I've fallen for them all.

I dive back into my book, hoping my heroine gives her first love a second chance after all these years. They've had to contend with the outbreak of war, losing contact, her marriage, his children. These star-crossed lovers deserve their shot at love.

Eventually Gigi shifts position and sits up. 'The salty air is doing wonders for my sleep-deprived brain.'

I raise a brow. 'That and the two-hour nap you just took.'

She glances at her watch. 'Wow, *two hours*, did I?' Gigi pulls off the sarong I draped over her to protect her from the bite of the sun. 'Thanks, Luna. I'd have been boiled crab orange by now.'

I grin; it's happened so many times before. Gigi can sleep anywhere, with no discernible warning. She's even fallen asleep mid-sentence. I'm sure it's a form of narcolepsy but she claims it's simply being attuned to knowing when her body needs rest. 'You were talking in your sleep again.'

'About eating?'

I laugh. 'How did you know?'

Gigi is obsessed with food. She'll try anything, no matter how eyebrow-raising. 'I've been hankering after those fish tacos I had in Tijuana. Speaking of which . . .'

'Let me guess, you're hungry?' And with that her stomach rumbles in agreement. 'How about some *Khao Niew Ma Muang*?' I offer.

'You pronounce the names so well, but I have no idea what that is, which is annoying since I'm supposed to be the fount of knowledge.' Gigi's a food blogger, and an up-and-coming influencer. It's been a lifesaver when funds have dwindled, and we've been invited to eat meals in return for a sponsored post. Aside from that, we pick up any work we can. Fruit picking, dish washing, car park attending, English tutoring, online surveys, you name it – we've done it.

'It's sweet sticky rice with mango and costs next to nothing here.' I picked up Thai language easily when I was young – as kids do – and I still remember bits and pieces as the signs around town have jogged my memory.

'Ooh, count me in. Shall we pack up and go find some?'

'Yep.' I shut my book and say a silent apology to the characters for making them pause their romance for me.

As I go to bundle up my towel, I feel a strange rumbling sensation. I glance around, but no one else seems to notice. Bikini-clad girls take selfies. Elderly couples soak up the sun. Kids gambol in the shallows.

The world tilts on its axis, upsetting my balance. I brace myself, but for what?

I do a mental stocktake but there it is again – the ground beneath me shifts. There's a roar, like a storm incoming. I look above and only see the bright blue sky and cotton-ball clouds. 'Did you feel that?' I ask Gigi, searching the faces of strangers around me whose expressions remain serene. Can't they sense it?

'Feel what?' Gigi asks as she packs her belongings.

My first thought is a tsunami, but none of the alarms have sounded and it feels more subtle than that. It seems almost *internal* somehow because no one else reacts. Not even to bat an eyelid or take a second glance.

'Nothing.' I paste on a smile but a sense of foreboding washes over me. Should we get off the beach? I watch the water recede and return. It's flat, unthreatening, so why do I suddenly feel so ill at ease?

Gigi surveys me, her eyebrows knitted. 'Are you OK?'

'Yeah. I'm fine.' I avert my gaze and stare out to the water, wondering what it means, because it *always* means something. I get these premonitions every now and then but they're never decipherable when it matters. You can't grow up as the poster flower child and not have some kind of *knowing*, I guess.

'Let's fill up our bellies before the rest of them get out of bed and hit the streets to cure their hangovers.' Neither of us are big drinkers, which helps when you lead the lifestyle we do. Last night's partygoers certainly gave it a good bashing and I bet there's a few waking up with sore heads today.

We find a street food vendor and order two plates of *Khao Niew Ma Muang*. The air is thick with humidity, as the sun crescendos high in the sky. We thank the vendor, a tiny woman missing her two front teeth, who wears a wide smile. 'Pretty girls,' she says, and we thank her once more. I'm too distracted to pay much attention.

'I need shade,' Gigi says.

Our humble bungalow beach hut isn't far from here. A headache looms and I'm unfathomably out of sorts. Cars whiz by, the road a cacophony of noise. 'Or head back to the bungalow?'

'Yeah,' Gigi says, sweat beading her brow. 'You look like you could use some time alone. How about we eat, and then I leave you in peace for a bit?' Gigi can read people like no one I've met before. She senses I'm unsettled. Whatever it is lingers, following in my wake. The world shifts, but I don't want to untangle its meaning. By the time I've figured it out, it'll be too late to do anything. What kind of gift is that? Tarot cards usually bring clarity, so I'll give those a go in the coolness of the bungalow.

'A bit of quiet sounds good. I'm beat,' I say to Gigi. Maybe it's just my body reacting to a late night. I'm usually the early to bed, early to rise type. Morning mediations and a spot of yoga and I haven't done that since we've been here, so my balance is out of whack.

'Thailand is great, but it sure is hectic. Maybe we need an ashram after here? Somewhere we can chill out for a bit,' Gigi suggests. 'I could do a feature on vegetarian food for those who are plant-curious.'

'It's all the rage right now but funds are low. We'll have to get work fairly soon.'

'How utterly boring.'

'Right? And I'd love to go see my mom. We can pick up work in Missoula easily enough.'

'Now you're talking! I'll finally get to meet our queen.'

Gigi and I connected at a hostel in Bondi, Australia, and have been together since. She texts Mom almost as much as I do now. We did a lap of Oz in a rusty old campervan whose nickname was Rusty Rust Bucket. If a friendship can survive living in close confines like that, it can survive anything. Sure we squabble over petty stuff sometimes, but we get over it just as fast. Gigi's the say-it-as-it-is type with a ready laugh and doesn't take life too seriously. Once we finished our epic road trip around Australia, we went to New Zealand, the land of the long white cloud, before heading here. I've seen so much beauty, sometimes I wonder if it's real.

Back at the bungalow we eat in companionable silence. The fruit is juicy and sweet and brings back so many memories of the children of the commune, feasting on fresh mangos from the tree, our faces sticky from our gluttony.

12

We fall silent for a bit and then I ask, 'Are you going to be OK exploring on your own?' We've grown protective of each other, always on high alert in a new place until we find our feet. While I'm vaguely familiar with Thailand, it was a long time ago – and Gigi has never been here before.

'Sure am. I'm going to take some content for the 'gram. Relax, Luna, and we'll head to the beach for sunset later, yeah?'

'OK, good plan.'

With a backwards wave she's gone. I find my tarot cards and cleanse them by lighting some incense and letting the smoke undulate in the air above. With some centring breaths, I get myself into the right mental space. I close my eyes and shuffle the cards, asking the question: *What does the shifting sensation mean? Why did the earth tilt on its axis?* I'm silently begging them not to tell me what I already know. My body knows. My heart recognises the break.

I lay out the cards. As I'm translating their meaning my cell phone rings, startling me. Holding my breath, I survey the cards once more. The ache in my chest tightens as the phone bleats incessantly. I don't want to answer it because I know I'm right. I've known since the ground moved beneath me at the beach, since I felt the rumble of change.

Chapter 2

'Hello?'

'Baby girl.' The only other person in the whole wide world who calls me that is my Aunt Loui. My honorary aunt, one of those women who danced into our life and never left. 'Luna?' her voice shakes. 'Can you hear me, all right?'

Aunt Loui is usually loud, strong, protective, with her Janis-Joplin-esque gravelly voice and straight-shooting persona, but now she sounds like a hollowed-out version of herself. Meek, somehow.

'Aunt Loui, I'm here.'

There's a snuffling sound, like she's trying to compose herself. How long has it taken her to work up the courage to call?

'It's Mom, isn't it?' As soon as the words leave my mouth, the ground beneath me moves once more. The shift is so *seismic* that I grab the wall so I don't fall.

'She's gone. I'm so sorry, Luna.'

'Gone?' We only spoke two days ago just after I'd landed in Thailand. She said she had something to tell me, but I'd been stuck in the customs queue and ordered by an official to hang up the phone. Mom told me not to worry, she'd call back later. 'But . . . ?'

There's a pause and then: 'The decline happened so *fast* otherwise I'd have called you home. It took us all by surprise.'

'Was she in pain?' How can this be? While she didn't sound like her sunny self on our last call, she didn't sound like she was actively dying either.

'No, it was a peaceful passing. We were all with her, hoping against hope we were wrong. The day before she was up and about, so we thought . . . we thought . . .' Her words peter off. 'She was such a fighter, baby girl, that none of us expected this.'

Was. We're already talking in past tense about a woman so vital I'd presumed she'd live forever. A woman whose spirit was at times so boundless, a brightly lit flame that would never expire. This cannot be happening.

'I wish I'd been with her.' We'd roamed together for so long. I'd lived inside her pocket my entire childhood. And then I took off again, knowing I had a place to go back to whenever I needed it. Her human experience is over, just like that? What had she wanted to tell me that day on the phone as I was trying to get through the chaos of the Thai airport? That her journey earthside was coming to an end?

'Me too, Luna. Me too.' It's why the ground shifted, the sky rumbled. The air thickened as she drifted to the next place. Saying last goodbyes as she floated the celestial path to beyond. Will she wait for me there?

Tears fall, silent streams running down my cheeks till I think I might die from the pain. This sudden shock to my system feels almost like my death too. A part of me is blackened, charred, dead. With no warning, no word, I'm suddenly untethered. The thread that binds us is broken. It doesn't *exist* anymore and how can that be?

Ruby, free-spirited earth mother, took strays under her gossamer wings, the lost and broken, the damaged and bruised. Did she see herself in them? Those wings, they were wide; there was enough room for everyone who needed shoring up. How will we cope without her?

Mom sang, she taught watercolour painting, she knitted, she created. She sunned her crystals. Wrote poetry and read aloud at slams surrounded by broody artists half her age, who cheered her on. She was ageless. Everyone wanted to be in her spotlight, even me. Even with her complicated moods. Her about-faces. Her ups and downs. I loved her with every breath in my body. How is it possible I'll never see her again?

'Will you come home, baby girl? We'll celebrate her life the way she deserves.'

How can I go home when there is no home if she's not there?

'Come home, Luna.' Aunt Loui's voice breaks. Losing Mom isn't only hurting me.

'I'll be there as soon as I can. Love you.' Tears fall so hard my eyes blur. How could that soul, that spirit, that rock star of a woman up and leave this world, just like that? Sure, she had her faults, but don't we all? She made up for it when she found the light once more.

'Love you too. Get home safe.'

I end the call and sit back on the bed, stunned at this new reality. I try to connect to her, across all these oceans, spiritual planes, the goddamn ether and wait for a sign. Nothing comes but a murky darkness. Mom's taken all the light with her. I can't feel her or sense her here.

I text Gigi to come back to the bungalow and attempt to make a plan of what I need to do in order to leave.

A metaphysical goddess has transitioned to the next phase, gone in so much stardust.

'I'm coming with you,' Gigi says and envelops me in a hug. She squeezes me tight, and I let myself cry until the tears run out. I must fall asleep because when I wake, the room is spick and span, and our backpacks sit forlornly by the bungalow door.

'Hey,' Gigi says, sitting at the foot of the bed, phone in hand. 'I've booked us a boat out of here and two flights to get back to

Missoula. I've cancelled the rest of the bungalow stay and packed our things. What do you need? What can I do?'

My eyes are sore from crying, and Gigi's love and support is enough to tip me over the edge again. Mom adored Gigi for her ability to read people and not settle for second best, made better still by her big heart. 'I'm . . .' I go to say fine, good, OK, but none of those things are true. 'I don't know what I need. I don't know who to be now. Where do I go from here?'

She pats my leg through the thin, itchy blanket. 'You listen to your heart. That's all you *can* do. If you want to wail, then wail. If you want to punch the pillow, be my guest. If you want to drown yourself in kombucha, I will do my level best to find some. Or we can chat about your mom. Will that help?'

I consider my options. Reading is where I go when the world gets too heavy but even that seems impossible now. What do words matter? 'Sleep, I think I'll sleep.' And maybe I'll wake up to a new reality. Or at least forget this one for a while.

She kisses my forehead, just like my mom used to do. 'Sleep, Luna. And I'll make sure we're up in time to head to the port.'

17

Chapter 3

I'm hollowed out and numb from the interminable travel and grief when Aunt Loui meets us at the airport. I run into the comfort of her outstretched arms. As always, she smells of sandalwood and patchouli, and earth from her garden. Like home.

'Oh, baby girl, is it good to see you!' Her voice sounds muffled through my hair.

'You too.' After an age we let go, but I clasp her hand tight. Aunt Loui is almost like an extension of Mom and I need her close, like I need air to breathe. 'This is my friend Gigi. Gigi, this is Aunt Loui.'

Gigi grins at her, her eyes shining with excitement. She's heard so many tales about Aunt Loui's escapades. '*The* Aunt Loui? The one who went running naked down the main street of Missoula?'

Aunt Loui turns to me and raises a brow. '*That's* the story you chose to tell?'

I laugh. 'Your reputation precedes you. What can I say?'

She squeezes my hand tight and turns back to Gigi. 'Well, I do hope Luna told you the full story?'

'Where's the fun in that?' I joke.

Aunt Loui hoists my backpack on her shoulder, as if it weighs nothing, and leads us outside. 'True. Well, I was protesting the live meat trade. I don't know about where you're from, Gigi, but around here it's impossible to get people's attention. I mean, you literally need to be naked to get a second glance, and even *then*, it's hard.'

'Did it work?' Gigi asks.

Aunt Loui grins. 'I got my point across, I guess. I also got arrested. But hey, anything for the animals, right?'

This isn't the time to tell her Gigi is a food blogger and far from being a vegetarian. Being plant-curious will be good enough for my aunt. 'Right,' Gigi agrees as if it's one of her core beliefs too.

'Let's get home, hey? There's a bunch of people waiting to see you.'

Cushioned by my aunt's love and energy, I feel less shaky.

We drive home in Aunt Loui's beat-up pick-up truck. How the panels still manage to cling to the body of the vehicle with the amount of rust is beyond me. She doesn't use it often, only for trips into town for supplies every now and then. Just like on the communes, they all live close here and grow or forage for what they need.

Mom was the creative, whimsical one of the pair, while Aunt Loui is practical. She's the kind of woman you want beside you in an apocalypse. She cans fruit. Ferments vegetables. Mills her own flour. Can throat-punch in a pinch if called for, but she's mainly a pacifist unless pushed.

As I drift down memory lane Aunt Loui regales Gigi with gossip about life in the town of tiny homes and I wonder how she's going to survive without Mom. She is the yin to her yang. They've been best friends for so long it's hard to remember what life was like before Aunt Loui was around. There's always been a steadiness about her – I like that I always know where I stand and that she'll always be on my side, no matter what.

That's largely the case with so many of our friends. No matter where I am in the world, there's a network out there that would drop everything in a heartbeat if I asked for help, and vice versa.

Soon the conversation fades away, and the silence grabs my attention. I glance at Aunt Loui as her bottom lip trembles. 'Let it out,' I say, rubbing her arm as she stares at the desolate road ahead. 'You don't have to act all strong and tough for me.'

'Baby girl, the world just got so dull and grey.'

Like winter.

The town of tiny homes come into view. When they hear Aunt Loui's rust bucket spit and curse, friends spill out onto the grass to come and greet us. I'm beat from being in transit and bed beckons, but when I see all the familiar faces my heart expands.

They gather round the truck and line up to hug me. I breathe in the life, their vitality, and what they meant to Mom. It's not until I've hugged every last person that I remember Gigi's here too and it's bad manners on my part not personally introducing her. But Gigi isn't the kind who needs an introduction; she's already off with one of the neighbours inspecting the raised beds and chatting about fermented vegetables. I wonder if the hippy life will rub off on her, being exposed to it here, almost like a modern-day commune, one designed in the spirit of those who came before.

Sadness is painted on so many of their faces; they wear wooden smiles, the same as me, though we're all pretending to be OK. As enlightened as these people are, no one quite knows quite what to say. Death is like that, I guess. It makes the atmosphere heavy. Stilted words and mumbled platitudes. What *can* anyone say? They're as heartbroken as I am.

I motion to Aunt Loui that I'm going into the tiny home for a breather. When I step inside, I'm assailed with flashbacks of Mom. The space is full to bursting with knick-knacks and art endeavours. It's clean and tidy, although with each passing year it seems she learned to spread out a bit more – as if she truly knew she wouldn't need to fit everything into a backpack ever again.

Her watercolours are strung up wherever there's wall space. There's a new one of me, a side profile, blurry and indistinct, but I'd recognise the backdrop anywhere: the canals of Venice. The glint off the water reflects on my hair, turning it golden under the sun when in reality it's much darker. Perhaps she saw me that way, a little brighter, a little sunnier than what I really am.

Before she settled in Missoula, Mom and I had one last adventure in summery Venice. We took a ride on a gondola, ate oysters at some fancy place, filled our bellies with wood-fired pizzas. Spent more money in four days than we usually did in a month.

But in hindsight, was it more than that? She'd cut our Venice trip short, which I've always found strange. Out of the blue, she'd told me about her plans to settle in Missoula so I figured she didn't want to dip into the deposit for her tiny home and I too wanted to hold on to what I had for whatever came next.

Then we moved to Missoula and got her settled in. Mom was quieter than normal. Aren't we all more subdued in a new place? There'd been much to do. We'd painted walls, potted flowers, helped in the communal garden. We made her a home and once I knew she was set, that she didn't need me, I took off again. Did something happen in Venice that I wasn't aware of? In hindsight I sense she'd been rattled, but by what? We were together most of the time. Once again, I'm looking for answers I know I won't find. I let the thought go.

The tiny home is warm and cosy with kitschy décor. There are wobbly ceramic plates she made in a friend's kiln. Crocheted rugs adorn the sofa, tucked behind batik cushions she picked up in Bali a million years ago. I go up the ladder to her loft bedroom, which is open to the downstairs. The ceiling is so low I drop to a crawl. I fall on to her bed, a too-soft mattress that takes up all the space. It's loaded with pillows, as if she needed to feel boxed in, safe. Dreamcatchers are fixed above, feathery beaded talismans that she insisted were crucial to a good night's sleep and protection from bad dreams.

I reach up and run my fingers through the feathers. Why did she need so many? Was she plagued by nightmares? Through the porthole-like window, darkness falls. Stars blink awake. I hug a pillow to my chest, as the scent and sound of a bonfire drifts by. Everyone is waiting for me outside. I'll just rest for a moment.

Chapter 4

As I slowly come to, I hear murmurs and try and make sense of where I am. In this transitional space between asleep and awake, I forget for a moment she's gone. It's Mom's perfume, a homemade concoction of orange and juniper, which reminds me. The crushing blow of it. Her pillows hold her essence, the shape of her head, her very soul. It's as close I've come to feeling her, here in this space.

It's still dark outside. Can it really be the same interminable day? I can't even run from time and sleep the sadness away because it's right there behind me, like my shadow.

My poor baby girl's exhausted. Let's leave her be and see how tomorrow goes.

I drag myself up on the pillows. I should go down and see Aunt Loui, and help Gigi settle in at least. They won't know how to get the sofa to unfold; there's a trick to it. And have they eaten? Gigi gets hangry when she doesn't eat. But that same listlessness washes over me. The thought of moving seems like too much effort, as if my body suddenly weighs double and everything is hard, like wading through mud.

Yeah, she needs her rest. I'll sleep on the sofa so I'm close if she needs me through the night.

They go back and forth for a bit, their voices droning like the sound of a thousand bees and I drift off again.

I sleep for a full sixteen hours. When I awaken the sun is high in the sky and it's hot in the loft. My stomach rumbles as I make my way down the rickety ladder and find Gigi nursing a mug of tea, flipping through an art magazine.

'Good afternoon, sunshine,' she says.

'Hey. Sorry I checked out like that. I just . . .'

She waves me away. 'No apologies. You do whatever you need to do, and I'm simply here to help where I can. Aunt Loui fetched some fresh eggs and brought over a loaf of sourdough she baked this morning. There's fresh churned butter from . . . oh what was her name? Pilar? The one who lives on a houseboat! An actual *houseboat* on land!'

There's all sorts of weird and wonderful here. They make it work. 'Yeah, that's Pilar. She makes amazing cakes too.'

'I see now why they don't need to leave. They have everything they need right here. So what . . . do they use a bartering system to swap goods, or how do they do it?'

I shrug. 'They just share. Aunt Loui is the foodie. Everyone's pantries will be full of her fermented goodies. Mom made art and textiles, so if you take a look inside everyone's homes you're bound to find the exact same décor.' The thought makes me smile that Mom's creations will live on. 'Everyone will have at least one of her crocheted rugs, some of her screen-printed cushion covers. She was an alchemist too; she ran the apothecary with Jillian. There's a whole lot of homeopathic remedies on hand for those who prefer a more natural approach to medical care.'

'I've got to see that. Where do they keep it all?'

I scratch my chin. 'It was all stored here but by the looks of it

24

Mom moved it elsewhere. There used to be a medicine cabinet full of all sorts of bottles, lotions, potions and powders.'

'Maybe Jillian has it all?'

Perhaps Mom didn't want the intrusion of people coming and going when she wasn't well. 'I'll have to ask Aunt Loui.'

'How about eggs on toast? You must be famished.'

When did I last eat? Sometime in Thailand. Which seems like another life now; seems like a different person walked that path, a carefree girl with hardly a worry in the world. 'That would be great.'

'Go get some fresh air, and I'll bring it outside when it's ready. Go soak up some vitamin D.'

'Oh Lord, you sound like us already.' Her laughter follows me outside. It's a beautiful sunny spring day, so bright I squint until my eyes adjust. The previous night comes back to mind, and I hope everyone didn't think I was rude, shuffling off like that.

I spot Aunt Loui tending her vegetable patch. The sight of her curved back, her hands plunging into the fertile soil is comforting but also slightly jarring. Life goes on . . . But how can it, so soon? Shouldn't we be fists in the air, wailing to the gods about Mom being snatched from us? When I get closer, I hear her sniffles. Maybe life goes on, but not in the same way it did before. The whole putting on a brave face thing is so out of the ordinary here, where usually feelings are *felt* and discussed openly. Death is different.

'Aunt Loui, can I help?'

She wipes her eyes with the sleeve of her shirt. 'Oh, baby girl! No, I'm just pottering. How did you sleep?' She stands and removes her gloves, pulling me in for a hug.

'Out like a light. Sixteen hours straight.'

'You needed it.'

'Yeah. What about you?'

She waves me away. 'Fine, fine.' There are dark shadows under her eyes that say otherwise, but I let it go, brave face and all that. 'Where's the apothecary these days?'

25

'Jillian's place. She's got your mom's medicine cabinet and they made an outpatient area. There's more space there, and they planned to extend the alternative side of things. Jillian's practising reiki and shiatsu massage. I swear to God she tried to poke my soul clean out of my body – but don't tell her I said that. She's a little touchy about it. Had a few complaints about her shiatsu technique but reckons it doesn't work unless it hurts.'

I laugh. 'I won't line up for one then?'

'No, I wouldn't recommend it. But feel free to go visit, and if you want your mom's cabinet back and her apothecary stuff, I can ask?'

'Oh no, no. I was just wondering, that's all. I'm glad Jillian's here to keep it all going.'

I know it might seem woo-woo to a lot of people, but natural and alternative medicine has always fascinated me. These tonics and tinctures are made with organic products foraged around the place with recipes that go back aeons in time – there's something almost magical about it. I'm not against modern medicine – anything but – however, I'd always try Mom's remedies first.

Gigi wanders out with our breakfast. 'Luna, your feast awaits.'

Aunt Loui taps me on the butt. 'Go have your breakfast. And I'll come over in a bit.'

I take my place at the outdoor table. 'Thanks, Gi.'

We sit and I do my level best to eat but it's as if the food won't go down. Almost like there's a blockage, and I guess it's just another part of grief. While so many emotions are flooding out, nothing can go in.

Gigi stares at me under her lashes, and I know she's worrying so I cut my portions smaller and try to eat, washing each mouthful down with a sweet tea.

A while later, Aunt Loui joins us, dressed in clean clothes, the garden abandoned for the moment. 'I know it's soon, baby girl, and it's going to be hard to talk about, but we need to arrange the funeral.'

'Yeah. I guess we do.'

'Jillian is going to cleanse and ritualise the body, and she'd love you to be involved. It might sound confronting, but it's a beautiful experience. Ruby's soul has transitioned so Jillian will perform this sacred rite so that we can say our thanks to the heavens for giving us our Ruby and prepare the body for burial so she can continue on her celestial path.'

A lump forms in my throat. 'Of course I'll be there.' Part of me worries I won't want to let her go, but I know Jillian will guide me. Mom and Jillian have done this for other women, many times, and I've heard about the singing, the chanting, and the way they prepare for the next stage. And as heartbreaking as it will be, it's an important part of letting go and assuring Mom's transition is a smooth one.

With a pat on my knee Aunt Loui says, 'So for the funeral itself, I know it's a cliché, but Ruby'd want it to be fun and a real celebration.'

I take a deep breath. It's true. She'd hate us to be maudlin, but it's impossible not to be. 'You're right. We'll have to play her favourite *luk thung* traditional Thai music.'

'And we've got to play "Ruby Tuesday".'

'Oh yes we do!' Aunt Loui called Mom Ruby Tuesday after the Rolling Stones song for as long as I can remember.

'You won't believe how apt those lyrics are right now. Like that song was written for her.'

I can't recall the lyrics, so I pull them up on my phone and read. *Whoa.* It's Mom in a nutshell and so fitting for this sombre occasion.

'It's perfect.' I'm going to blubber my way through that song, as I'm reminded of their friendship and what they meant to each other. Soulmates can come in all forms, and I truly believe they were connected on a deeper level, despite it being platonic. Female friendships are just as important, if not more, than true love. Well, that's what I've grown up to believe and it's evident on every line and plane of Aunt Loui's face. Her loss is great; her soulmate is missing forevermore.

She gives me a sad smile. 'And what about photos, baby girl? Do you want to make a montage we can play on screen? I can borrow Jillian's TV and there's solar power in the temple.'

I give her watery smile. 'Yeah, I do. If there's one thing we have in abundance, it's photos. I even have a box somewhere full of Polaroids from my childhood. I'll have to have a hunt around for them.'

We discuss our ideas to celebrate Mom's nomadic life in depth and come up with a plan. 'OK, you find the photos and I'll arrange the rest.' Aunt Loui pats my hand and blinks back tears as she stands to leave.

It all seems so real suddenly. So final. I want Mom's send-off to honour who she was, and I focus on that for now, so I can get through this stage. But internally I rail, I choke, I scream at the thought of being left behind. There's a feeling of abandonment. Maybe it stems from not getting to see her one last time. To kiss her soft pillowy cheek. To tell her what she meant to me.

Did she know the end was near and not tell me? That was always Mom's way, shielding me from hurt if she could, but I didn't always agree with her keeping things from me. It often felt evasive, as if I only knew one part of her, the part she chose to show me. I'm probably overthinking things. My brain feels like it's misfiring, running too fast for me to make sense of anything.

I can't sit here and obsess over it but it's hard to let that thought go, in order to feel everything else that *demands* to be felt.

'Want me to help look for the photos?' Gigi says, picking up our plates, dragging me back to the now.

'Sure. But let me take those. I'll wash these up and throw myself in the shower and then we'll search.' *Pretend, Luna. Pretend this is all OK.* One foot in front of the other.

Chapter 5

We sit on the floor of the tiny home, knee-deep in memories, photos spread all around us. How will I choose when so many of them capture her wild and wonderful spirit? This is the woman I knew and loved – this carefree globetrotter who told rude jokes and cackled like a witch.

'Look at this one!' Gigi says and flips the photo to show me. It's Mom and I with a slice of orange as our 'teeth' staring goofily at the camera.

'That was in Sumatra.' I think back to the trip. 'We stayed there for a few months in a friend's hut in the rainforest. I must have been about nine or ten by then. It's where I saw my first Sumatran tiger just loafing about! I wanted to go play with it but Mom had other ideas. They're endangered now because of deforestation.'

'Oh God, that's so sad.'

'Yeah, awful.'

Gigi digs through another shoebox full as I add another picture to the montage pile. There's Mom atop some mountain range, arms splayed in triumph. There's one of Aunt Loui and Mom in full Eighties regalia; leg warmers and sweat bands, bent double laughing. I flip the photo. Scribbled on the back is 'First and last aerobics class 1987'. That explains the sweat bands.

There's one of us together in Venice, standing by a gondolier who wears the obligatory black and white striped shirt. He's busy ogling Mom, who stares off into the distance totally unaware of how he's zeroed in on her.

'Ooh look at this, Luna.' Gigi hands me a stack of envelopes held together with twine.

I unwrap them, wondering who the pen pal was; by the looks of it, the correspondence went for quite some time. The parchment is yellowed with age, so maybe they're from her teenage years? The writing is formal, cursive. Would Mom want me to read these? I have a moment of indecision. They feel private somehow, hidden away in a bundle. I don't remember ever seeing Mom read such a thing or mentioning letters arriving. I can't recall ever seeing her writing back to anyone. If she did, it was usually a postcard sent to one friend or another. A quick scribble with a forwarding address and that was it.

The bundle feels weighted. They hold a gravitas that pulses from the page. Nothing is the same anymore. Maybe these letters will provide some clarity.

There's only one way to find out.

I take a letter from the top envelope.

My dearest Ruby,
  The days are so long without you. So empty. I'm desperate to know you're OK. I woke to the sound of crying and you were gone. Think about what you've left behind . . .
  Please come back.
  Forever yours,
  Giancarlo

The air in the room leaves with a whoosh. Another mystery left by Ruby Hart.

'What is it?' Gigi asks.

'Looks like Mom up and vanished on this guy.' The hairs on

30

my arms stand on end. Instinctively I know there's more to this. The *knowing* pulses but not enough for me to gauge why.

'Show me.' I hand her the letter and she skim-reads it. 'What's this part mean: *Think about what you left behind?* Her heart? Him? Their love? What do you make of that?'

'All of the above, maybe?'

I pull out another letter.

You say I'm trying to clip your wings, hold you back from being free – and maybe that's true but not in the way you think. I presumed our love and what we made together would be enough to hold you here and that you'd want that too. I never meant to make you feel trapped. That's the last thing I'd do to my farfalla. If I could turn back time I would and I'd do it all differently.

'*Farfalla*, what is that? Italian or Spanish?' I ask.

Gigi brings up Google translate. 'It means butterfly in Italian.'

'You don't think . . .' The words dry on my tongue.

'What?' Gigi asks, eyes wide.

This woman, this saint who I loved more than life itself kept these letters hidden. Was this a love affair gone stale for her? Under the cover of darkness she left this man? Or is there more to this . . . ?

'For some reason I have the strangest feeling when I hold these letters. Like there's a secret that needs unearthing here. A big secret. But I don't want to overthink things. Maybe I'm wrong. Could be a simple explanation. She was young, dated a guy and it ended. Mom wasn't the kind to hang around if the vibe was off, you know?'

'That's the thing though, Luna. You're never wrong when you get these premonitions, are you?'

'As usual, I can only guess at the meaning.' And I do have a theory but I don't dare tempt fate by voicing it.

I pull out another letter.

Dearest Ruby,

Thank you for the pictures. I've sent you some in return. How can you stand to be parted? I'm trying so hard not to pressure you, but as time goes by and the distance between us expands, I wonder if you'll ever come back. Worse is thinking you won't. And then what? My heart is broken. But I guess that's the price I pay for falling in love with a rolling stone. Is there any chance for us? Just tell me there is. I can wait. I can wait a lifetime for you. And I will.

Forever in love,
Giancarlo

I search the envelope for clues as to where he lives but there's no return address. There's nothing on the letter either. Italy is a big country; he could be anywhere. And here are a bunch of handwritten love letters that need returning to their sender. I recall our trip to Venice. This has to be tied to it. It *has* to be. Why did we leave in such haste? And by the sound of these letters, it's not the first time Mom did such a thing. Why? What pictures did they send each other?

'Let's look for pictures of this guy while we're going through these boxes.'

'How will we know him though?'

'Well . . .' I tuck a strand of hair behind my ear. 'These photos are mostly of women; a man is bound to stand out.'

'Right.'

There's a whole mystery to unravel but we're interrupted by a knock at the door and a small head appears, with a bright pink pixie hairstyle.

'Luna!' she says and pulls me into a hug, standing on her tiptoes.

'It's good to see you, Jillian. I love the new hairstyle. Suits you.' She's always reminded me of a fairy, so sprightly and full of verve.

There's something utterly compelling about her, as if she's truly enchanted and not of this earth. When it comes to apothecary work, she's got a gift like Mom did. It's why they got on so well, each sharing their wisdom with one another.

'I'm so sorry about mamma bear. You know we tried everything, we truly did. It worked, for a long time too. We really thought we'd made a breakthrough.'

'Thank you for helping her. I know she was in the best hands.' I don't want Jillian to hold on to any worry over it.

'We did the best we could and we thought we'd proved all those fancy doctors wrong.' Mom wasn't against traditional medicine either, and she did go ahead with chemo in the beginning, until she felt like the apothecary medicines would work better for her needs longer term.

'You made the end of her life better, Jillian.'

She lifts a palm. 'I'm a little stuck on the *if onlys* but that's grief pulling me into the vortex. Grace helped me with a chakra cleanse and honestly, Luna, you need to try it. It's not going to make the pain go away but it'll make it easier to sit with. Want me to see if she's free today?' Oh how I love these women. There's a cure for everything, if only you have an open mind. Heartbroken? Have a chakra cleanse. Feeling sad? Sit in on a drum circle, to raise your vibration.

'Maybe later. This is my friend Gigi. Gi, this is Jillian who worked the apothecary with Mom.'

'Ooh, hey! I've heard all about you and your skills.'

'You have? That's plain old made my day. I've just started shiatsu. Why don't you come over for a session? I heard you girls had a long journey home and it'll free up those muscles that were cramped for so long on the plane.'

I remember Aunt Loui's warning about poking her soul clean out of her body. How can someone so small and delicate have enough strength to poke that hard? Perhaps Aunt Loui was exaggerating.

'I'd love to,' Gigi says, always willing to give new experiences a try. There's no way to warn her about her body being potentially separated from her soul without Jillian hearing so I leave it be, hoping it won't be as bad as Aunt Loui claimed.

'Great! And, Luna, you'll come another time?'

'Sure will.'

Jillian takes both my hands and looks deep into my eyes. 'Aunt Loui is sitting with Mom now and if you're ready tomorrow morning we'll perform the rituals?' When a woman dies here, the body is never left alone, right up until the burial. They take it in turns to sit in the candlelit room and sing, dance, pray, chant, whatever their beliefs are. I haven't been able to go see Mom yet. To make it real. Truthfully, I'm terrified I won't be able to physically let her go.

'I'll be ready.' My last moments with Mom will be special. I silently promise her that.

Jillian takes Gigi's hand and leads her away, talking all the while. Maybe Gigi will come back relaxed and refreshed while I find out more about this mystery man and why Mom left him so abruptly.

A few hours later, Gigi returns limping. Oh no. 'What happened?'

'For a woman who is the size of a twelve-year-old boy she sure is strong! I thought her fingers were going to go straight through my body. I mean, maybe they did! Am I bleeding?'

I twirl her around. 'Not that I can see. Maybe it's one of those pleasure and pain things.'

She groans. 'Yeah, yeah, release the muscles. I've heard it all already.'

'Can she give you something for the pain?'

'Wouldn't that defeat the purpose? Plus, I can't tell her it hurts. Well, she might have surmised by my screaming . . .'

'That was you? I thought someone was in labour.'

She grimaces. 'That was me. And it felt like I *was* in labour. Felt like the devil was being torn from me. It was like an exorcism.'

I can't help but laugh at Gigi's description. 'Oh dear. Well how about a nice refreshing lemon water?'

'You knew, didn't you? That's why you didn't go.'

I cast my eyes to the floor. 'Yes. Aunt Loui warned me. But thanks for taking one for the team. I owe you.'

'You do owe me. And yes to lemon water. Jillian said I need to flush the toxins out.'

I go pour Gigi a glass of water from the jug and cut up some fresh lemon slices.

Whilst I'm fixing the drinks a voice comes from the door. 'Hello! Luna it's me, Maggie.'

'Maggie come in!' I introduce Gigi.

We hug and Maggie swishes me from side to side like she used to when I was a child. She's been in my life the longest, meeting Mom way back when they were in the Thai commune. After Thailand she drifted to India for years until returning here and starting what would become known as the town of tiny homes.

'Sorry I missed your arrival last night. I was helping Lhama with his Buddhist retreat in the next town over.'

'I remember Lhama. How's he going?' Maggie practises Buddhism and has travelled the world hosting at various retreats. She connected with Lhama about a million years ago and somehow the two never seem to age, like they've found the fountain of youth.

'As cheeky as ever.' She grins. 'We were fasting to purify our bodies and clarify our minds. But of course, Lhama didn't tell me it was a fasting retreat until I got there because he knows how tedious I find those. What can I say, I'm a failed Buddhist most of the time because I live to eat and not eat to live.' She shrugs as if it's just a cross to bear. 'They weren't wrong about the four noble truths.' She's referring to Buddha's teachings. 'There's always suffering when you want to be enlightened.'

'For what it's worth you look purified *and* clarified,' I say smiling. It's so good to see her bright sunny face. Maggie is one of the good ones. Mom used to joke if she was any more laid-back, she'd be dead. Nothing bothers her, not even a fasting retreat. She truly is Buddhist, no matter how much she jokes about it, and it's made her the woman she is – which is this peaceful joy-spreading human whose goal in life is to connect to people on a deep spiritual level.

'If you're up for sound mediation, I'm hosting a small group later tonight. Might help relax you, clear the mind?'

'I'd love to. What about you, Gigi?'

Gigi's eyes go wide, and she holds her hands up. 'Not for me, thanks. I'm er . . . busy tonight.'

'Oh?' Maggie says. 'We can put it off until tomorrow?'

'Please don't change it on my account. You just go right ahead.'

Poor Gigi is still stiff and sore from the shiatzu massage. 'Are you *sure* you're busy tonight? Sound meditation is truly peaceful,' I say. 'A great way to unwind and just be.'

'Extremely busy. These romcoms won't read themselves unfortunately. I'll have to take your word for it.'

Maggie nods to Gigi with a smile and pulls me in for one last swishy side-to-side hug. 'OK, my darling, see you tonight. I'm going to go meditate with my Ruby for a bit.'

Dear Ruby,

Some days I think you're a product of my imagination. A dream woman, a figment. You walk this earth, you're real, you simply don't love me as I love you. I'm trying to understand. Unrequited love feels like a curse some days. Like a punishment. And for what? I wish I knew how your mind worked. Wish I knew why I can't let go of the thought of you. I wish I hadn't agreed to your idea. That's where this all fell apart.

Love always,
Giancarlo

What idea did he agree to? This seems more complex than a simple break-up. I'm desperate to know more. I'll have to ask Aunt Loui what she knows about this.

Chapter 6

With a heavy heart, I spend the morning helping Jillian cleanse and ritualise Mom. It's bittersweet seeing her like this. The animation in her face is gone; there's no light left. With tears streaming down my face, I hold her one last time and tell her what she means to me.

Thank you for loving me so fiercely.

I know Mom hears me, wherever she is. I will carry these last moments holding my mom's hand forever.

Once again, I'm grateful to these women for the love they show their dead. Like Mom made me promise all those years ago, I'm not supposed to run away from hard things. And as hard as it is to see her like this, there's such a desperate poignancy to it, and a sense of her life coming full circle, with me and her community of women right beside her for the end of the journey: dressing her for burial, performing sacred rituals and telling her how much I love her and will carry her in my heart for the rest of my days. When I let go of Mom's hand for the very last time, Jillian holds me tight and whispers a prayer in my name.

Why do you run away when things get hard, Ruby?

That one line is enough to cement this fact in my mind. That this, whatever it is, needs exploring. All those years ago when Mom moved to Missoula, I remember us sitting in the grassy meadow, the rocky mountains in the distance. She set me free, that day. And she insisted I make her a promise: that I'd never run from hard things because running never solves anything. And here is a sentence from some man that shows she did just that. What was hard? Why did she run?

As evening falls, we're all sitting around the bonfire. The spring days are warm here but as night comes it cools.

Sitting in a circle around the flames, it feels like Mom is still here, like she's just stepped out to replenish her tea.

It's easier to pretend I'm here waiting for her. The group dynamic in the town of tiny homes has shifted. There's not as much laughter and people talk quietly as if a sudden burst of boisterous conversation would be inappropriate.

If Mom were here she'd admonish them and explain life is for living and laughter, and good conversations are crucial especially when you're grieving. But I'm not my mom. Not as vivacious as her, so I stay silent and feel cocooned by their love and the way they show it, through little homemade gifts of food and tight hugs, the willingness to listen if I need to talk.

The sound meditation class the previous night was so relaxing, I almost felt back to myself and centred, but as this next day has turned into night once more, that sense has vanished. It's to be expected. This *will* hurt and I need to sit with the pain and feel it.

Gigi stares off into the distance, her blinks getting longer by the minute. 'Nearly bedtime for you?' I ask.

She lets out a sort of *huh . . . mumph?*

'Did you eat one of Francine's brownies or something?' I forgot to warn Gigi that they're not your average brownie, but Francine's answer to everything. Can't sleep? Have a brownie. Sore back? Have a brownie.

38

'What? No,' she says sleepily. 'I think it's the shiatsu. Yeah, the exorcism hurt at the time, but now I feel almost boneless. If I was any more tranquil, I'd be liquid. She's got magic hands, that Jillian.'

My eyebrows shoot up. 'Well, you see? And there you were complaining about it.'

'Right. So, what exactly is in the brownies?'

'Let's just say they're "medicinal" and leave it at that.'

She laughs. 'Noted.'

Aunt Loui joins us and pulls up a chair next to me. 'You did good today, Luna.'

'As sad as it was, I'll never forget how I felt in that moment.' It had been a such a pure spiritual experience, with singing and keening and smiles and tears as we paid homage to my mom as we prepared her body to become one with the earth once more ahead of the funeral.

These women teach me there's beauty everywhere, even in death.

'I'm on autopilot now but maybe I'm just spent.' The way I miss Mom is so fierce, it's as though every cell in my body feels the shock. The deep loss.

'Grief is like that.' She takes a swill of kombucha, the scent of ginger perfuming the air between us. 'You're like a robot going through the motions, trying to think of every little thing that needs doing and all the people you need to tell, commiserate with, reassure. Soon it'll be over and you'll fall into a bit of a void. But that's where the true healing starts, baby girl, so I don't want you to be scared of it.'

Aunt Loui is a great truth teller, so I know she's probably right. This waiting, this pause feels like treading water, holding myself tight, holding myself together and waiting for the inevitable so I can fall apart in private later. But the thing is, this community won't let me fall apart. It won't let me do this alone, and I thank my lucky stars that Mom chose this life for us. Even without her, and the gaping yawning chasm she's left, there will be others who help slowly fill that void. It'll never be the same, but I'll be surrounded by love.

Which makes the next part hard. Because I don't want to stay here. Not when there's the mystery of the letters calling my name. Will Aunt Loui understand my reasons for acting on a whim? Acting so rashly based on nothing more than a feeling? Even I question myself, until the next time I hold those letters full of beautiful penmanship and feel them pulse, almost as if they're alive and sending me a message.

I scooch closer. 'Aunt Loui, I found some letters.' I survey her face, but she doesn't react. She does have a good poker face. I've lost money to her on several occasions, playing cards under the moonlight.

'Letters?'

'You don't know about the letters?'

She purses her lips, as if thinking. 'I can't say until you give me some more information. Letters from who?'

'A man named Giancarlo.'

She contemplates it. 'Never heard of a Giancarlo. Why? What are the letters about?'

'He mentions my mom leaving because she didn't want her wings clipped, didn't want to be trapped. He's in Italy, but I don't know where. I get the feeling he's tied to our Venice trip, all that time ago. But I don't know for sure. When I hold the letters, I have this overwhelming sense I need to act on them. Untangle the nebulous thread that lies within.' I let out a strangled laugh. It sounds odd, even to me. 'Why didn't she stay with him? She didn't want to stay in one place because she had the heart of a nomad, so it could be that. I need to know why, and who this guy Giancarlo is. What their relationship was like.' I don't mention the promise I made to Mom, not to run away from hard things, but it hums inside of me.

'If you feel this needs to be explored, then why not? I trust in you, Luna, and if there's something you're sensing with all this,

40

then you know you have to follow that path and see where it leads.' Aunt Loui stares into the fire as if she's lost in thought. She doesn't speak for an age. 'Makes me wonder too. I haven't heard of a guy called Giancarlo. Ruby always had her secrets though – you know as well as me there were times she went to another place inside her own mind and everyone else was locked out. She always came out of those funks eventually, and she was best left alone to deal with them in her own way . . .' Her words trail off.

She's right. Mom had these moods that would catapult her to great heights and just as quickly cause her smile to fade and she'd hide herself away. These spells didn't last long. She'd use her apothecary of potions and be back with us in her own time. We learned to recognise the signs and leave her be, as requested. Are those moods connected to this?

Aunt Loui taps my knee. 'And I'm guessing you don't think it's just some old love letters from a holiday fling then?'

I shake my head. 'There are so many letters. By the sounds of it, she wrote back many times too. There's more to this. Or it could be me holding on tight to some kind of hope, something that will bring me close to her again – but I don't rightly know.' I'm not one to doubt myself when I get these premonitions. Usually, I have blind faith that if I listen hard enough I'll be guided the right way, but everything feels up in the air since Mom left. And doubt is always right behind me.

Aunt Loui exhales a long breath. 'Baby girl, you know what you have to do, right?'

My heart thrums at the thought. Trust Aunty Loui to be so prescient. She's an extension of my mom, another mother really, and I'm so lucky to have her when the loss I face is so great. She knows my heart. She knows I have so many questions and that for me, as much as a gift as Mom claimed I was, I needed more than the brush-off I always got about this one important thing. Could this be linked to me? Maybe. Maybe not.

41

'I have to go to Italy and find him. There are hundreds more letters. If I pore through them maybe there'll be a clue.'

'Promise me one thing, you'll come back and visit when you've found what you're searching for. That you won't forget your family here?' Her strong voice breaks and I know she needs me as much as I need her.

'I might flitter here and there but I'll always come back, Aunt Loui.' A soft landing into Aunt Loui's arms gives me the courage to go. If I didn't have her to come running back to, I don't know if I'd be brave enough. What if this Giancarlo *is* someone best avoided? My mother didn't have a mean bone in her body, yet she was furtive at times. 'Part of me wonders if Mom left those letters knowing I'd find them.'

'Could be. Ruby was a wily one when she needed to be.'

I exhale all the angst. 'First, we've got the funeral, then I'll do some research and see if I can find out where this guy is and if so see about visiting Italy.' I've got a small amount left in my emergency fund but it might not be enough.

It's best to put space between me and the town of tiny homes while it's still so raw and immediate. I'm hoping this'll be the distraction I need to cope with the hard road ahead.

'Your mom left you some money, you know. It's not a lot, but it'll help tide you over.'

'She did?' Mom never had a lot, just like me. We had enough to get by but usually there wasn't any surplus, and I'd promised Aunt Loui I'd start an emergency account, in case I ever needed to get home.

'I can't help but feel she wanted me to follow this trail . . .'

'Sure, seems that way now, doesn't it, baby girl?' Aunt Loui, who's always so wise, seems to think the same way I do. Did Mom know I'd find the letters and then want to explore the mystery? And leave me some money to assist? Is that what she wanted to tell me when I landed in Thailand? Maybe Mom knew all along that this would be the perfect tonic to help heal my broken heart . . .

Dear Ruby,

Letting go is the hardest part. I don't even think I can let you go, at least not the memory of you. Our letters are my life blood but they also set me back for days. I want to tell you not to write but silence would be worse. I can't sever that connection. I don't know how to say goodbye to you.

All my love,

Giancarlo

Inside the temple where I usually partake in sound meditation and yoga, I step up to the pulpit to speak. My hands shake; my heart races. I take a centring breath and remember the strong, brave woman who gave me life.

I clear my throat and focus on the assembled crowd. They give me encouraging smiles. 'It feels like a lifetime ago I got the call from Aunt Loui about Mom. Life as I knew it got flipped upside down. I felt adrift, like my anchor to the world had snapped clean off and I was lost at sea.

'But I should have known better. Mom would never leave me alone. Never leave me lonely. While my heart aches for her and the space she leaves behind, she left me with a roomful of mothers. Women who will always strive to lift me up and love me. Help me when I fall. In the days leading me to here, I spent a lot of time thinking about Mom's motivations. Mom lived a life less ordinary, and she did it on her terms. Always. She did it for me. For us. For a way of life that so many try to tarnish, to pull apart.

'So why did she go against the tide? It can't have been easy, a single mother travelling the globe searching for her own version of nirvana. Not many people can say they experienced a hundred different lives in one lifetime, but that's what she did. Firstly, as an adventurer, and then healer, painter, spiritualist, creative, friend and mother.

'She picked tropical fruit in balmy Thailand and grew to love their customs, their music, the language. I'll never forget her at

43

the fish markets, haggling away in Thai like she was a local. In Indonesia she studied Hinduism and learned how to make batik prints. She fell in love with a temple monkey who stole her shoes. There was a trip to Cambodia where she volunteered at a refuge that helped children hurt by landmines. She never showed them her sadness, but she'd come home and weep for them at night – that place and so many others indelibly changed her. In each new city, there was a new experience, new people to love, new faces to hold on to.

'Mom might have only had fifty-eight years earthside, but her human experience was nothing short of extraordinary. When the hurt feels too heavy, and the pain makes tears well, I'm going to remember her as she was: a gutsy spirit who valued the women in her life above all else. Who valued friendship and the bonds that tie us together. She leaves behind her greatest legacy, the community I have with you, and I am truly grateful for that.

'I'll miss you, Mom. Thanks for loving me.'

There's a mixture of tears and laughter as the montage of photos of Mom plays across the big screen to her favourite *luk thung* music. Love swells up inside as the photographic memories flip past. She and Aunt Loui chained to a big old cypress tree that they were adamant about saving, a fierce determination in their eyes. Mom and Jillian, faces illuminated by candlelight as they mixed their many potions. In each picture Mom is with a woman who lifted her up, added value to her short life. There's one of Mom in Venice, a book held tight to her chest. I can't remember what she'd been reading. Ruby Tuesday plays loudly from the speakers, and Aunt Loui looks up, as if she can feel Mom here.

Later that night, body running on empty, I read by filmy light in the loft so I don't disturb a softly snoring Gigi, who sleeps on the pull-out sofa below. My eyelids are heavy after reading so many of the love letters. I'm about to call it a night when I spot something.

This bookshop on the canal of Venice was once my dream, but without you, it seems so hollow. I find customers tedious. Their requests for romance novels a stab to the heart. When you worked here, every day was glorious. Reading poetry together by the softly lapping water, as you expounded about why you were so moved. I could have listened to you all day, even when time lost all meaning, or you spoke too fast for me to untangle your English words.

I'm stuck here though, as my parents rely on whatever income this place produces, and I can't break their hearts and leave to meet you. And, of course, a family needs stability so I have to be the one to provide that. And truthfully, I love my new role. But we're only half a family without you.

My hands shake as I drop the letter and grab my phone to open Google and search for bookshops on the canal in Venice. Only one pops up. A second-hand bookshop called *La Librería sul Canale*.

I sift through various sites, trying to find a face, a name, but nothing comes up. There's a few blog posts about a wonderful quirky second-hand bookshop on the banks of the canal in the San Polo district. I scour the posts quickly and learn that the Canale Bookshop is a jumble of books in no particular order and has many languages and genres on offer but specialises in English books catering to the many tourists who visit Venice. There are photographs of what looks to be one of the world's most unique bookshops. One blogger has pictures as she arrives by gondola. It's feels like a dream for a bookworm like me, and once again it feels like fate has intervened and put me on the right path. Books have always been my salvation. For the first time that day, I'm renewed with a sense of purpose. And this strange compelling feeling. *Hope.*

I stash the letters aside for the night and switch off the light. It's Gigi's birthday tomorrow. She hasn't mentioned it because she doesn't want to intrude on my grieving. That's the mark of the kind of person she is. But there's no chance of visiting the town of tiny homes and not celebrating another trip around the sun in true communal style. Aunt Loui and I have been making secret plans, so Gigi will experience a birthday she'll never forget. And it will all start with a refreshing mineral mud bath and progress from there.

Chapter 7

Gigi and I stumble from the boat, our top-heavy backpacks making us teeter like turtles at risk of tipping over. We thank the driver and pause on a cobblestoned road in the lagoon city. I blink back tears at the memory of Mom and I taking this trip long ago. Did she bring me here to meet Giancarlo then change her mind? Is that why we left in a hurry, our plans cancelled like a broken promise?

Mom would be admonishing me for being lost in memories when I have this vibrant city in front of me. Venice is like no other place in the world. The lover Casanova lived here. It's a city of over four hundred bridges with no cars: rush hour is foot traffic or water taxis. While it's slightly jarring not having the usual beeps and groans of car noise, it's replaced with a sort of water theatre. Gondoliers shout to one another across the canal, the lapping of water accompanying their back-and-forth banter. Water taxis zoom in and deposit goggle-eyed tourists. Sunlight gleams from the gold on ornate buildings that are so beautiful it's almost hard to believe they're real. People sit on balconies, sipping wine and eating cheese as their freshly washed linen blows in the breeze beside them. The place is so *alive* it hums.

Another water taxi arrives at the dock, and people spill out.

It's a hub of activity and for a moment I'm lost watching it all unfold.

'We better get out of the way!' Gigi says as a little boy runs over her toes with his tiny suitcase on wheels.

We press ourselves hard against the cool stone of a building as the newly arrived tourists edge past wearing determined faces as if they're on the clock, not like me and Gigi who spent too long revelling in the vista and are now stuck as the queue of people hurry past.

A guy with a head full of messy curls is the last to pass, so we patiently wait for him. He's lost in a book; he's too far away for me to tell if it's a guidebook or a novel, but there's something magnetising about a person who is too absorbed by words to pay attention to the beauty and bedlam surrounding him. As if he's in his own little bubble and the world does not exist as we know it.

As he approaches, I try to make out the title of the book he holds aloft, when he catches me staring. My breath catches at being caught being so overt, and I quickly look the other way. In my haste to appear nonchalant, I hoist my backpack and hear an *oomph!*

I turn to see where the noise is coming from and see the messy-haired guy on the ground. Did I do that? I forget how big my backpack is, sometimes! 'Are you OK?' I ask, reaching out a hand to help him up. His hand is warm, and I get the strangest spark when our skin meets. A momentary vision but it's gone before I can grasp it. His book lies splayed and drenched in a puddle left from the water taxi. 'Oh no, your book!' *Into the Wild* by Jon Krakauer. A great read – who can forget Alexander Supertramp! I bend to retrieve it but it's no use – the pages are soaked and stick together as one. Not salvageable.

'It's OK,' he says, and takes the book from my hands.

'It's really not. I'm so sorry. I can try and find a replacement for you?'

He checks his watch as if he's got somewhere to be. 'No need. I can find another.' And with that, he continues past, surreptitiously wiping the pages of his book on his jeans as he goes.

'I just killed a book!' I'm quite grieved by it. There he'd been, so wrapped up in the story until I sideswiped him with my ridiculously large backpack. It's lucky he didn't end up in the canal. It would be just my luck he'd then get run over by a water taxi or something.

'You . . . what?' Gigi asks, only half listening. Her gaze is locked on a gelato place that's doing a roaring trade in the bright sunny day.

'You didn't see him?'

'Who?'

'That guy with the messy bed head, curls hanging over one eye, as he shuffled along reading his book as if he was the last human on earth?'

She laughs and puts a hand to my forehead. 'Are you feverish? Sounds like you're describing your perfect man, but alas I did not see such a dreamboat or I would have remembered it.'

I shake my head. 'Poor guy. Now he'll never find out what happens in *Into the Wild*.'

'Yeah, tragic. Right, so let's move before the next water taxi arrives. I'm downright salivating over that gelato over there.'

While dodging slow-walking tourists with cameras slung around necks, and guidebooks in hand, I take my phone from my pocket and try and find free Wi-Fi as I shuffle behind Gigi who is keeping up a one-way conversation about how pretty the ancient town is and all the foodie delights that are on offer.

I connect to the Wi-Fi of an adjacent café. 'Wait, Gigi,' I say, leaning against the sun-warmed stone wall, as if I'm a tourist checking her phone and not someone stealing their internet without the courtesy of even buying an espresso. 'I've got a couple of bars of reception here.' I type the hostel address into maps and take screenshots of the directions. We're not too far, but all the twists and turns and many waterways make it hard to gauge. We need to check in and dump our stuff before it gets dark. I can't imagine trying to acclimatise under the moonlight, especially with all these alleyways that are in no discernible order. While I've been here before with Mom, it was only for a few days before she pulled the pin and we left almost as quickly as we came, so nothing much looks familiar to me.

'OK,' I say. 'According to Google Maps we're about ten minutes away.'

'Let's do it. I'm going to need me some watermelon gelato in my life, stat. Let's stay here forever – I'm already in love.'

I smile. Gigi has come to a culinary paradise, and I know she'll spend many a day eating her body weight in delicious creamy, garlicky foods while I . . . do whatever it is I need to do.

We zigzag, getting lost like Alice down the rabbit hole until we finally see a sign advertising the hostel. There's a balcony filled with young travellers, drinking wine and smoking cigarettes.

'Here we are . . .'

We check in and are shown to a female dorm room. The floor is a mess of women's clothes and shoes. Backpacks and suitcases are stuffed under the bottom bunks. The air reeks of cheap perfume and cigarette smoke. We've been in worse places though. And it suits our budget.

'Rock paper scissors for the top bunk?' Gigi says.

'What are you, like twelve?' I tease but do it anyway. The top bunk is always better as it feels like there's more distance between you and all the snoring and night-time sounds that are rife in a dorm room.

Gigi wins the first round. 'Best out of three.' I win the second and third.

'Dammit.' She grins. 'Like the fairy tale, you get to be the princess sleeping on the pea, up high while I'm kept below with the peasants.'

I laugh. 'Not for long, I hope.'

'Yeah, I hope so too. This mess is not exactly giving me namaste vibes.' Gigi is likely to gather the women who sleep here and appeal to them to clean up their living quarters. She likes things orderly and neat. As you can imagine, some people don't like being told what to do but Gigi has a canny charm and usually gets her way. Our plan is to find jobs and then a cheap apartment, or flat-share if the prospects look good.

'Do you think our stuff is safe here?' Her forehead wrinkles.

'Take your iPad just in case.' Gigi's whole life is on that iPad. She's already had one stolen once at Bondi beach, where we'd left our belongings under a towel and went for a frolic in the water. A rookie mistake – we should have known better. Beaches are easy pickings for thieves.

Once, I had a romcom stolen in Corsica, and I'm still bummed about it. Who'd steal a well-thumbed second-hand novel and prevent me from knowing if the enemies soon turned to lovers? It's not as expensive as losing an iPad but I can't remember the title of the book to rebuy it, so it will haunt me forever.

'You're thinking about that bloody book you lost again, aren't you?' Gigi gives me the side-eye.

'Maybe.' I laugh. 'It plagues me, Gi. *Plagues* me. I'll look for that book for the rest of my life until I find it. It had a blue cover with a . . .'

'Stop, I'm not doing this again. You and your books! Don't they all end up the same, anyway? The guy gets the girl and everyone lives happily ever after?'

I make a show of rolling my eyes. 'It's about the *journey*, Gigi. And if you continue talking in such a way, I'm going to be forced to give you the silent treatment until you admit romance novels are a guide to life and not just a way to pass the time.'

She grabs her heart theatrically. 'Please don't. I will never speak harshly about happy ever afters again. It's the jet lag. It's the low blood sugar because I'm hangry. You know I love your romcoms.' We burst out laughing. In truth, I catch Gigi stealing

51

my books all the time, but she pretends romance isn't her thing so she can uphold her reputation as an ice maiden who only reads true crime and then sleeps soundly.

How she can devour such a thing and then fall into a deep slumber is beyond me. Especially when we were in the Australian outback and Gigi insisted that we watch a serial killer movie called *Wolf Creek*. She backed that up with a non-fiction book about murders that happened in the same area and told me every gritty detail. Let's just say, I kept my sleeping for the daytime, when Gigi drove Rusty and night-time was spent clutching my blanket and staring out into the black void hoping no one was out there.

We take a few things from our backpacks and then stuff them hard under the bed and pull the blanket down to cover them. It's always good practice to try and hide your things as best as possible in a share scenario like this, but if a thief is in the midst, there's not much you can do about it. I take the love letters with me; they're not replaceable and I'd be devastated if they went missing.

'So where to now?' I ask, itching the back of my neck.

Gigi ties her long blonde curls into a loose ponytail. 'Surely we have to do a reconnaissance of the bookshop?'

'Yes, seems like the best course of action.' I've spent the last couple of weeks planning this trip until it's consumed my every waking thought. March soon drifted into April and here we are. No one tells you when you grieve you sometimes lose days sleeping. It's like my body just gave up and I had to retreat. I'm lucky to have had that time, to have been coddled and cuddled by so many women while the healing process began.

I check the time; it's almost eight p.m. Would the bookshop still be open on a Wednesday night? Probably not. Which makes it the perfect time to wander past and acquaint myself with the place where Giancarlo penned those love letters to my mom. We head outside but I stop short once we hit the cobblestoned street.

'What if he's there?' I need to prepare myself for any scenario and not blurt out anything because I'm nervous.

'Then I'll go in, buy a book and have a chat, see what vibe I get from him and report back to you.'

I gulp at the thought. 'OK. What will you say?'

'I'll say how lovely the spring weather is, and can he recommend a book. What else is there to say?'

I nod, distracted. Now that I'm here I'm not so sure.

'What if he's *not* here? What if he sold up and moved to Mexico or something?' The thought is a worrying one. Perhaps, I should have called first and pretended to be looking for a book.

'Then we move to Plan B. And who doesn't love Mexican food?'

I smile. Gigi would go to the ends of the earth for me, so I relax into the support.

It's hard to know exactly what the game plan will be though, because I don't really know anything about this guy. What if he's married and has a family? He might not appreciate a stranger appearing with a handful of letters from an old flame. This needs to be handled carefully.

Gigi must sense my hesitation continues. 'Hey, *hey*, Luna.' She rubs my arms. 'We're just going to walk past. If it's open I'll step in, and that's all. OK? We can take this as slowly as you want.'

'OK.'

'OK, good.'

Still my feet remain firmly planted. 'Mom always said we didn't need anyone; we had each other. And we had our community. But just who was this guy to her? What if it blows up in my face?'

'And what if it doesn't?'

I nod. 'There's so much mystery about this and I want to know why. None of it makes sense. And I guess I'm saying if this backfires, I'm concerned that another knock to my psyche will push me over the edge. If only I had a bit more information, something, anything to go by that shows me that my mom would approve of me doing this.'

'Your mom made you promise you wouldn't run away from hard things. Maybe this is that hard thing?'

Goose bumps break out over my skin. 'Yes, Gigi, that's exactly what I've been thinking. I'm going from what the hell am I doing – to this needs to be solved. I just wish I knew a little more information. Is this a wild goose chase?'

'It's an adventure!' She pulls me in for a hug. 'Your feelings about this muddle are valid. You're just going to have to roll with them.'

'OK.' I consider the worst possible scenario. Not finding any answers. And if so, well I'll still be where I'm at now. 'It's that last phone call with Mom that bothers me.'

'Because she wanted to tell you something?'

I nod. 'There was . . . an urgency in her voice but I ended the call abruptly. I don't think I'll ever forgive myself for that.'

'Luna, it's not as if you had a choice. You were told by the customs official to hang up the phone that very second.'

My mind goes back to that day, the sweltering heat, the bustle of customs, being yelled at, my phone snatched from my hand because I hadn't realised what he meant. 'But I should have called her straight back.' By then we were trying to work out how to get to Ko Pha Ngan island by boat and after that looking for accommodation. Mom's call slipped from my mind as jet lag caught up with me and I slept, ahead of the full moon party the following day.

'Your mom said she'd call you back. So don't do that, Luna. Don't play the blame game with yourself.'

I wish I'd stopped in that moment and seen it for what it was. I wish so many things. 'OK, it's time for an energy change or I'll be stuck on this loop forever.'

'The macarena?'

I laugh in spite of it all. Usually, I do an aura cleanse or meditation when I'm feeling zapped but since Gigi came along somehow that's morphed into doing a silly dance like the YMCA or the Time Warp, which has been strangely effective.

'The Macarena is new, but why not?'

She finds the song on YouTube and plays it out loud; we draw the eyes of many a passer-by as we do the moves to the Macarena. Gigi jiggles and dances as if her life depends on it, and it's hard not to follow suit and be totally present in the moment. When the song draws to a close we're out of breath and smiling and have managed to draw a small crowd.

'They think we're busking,' she whispers, giggling as a few people throw coins at our feet. We dash off in fits of laughter before we're arrested for it or something wild. As always when Gigi suggests a dance-off, my mood lifts and I let all the angst drift away like so much fairy dust.

We head to the bookshop, twisting and turning through various alleys and over small Venetian bridges. We turn yet another corner, and it comes into view. If you didn't know it was here, you'd never find it.

'Right, I'll drop a pin so I know how to find this place again,' Gigi says. There's a guy obstructing the frontage. He types something on his phone and then turns to us, still tapping away. His messy curls fall over his face and I wonder how he can see what he's doing. When he glances up, my breath catches. It's the guy from the dock, whose book I drowned. Is he here looking for a new one? Guilt rushes at me, and I only wish I had a novel to give him in lieu. Before I can say anything, he spins the other way and walks deeper into the dark laneway.

'That was him!' I whisper to Gigi who is still chin down, lost in her phone.

'Who?'

'The guy from earlier today with the floppy hair!'

'I missed the dreamboat again?' She shakes her phone as if it's the cause for all her troubles.

'Dreamboat? Not exactly! He must've come here looking for a replacement for the book that was tragically murdered.'

'Bookworms, eh? Lucky it wasn't a Kindle.'

'Yeah, lucky.' He might not have been so kind if it was.

'Wow, look at this place . . .' Gigi says, awe in her voice.

A yellowed lamp shines down over the façade.

There are dusty arched windows at the front with books stacked atop one another. They're weathered from sunshine, faded and cobwebby as if they've been there for aeons. A red and white striped awning is concertinaed open but the middle droops down as if it's tired. A sign saying *La Libreria sul Canale* creaks backwards and forwards in the breeze. The bookshop has almost an abandoned feel to it, as if the owner just got up and left one day.

I have the oddest sensation, as if time has truly stopped here and nothing has moved on since that very moment. Was it when my mother left? Is it possible these displays have been here all that time? The shop is already shuttered up for the night, which gives me ample time to gauge the surroundings and have a moment soaking up the space to see what I can intuit.

My mom worked in this very shop, walked on these cobblestones beneath my very feet. She and Giancarlo fell in love here. And then something happened that drove them apart. I touch the cool stone wall and feel the life of the books that pulse inside. Crazy, I know, but books have their own life-force, like a hum, a purr, that most people can't discern. It's an almost imperceptible vibration that makes a person stop and pick up a book. Did my mom feel the energy of this bookshop too? While it has a neglected air, inside is alive; it practically whirrs right through to the stone outside.

'It looks like it's been closed for a hundred years!' Gigi says. 'Let me check the opening hours.' She approaches a sign on the door. It's then I notice a handwritten sign affixed to the window. I'd recognise that penmanship anywhere. It's exactly the same as the letters. The sign is written in Italian, but I can guess at its meaning.

'Gigi, look!' I point to the words. 'Is that a job opening?'

'I have no idea.' She takes a photo of it. 'Let's go find a restaurant for dinner and get on Wi-Fi to find out. That could very well be your way in.'

'I was thinking the same! I can get a job there and see what Giancarlo's like. Wouldn't that be a much easier way to go about things? The bookshop sells mainly English books and caters to a large number of English-speaking tourists so I don't think the language barrier will be an issue.' I'd get a feel for the guy and decide whether to share the letters and ask about what Mom left behind in Venice. Why she made me promise not to run away from hard things, when she had so clearly done exactly that. 'We have to be open to the possibility she cut him out of her life for a very good reason. After all, he didn't exactly come looking for her either, right? He might have penned some letters, but that's it.'

'Yeah, but he had his reasons. Didn't he say he was looking after his parents?'

'He took over the bookshop from them. But maybe there was some pressure there.'

'When all we've got is the letters from his point of view to go on, we don't really know for sure. Let's find a place for dinner and work out what this sign says.'

57

Chapter 8

We find a place called *Nonna's Trattoria*. It's bustling with formal-attired waitstaff and loud with the sounds of diners chatting and laughing away as cutlery clinks on plates and the odd prosecco cork pops and is met with fanfare. It's got a rustic family feel about it, as if we truly are at someone's grandma's house, surrounded by a boisterous extended family. We're shown to a table by a person who looks like a nonna. She's sprightly despite her advancing years and we have to dash to keep up with her as she guides us to a table. She speaks in rapid-fire Italian, so I mumble *sì, sì*, in the hopes it was a yes-no question before she dashes off to greet a new wave of patrons.

I really must try and pick up some of the language while I'm here. It's one of the best parts of exploring a new place, trying to learn the words, their customs. Some of the best moments I've had roaming are when I've used the wrong word in the wrong context and had people doubled over laughing while I'm still trying to pinpoint what I got wrong.

'I hope I'm as nimble at that age,' Gigi says watching Nonna bustle around on high heels as if she's floating on air.

We're momentarily distracted watching the theatre of the trattoria before Gigi motions to a waiter. 'Excuse me, would you mind translating this for us?' She pulls out her phone and shows him the picture of the sign in the window at the bookshop. Instead of focusing on the phone Gigi holds aloft, he stares at me. I blush under his gaze, unsure as to why he's so overt about it.

Gigi wiggles the phone in front of his face to get his attention. He drags his gaze from mine and takes the phone. 'It says they're looking for a staff member. Thirty hours per week, for the right applicant. Must speak English. Enquire within.'

'Perfect!' she says and then looks from him to me with an eyebrow raise. She tries to ease the phone from his hand but he's too distracted to notice. Does he recognise me somehow? My hands shake as I run a hand through my hair. For a moment, I'm lost in the waiter's gaze, in his unfathomable brown eyes. There's some connection, some link, I'm sure of it, like he's trying to gauge where he knows me from. Am I linked to Venice somehow? At times like this it really feels like it.

Gigi interrupts. 'Could we have some menus, maybe? The wine list?'

He blushes. '. . . *Sì, sì.* I won't be a moment.' He strides off into the busy trattoria.

'Oh my God!' Gigi says. 'What the hell was that?'

'He recognised me!'

Her eyes go wide. 'Yes, he sure did! Cupid sent that dart straight into that poor fool's chest! I didn't know love heart eyes were a real thing. He's gorgeous, Luna. You might just have found yourself a husband.'

'What?'

'What *what*?' Her eyebrows pull together. 'Is it the husband thing? I know you're wild and free, but I'm just saying, hot Italians with moody eyes and sultry lips don't come along twice in a lifetime, surely? It might be worth matrimony is all I'm saying. That guy is hot, hot, hot!'

I try to unscramble her words. 'You think he's interested in me?'

She groans. 'I don't think, *I know*! Jeez, Luna, every fish in the sea felt that jolt. The poor guy couldn't form words! Talk about lovestruck. Did you not notice?' Concern rushes across her features, though it appears we're reading this situation completely differently.

'Shush,' I say. 'He's coming back.'

The waiter seems to have gathered his wits and smiles as he hands us the menus. Gigi has pegged this all wrong.

'What can you recommend?' Gigi says, confidently, as if we eat at these types of places every day, not once in a blue moon.

He rattles off some dishes in Italian and I take a moment to survey him under my lashes. His voice is velvety. The beautiful poetry of the Italian language rolls off his tongue and I'm momentarily distracted by it. I want to tell him to keep talking, let those silky words slide on out, but of course I don't. It's not that I'm keen on the guy, it's that I love the sound of foreign words, all jumbled up in a sentence.

Besides, I'm not going to let myself be distracted, no matter how sultry his lips are. And as far as lips go he has the perfect men's pout, the kissable type you usually find on movie stars. But I'm not looking. I don't care. I'm here for the food.

'I'll have the gnocchi funghi,' I say with a neutral smile and hand the menu back.

'Same,' says Gigi. 'And a bottle of chianti. Is that OK with you, Luna?'

I nod. We're not big drinkers, but we have a tradition that on the first night in a new town we splurge on a fancy dinner with wine before we're back to our frugal ways.

'*Perfetto. Perfetto.*' He dashes off again.

Gigi pretends to fan herself. 'Is it hot in here, or what?'

I roll my eyes heavenward. 'Oh stop. You're hamming this up.' Truthfully, alongside Gigi with her long blonde California curls and beach body, I pale in comparison. I'm still a little wary of trusting my heart to anyone at the moment. 'It's not that he's interested in me in that way; it's something else. Do you think I look familiar to him, that he's wondering who I remind him of?

There's a whole untold story about my mom in Venice, and I'm starting to wonder if I'm tied to it somehow.'

She considers it. 'The guy looked at you like he was hit with a thunderbolt! You don't see that kind of thing very often, so it stands out when it *does* happen. You're looking for signs and symbols like you always do, which is fair, but in this instance it was a pure zap of longing, written all over his very symmetrical features.'

'Maybe I am looking for things that aren't there.'

'Lusty Pants here took one glance at you and boom – love at first sight!' Gigi cries. 'I can see how this is going to go – third wheel Gigi, that's going to be my new moniker. *If* you give love a chance.'

I gaze at Gigi who seems stuck on this crazy notion. 'Lusty Pants? Oh please. You're the last person who believes in love. You've burned many a hopeful with one nuclear glare.'

She flicks her hair over a shoulder. 'True. But that's because I haven't yet met the person who sets my world on fire. I'm not going to waste one moment of angst on someone who doesn't. I'll know when I find the one, and we'll settle down and have bambinos as soon as possible.'

I cock my head. 'OK, so why do the same rules not apply to me?'

'Ahem, did that Italian god not set your heart aflutter? That scorched gaze of his didn't melt your icy heart? Are you sure?'

'My icy heart? Spoken by the queen of ice herself.' I laugh at her dramatics. It's so out of character for her to push romance on me. I sense she thinks it'll take my mind off my grief. But it won't. 'Look, he's a very attractive guy, in a city full of very attractive guys. So what?' To be honest, he's downright heart-stopping but eh, who cares? I prefer a more bedraggled guy. Someone not caught up on aesthetics. Theirs or mine. I'm scruffy too, most of the time. Roaming isn't conducive to fine clothes and immaculate hair and make-up. And I couldn't be bothered with such a thing, even if I lived in one place.

Gigi lets out a lengthy sigh as though I've disappointed her. 'I see what you're doing, you know.'

I raise a brow. 'Oh, yeah?'

'This is your classic case of avoidance. But you can't fool me, Luna Hart. All your woo-woo has rubbed off on me, therefore I feel obliged to inform you that guy has raised your vibration and your interest is piqued.'

I shake my head. She really has lost the plot. 'Raised my vibration?'

'Yes, you feel lighter, happier because your soul recognises his, but you're too stubborn to admit it because you think it'll get in the way of solving the mystery of the letters.'

'What did you do with my friend, Gigi? Who even are you?'

'Deflecting, case in point.'

'Now you're a psychologist too? Are there any limits to your talent?'

'Still deflecting, attempting humour.'

'Make it stop.'

'Avoidance.'

I throw my linen napkin at her but it falls uselessly on the table between us, so close to the candle that I'm forced to snatch it back. The waiter arrives with a bottle of chianti. He opens it and pours, all the while keeping a firm gaze on me. Now this just feels weird because Gigi has trumped it up so much. What's with the stare-down? 'What's your name?' she asks him, smiling coyly like a cat playing with a mouse. I kick her foot under the table for good measure.

'You little . . . !'

'Oops, sorry.' I give her the same coy smile insinuating two can play at this game.

'I'm Sebastiano. What are your names?' He's so formal it's hard to believe all the mumbo-jumbo Gigi is sprouting about raised vibrations and wedlock and just plain nonsense.

'I'm Gigi and this . . .' she does jazz hands – for crying out loud '. . . is Luna. We've just arrived in Venice and don't know the area all that well. We could use a tour guide . . .' She leaves the words hanging. I go to kick her again but the wily fox has moved her feet in anticipation of another attack.

'I'd love to show you around, Luna.' The full force of his gaze is on me again and it's quite disarming, like being under a spotlight. I feel exposed somehow. 'And you too, Gigi,' he quickly adds. 'I'm free tomorrow morning?'

'Perfect.'

I go to disagree. I need to get to the bookshop early. I want to apply for that job before anyone else gets hired and scuppers my plan. Who needs a man in the mix when all this is playing out? 'Gigi, I want to . . .'

'I know, you want the job. Perhaps, Sebastiano can escort you to *La Libreria sul Canale* and introduce you? Do you happen to know the owner, Sebastiano?'

He does a formal little bow that's really quite charming. 'I'd love to escort you to the bookshop. And *sì*, I know the owner Giancarlo. He dines here occasionally. I can definitely introduce you, Luna, if you'd like?'

I clear my throat. 'Um, yeah that would be nice, thanks.' I'm not sure if I need an introduction, but I can't see how to back out of it now that Gigi has orchestrated a morning with Sebastiano. Nerves flutter at the thought, reminding me we know virtually nothing about Giancarlo. Maybe safety in numbers is my best bet?

'What's he like?' I ask.

'Giancarlo?'

I nod. Sebastiano takes a moment. 'A regular guy. Quiet. You'll find him in his bookshop, reading. *La Libreria sul Canale* is not busy, despite it being of interest to some tourists who like taking photos inside.'

We'd done some digging and found some blog posts about the disorderly second-hand bookshop that looked like an Aladdin's cave for bookworms.

'Has Giancarlo always lived in Venice?' I ask, wondering if he ever did escape and look for Mom.

'As far as I know, yes. The bookshop has been in his family for generations. He took it over when his father retired. Sadly not long after that his father died.'

'That is sad.' His father died? Perhaps that's what stopped him searching for his lost love too if there was no one else to help run the bookshop? 'But I imagine owning a bookshop would be a lot of fun. Especially if you can spend the day reading – isn't that every bookworm's dream?'

Sebastiano shrugs. 'I don't think it's a secret that the bookshop is struggling. There have been whispers that he is thinking of closing down. It would be a shame for Venetians and tourists alike to lose the only second-hand bookshop here. He has a lot of stock but it's in a mess, which makes it impossible to find what you're looking for. And to be honest, Giancarlo isn't much help when you ask for it.'

I'm saddened at the thought that that beautiful, jumbled bookshop on the bank of the Venetian canal is struggling financially. Bookworms surely can't resist buying a book as a keepsake, if nothing else? But if Giancarlo isn't welcoming, I suppose that puts a lot of people off. And the bookshop is sort of hidden. It's not in a busy tourist hub so if he isn't advertising, which it appears he's not, then how does he expect people to find him?

'Why does he want staff then?' Gigi asks.

Sebastiano lifts a palm. 'Giancarlo is . . . reticent, let's say. He's not a sociable sort. Most of his time is spent nose pressed in a book, so I gather he's looking for help so he doesn't have to face customers himself and can perhaps do more of the behind-the-scenes work.'

It appears that Giancarlo isn't a people person and would rather read than serve customers. He did mention something about that in one of his letters, but I assumed that had been because he was heartbroken. I'd have expected he'd have pulled up his socks and got on with it by now, but perhaps the shine of being a bookseller has worn off.

Or is it that the bookshop was the reason he couldn't leave to follow my mother and so he holds a grudge? It could be he's just an old man who's set in his ways and doesn't want to move with the times. Venice is overrun with tourists so I can imagine that gets old quite quickly. Every day, another cruise liner docks, spilling thousands onto this tiny island, like ants scattering for crumbs before they board the ship and pull away again. It would become tedious. But Giancarlo could use that to his advantage to sell more books. So why doesn't he?

Sebastiano brings me back to the moment and says, 'Why don't I escort you there when the bookshop opens at ten tomorrow? Perhaps we can have an espresso first? Afterwards we can take a stroll and I can show you some hidden gems in Venice that only the locals know about.'

Tempting.

'You'd share your secrets just like that?' Gigi teases him.

'Only with Luna.' He winks. 'And you of course, Gigi, if you change your mind about coming too.'

'Work calls, sorry. The 'gram won't update itself, unfortunately.'

'I understand,' he says in a way that implies he has no idea what she's on about.

With Sebastiano by my side, maybe it won't be so bad meeting the mysterious owner of the *La Libreria sul Canale* bookshop and the man who's been writing to my mother for most of my life. Did he keep the letters she wrote back? The best way forward is to get myself hired and then go from there . . .

Chapter 9

I'm awake hours before my alarm. The snores and sleep-talking in the dorm room haven't been exactly conducive to a good night's rest. Various scenarios run through my mind about meeting Giancarlo. Will I know on sight if he's a nice guy? And that Mom always regretted leaving him, thus prompting the promise I made to her? Has he always hoped she'd walk in with the sun at her heels and an ache in her heart from missing him? Will giving him his letters back help or hinder? Is there more to this, and am I involved in the way I'm starting to think I am? It's too soon to tell, but I know when I lock eyes with the man, I'll probably have some kind of feeling . . .

The man I'm picturing held on to his love for my mother, despite knowing she didn't feel the same. An old-school romantic who pined for her and turned to books for comfort. I'm quiet and reflective most of the time too, so I can relate.

Or am I living in fantasyland and Giancarlo got himself married as soon it was clear Mom was gone for good? The letters stopped eventually, probably because he'd decided he'd waited long enough. There's a big chance he's got a brood of children who've made him proud, and Mom's a memory from a murky past where he once met a wild woman who would not be tamed. Not by anyone.

There's no point agonising over it – I know this. But my mind won't shut off.

I gently prise the blanket back and climb down the bunk. Gigi sleeps like she's dead, her limbs all akimbo like a starfish, her mouth slack. I envy her ability to fully let go, no matter where she is. In new places, I sleep stiff like a toy soldier, spare pillow hugged firmly to my chest as if protecting me from invisible enemies.

I take my backpack and head for the bathroom, hoping there's plenty of hot water to wash away these shadowy thoughts.

Once I'm done and dressed, I head back to the room. Women slowly come awake like ballet dancers, unfurling like swans. I wave hello and figure it's time to wake up Gigi. Unlike the graceful, quiet women near her, she shoots up, eyes wide and says, 'What time is it?' At the top of her lungs. Subtle, she isn't.

'Shush. It's eight-thirty. I'm going to meet Sebastiano for coffee. Are you going to be OK on your own or have you realised the error of your ways and that trying to set me up with him is an epic mistake?'

Gigi scrubs her face and groans, not caring one iota how loud she is. 'I will suffer alone in the morning damp of these lonely Venetian streets in order for love to blossom.'

Cue the eye-roll. 'You should have been an actor, Gigi. You've missed your calling, you know.'

'Venice one day, Hollywood the next!' The blanket falls to the floor as she stands and arches her back. 'At least kiss the poor fool and let him know what he's missing out on.'

'I will do no such thing.'

Bending, she retrieves the blanket and folds it into a neat square. 'When you speak prissy like that, I know I've got you.'

I heave a sigh as if I'm very busy and have far more important things to worry about, which I do, I remind myself. But it's nice to joke around after feeling so heavy-hearted lately. I'm missing Aunt Loui, worrying about how she's coping without her sidekick, Ruby Tuesday. And I'm missing Mom. Would she be happy I'm here?

'OK, well I'm off then. When should we meet up? Late lunch?' I check I've got everything that's dear to me. The letters, my phone, passport and my purse.

'Yep. Meet back here and we'll work out what we're doing for the rest of the day.' Gigi yawns again, not a pretty delicate sound, but one so loud it's like she is exorcising the devil himself.

'OK.'

She searches my face. 'You're nervous about meeting him?'

'. . . Yeah.'

'No one keeps up that amount of correspondence if they don't have love in their heart.'

I nod. She's right. Shoulders back, head held high. I can do this and I *will* do this.

'Want me to come with you for moral support? It'll only take me a minute to change.'

'No, I'm OK. I'll have Sebastiano there if all else fails. See you later.' I squeeze her arm goodbye, grab my handbag and go outside into the bright Venetian day to find Sebastiano waiting. His dark black hair turns silver under the sunshine and he's so heart-stoppingly handsome that I lose my train of thought for a moment. Gigi's constant barrages are getting to me, *obviously*.

Out of his formal work clothes he looks like a different person, more assured somehow and downright gorgeous. He wears a designer label T-shirt whose logo even I – fashion-phobe extraordinaire – recognise, which is cut low in a V to expose his chest. His jeans fit as though they were tailored for him, and he looks like he just stepped off the cover of *Vogue Italia*. He's wearing some alluring fragrance too.

What is it about Italian men and their fashion sense? They're so stylish and well groomed. It's all I can do not to question him about this sartorial mystery. But I'm dying to know. Do their mothers guide their fashion sense? Is it a subject at school? Or are they born intuitively knowing how to put clothes together and get their hair just so? Maybe it's their fathers who know these things.

It's a conversation for another day, but as I glance at my own outfit, denim cut-offs and a wrinkled tee, I wonder if I should have made more of an effort. Will Giancarlo judge me on sight for not being fashionably attired? Even my hair I just threw into a messy bun. And my nails haven't seen polish in years – who can be bothered with such things that all need constant maintenance when I've got books to read and countries that need exploring?

'Good morning.'

'*Buongiorno, bella.*' He leans in and pecks me on both cheeks. His scent hangs heavy in the air; it's almost swoon-worthy. I remind myself to be on guard. Of course he smells good, that's part of the charm offensive. And I can't fall for the guy just because he uses expensive cologne. I ignore the overwhelming urge to sniff him up close. What is wrong with me?

'Shall we go?'

'Yes, I could *murder* a cup of coffee.' He frowns as if he doesn't understand the translation. 'I'm very thirsty,' I add helpfully. 'For caffeine.' *Stop, Luna!* I'm grateful Gigi isn't here to witness my sudden lapse of intelligence.

I dart a glance up at the dorm window to find her hanging half her body out in a way that is clearly not safe. She gives me a wink I can only describe as salacious. I duly ignore her and take Sebastiano's hand to lead him away so he doesn't see her, but I quickly turn back and wave her inside and off the damn railing. She's incorrigible at times! I can imagine it now, death by falling off a balcony just so she can tease me later about holding his hand or some damn thing.

We head to a small bar that is full of locals standing at the bar drinking espressos and chatting to the owner in Italian. They speak loudly and gesticulate wildly, and it's so much fun to watch them and try and translate what on earth they could be talking about that's so very expressive.

'What is he saying?' I point to an older guy at the bar who wears a striped beret. He's enunciating every syllable with such force it's as if he's just won the lottery – or had a very big argument, it's hard to tell which.

Sebastiano listens for a moment and then says, 'He's saying that he got up late this morning and his wife hadn't made his breakfast because she's not talking to him because he stayed out late playing poker with his friends.'

'Oh!'

'The owner is joking that he must've lost a lot of money and that's why his wife isn't talking to him!'

'Did he?'

'He denies losing money, says he was on a winning streak and that's why he was late. He's going to buy his wife some peaches from the market to make it up to her.'

'Peaches – is that how people apologise in Venice?'

'Why not? If he gets the best peaches. Depends how well the fruit seller likes the man. If he's not in favour he won't get the best ones and the wife will be more upset.'

'Wow, I had no idea. You don't get to pick your own peaches at the fruit market?'

'No, the fruit seller will choose for you. You're not allowed to touch the fruit.'

'What? Why?'

'Because it's not for you to decide. It's their fruit and they will decide.'

'Wow. So me being new to town, what fruit will I get?'

'Depends.'

'On what?'

He gives me a wink. 'How flirtatious the fruit seller is.'

It's a whole new world! 'Well, I'll have to remember not to touch the fruit!'

'Please do. Otherwise you'll be blacklisted.'

'Really?'

'No, but they wouldn't like it, even though you're absolutely gorgeous.'

'Oh please.'

He lifts his palms in the air. 'You are, Luna. And you're going to learn that very quickly in Italy where men aren't shy about saying how they feel.'

Internally, I squirm. Overt displays of affection aren't my thing.

Around us, people chug back their coffees quickly like a shot of vodka, tip their hats, and head back outside, as if they just needed a jolt of caffeine to start their day. Sebastiano orders two espressos and we take a seat in the sun. Behind his dark sunglasses, it's hard to tell what he's looking at and the conversation is stilted. I let my mind drift as I drink the strong coffee, which gives me the much-needed caffeine jolt to handle this new day . . .

'I hope I get the job,' I muse, keeping to safe topics void of any mention of how I look.

'I'm sure you will. Giancarlo's been advertising for a while now and there are not many takers.'

'Why's that, d'you think?' Maybe he's an ogre to work for, with insisting standards and lofty expectations. Or the renumeration is pitiful – it happens a lot when business owners know backpackers are desperate for work. Usually, we grin and bear it as anything is better than nothing, but we tend to move on from that job fast. Is that what's happening here? If sales are slow perhaps he can't afford full-time staff and will settle for a backpacker who'll accept a lot less.

'I'm not sure why he hasn't found the right candidate; perhaps we'll find out when you meet him. Is it your dream to work in a bookshop?'

Sebastiano must wonder why I'm so obsessed with Giancarlo and *La Libreria sul Canale*. I hadn't thought about having to sell myself to get the job. Really, I should have figured this out in case I'm put on the spot. 'Erm, yes. I love reading. Love bookshops. Novels are like a portal into another world. No matter what's happening in my life, I know I can always escape into the pages of

71

a book and forget my troubles for a while. Reading is like therapy and you don't need great sums of cash to access books. I have library cards from all around the world. I scour flea markets and second-hand bookshops for forgotten beauties. I might not have much in terms of material possessions but I have those stories in my heart.'

He slides his sunglasses atop his head, his eyes sparkling with wonder. 'You should say all of that to him. *Wow*, Luna.'

I give him a shy smile. 'I *really* love reading. It saddens me to hear the bookshop is struggling in a city that's full to the brim of tourists.'

Sebastiano nods and takes up his espresso. Even the way he sips his coffee is artful. Arched backwards on his chair, as if he doesn't have a care in the world. I'm so awkward in comparison. Why are some people self-assured like this? Like they know their place in the world and exactly how they fit into it. 'The bookshop is a sight to behold but it needs to be organised.'

Maybe that's my way in? I can offer to help sort it out so customers can find what they're looking for. 'I don't know how it's possible to walk into a second-hand bookshop and leave without a book. Do you like reading, Sebastiano?' If he says no there will be no hope of friendship, and I'll know it's a sign from the universe that I really do need to focus on my mission and not . . . whatever this is.

'*Sì*. I love the classics the most. Oscar Wilde. Hemingway. The Brontës.'

The Brontës? Oh no, there goes my heart. Insta-love at the thought of him being a bibliophile. If I was into a holiday fling. Which I'm not. I play down my admiration of him being a fellow bookworm while my heart goes *ba-dum ba-dum*. 'Nice. What's your favourite Hemingway book?'

He considers the question. '*A Moveable Feast*.'

Nineteen-twenties Paris, what could be better? 'I love that book too. The last page gets me right in the heart, every time.

He should have stayed with Hadley; he really messed that up. She loved him for who he was not what he became.'

'You have strong opinions about it.'

I blush. He doesn't know the half of it! 'Well, yes. That happens to be a favourite book of mine too.'

Sebastiano gives me a slow saucy smile. 'I'll have to read it again, with fresh eyes.'

'Do that, and we can discuss!' Have I found a fellow book nerd? If so, that changes everything. I might have pegged Sebastiano all wrong. So what if he looks like a cover model; if he reads then I'll forgive him for that.

'Did you get swept away by the glamour of the roaring Twenties? Or were you more taken with his adventurous side?'

'Maybe a bit of both – why not?'

'Same for me. And what about the Brontës? Which novel do you like best?'

'It's impossible to choose.'

'Yes, quite the catalogue they've got.'

He doesn't seem to want to dive into a book critique so we quietly finish our espressos while my nerves ratchet up a notch about the impending visit. 'Let's go to *La Libreria sul Canale* and see about this job.'

'OK.' I take some euros from my purse and we bicker back and forth about who should pay before he finally begrudgingly acquiesces and lets me pay when I agree to another coffee date.

We come to the second-hand bookshop. I stop at the entrance hall and gaze around in wonder. The only light comes from the archways that open up to the canal at the back of the bookshop. Filmy fingers of sunlight land in soft shards on disorderly stacks of books as if pointing the way: choose this one! It reeks with the scent of old books, coupled with the brininess of the water, lapping gently outside. Everywhere I look a cat lounges lazily, some looking up through half-lidded eyes at me, as if I've interrupted their morning rest.

I take a few more steps. There's no direct route around the shop. Bookshelves lean against walls, drooping and sagging with the weight of the novels that overflow and are stacked on the mosaic stone floors in front. There are tables covered with novels, and vases that hold plastic flowers that are grey with dust. You'd think it was truly abandoned if there wasn't so much musicality to the place, from the canal babbling and boats whirring past to the murmuring of books and cats. There's a current, as if the bookshop is slowly waking from a deep sleep after the winter.

It's a spectacle to behold and quite the prettiest bookshop I've ever seen – and I've seen many. There are doorways that lead to other rooms and I can only presume they're much the same, with books creeping over every available space. Antique chairs are dotted here and there, their once rich velvet now pale and faded, their cushions softened with age. I feel connected. Almost like I've been here before, or I've seen it in my dreams.

A shiver of comprehension runs through me – the thing I haven't been able to voice to anyone but what has compelled me to visit Venice. Could this man be my father? I recall one of the letters saying: *I wish I hadn't agreed to your idea.* Had Mom taken me away and not returned? Did she tell him she needed a break, needed to feel the wind in her hair, the sun on her face in some tropical city? Or am I reaching for answers I'll never find?

Did she just run from this life? From the thought of being tied to one man, one place forevermore? Or did she make up the fairy tale about the full moon party, so she didn't have to face her actions? The thing with Mom is, I never quite knew her motivations. If I'm honest with myself, we spent our life running, roaming, until she stopped, right after our trip to Venice. Why?

For a few moments, I toy with the idea that the bookshop and I are connected. I see a man sitting on a worn-out sofa by the canal archway. He's lost in a book and only acknowledges our presence with a wave, not taking his eyes from the pages as he strokes the fur of a tabby cat who has wound itself under his arm. I study his side profile, looking for clues, subtle hints that he's the owner. He has a full head of thick grey hair and bushy eyebrows. In profile, it's hard to see much in the shadowy shop. He's bigger than I expected, tall and hulking, solid, as if he enjoys good food and wine. He's dressed well, stylishly like so many Italian men are here. I expect a jolt, a sign, the ground to shift, alerting me that I'm on the right path being here but my feet remain firmly on the floor. The earth continues its normal rhythm.

'*Buongiorno*, Giancarlo,' Sebastiano says.

I hold my breath as he turns to us, a frown marring his features as if he's annoyed: we've interrupted his book. And let's be honest, I can relate.

'*Sì*?' He doesn't even say good morning back.

Sebastiano and I exchange a furtive look before he says, 'This is Luna. She's just arrived in Venice and is interested in the bookseller position.'

'Hi.' Hi? *Way to sell yourself, Luna!* 'Your bookshop is beautiful. And so many bookshop cats – I wasn't expecting that.'

He stares me full in the face without a flicker of recognition. Is this dream, that there might be a link between us, just wishful thinking on my part again? I study his features. He's not what I expected. 'As Sebastiano said, I'm Luna, and very keen to interview for the job. I love reading and I'm prepared to work hard.'

'You have a work visa?'

Dammit. 'Not exactly.'

He turns back to his book. I'm disregarded just like that. Well, I happen to know a lot of people turn a blind eye when wanderers don't have the correct visas. And I'm not going to give up without a fight.

I scramble for an alternative. 'What about if I do a free trial? I can help clean up a bit here.' I point to a stack of fallen novels that sit close to a puddle near the canal entrance. While it's spring, the choppy winds lash outside and canal water continually sprays inside. 'I can . . .' It's no use. He's completely switched off. What kind of man is he? No wonder he can't keep staff. A rage boils that he's being so dismissive. 'Excuse me, did you hear what I said?' I try not to let emotion show in my voice but it comes out wobbly and I want to berate myself for it. Now that I'm here, I get a strong sense that I need to stay. There's something inside these walls I need to know. But what? Am I totally off track?

'I heard you. The answer is no.'

Sebastiano gives me a sad smile. 'Come on, there are other places.' He tries to lead me from the shop but I resist.

'But I want to work *here*.'

Confusion dashes across Sebastiano's face. Perhaps he wonders why I'd stay here when I'm being resolutely rebuffed.

I turn back to Giancarlo. 'Fine, I can see now is not a good time. I'll come back tomorrow.'

'There's no need,' he says, his voice gruff as he flicks another page. The cat beside him stares at me imperially as I dither about what to do.

'Oh I think there is!' I slink from the shop, Sebastiano following in my wake.

Outside Sebastiano shoves his hands deep into his pockets. 'Luna, I think that Giancarlo is not so happy for you to work there. You should look elsewhere because you don't have a working visa. There's plenty of other places that will pay cash for backpackers.'

I tilt my face up the sun. 'No, Sebastiano. That's the place for me. He'll see that eventually.' My mother's steely resolve shifts to me. I will not be told no. I will not be given up on again. I could tell him who I am but I'm not going to give him that privilege unless he earns it. I'm not going to share anything about my life until I feel comfortable doing so.

'OK, if you're sure . . . ?'

'Why is he so rude?' I feel a slow burn of rage build up. Why am I always forgotten, looked over, ignored? Because I'm too passive, too peaceful, unlikely to make waves? Well, that's not going to wash anymore. I'm here and I'm determined to find the answers I damn well deserve.

Sebastiano shrugs. 'A life of disappointment, I guess. Why is anyone rude?'

'A life of disappointment? What do you mean by that?'

'I've always had the feeling that life sort of passed him by. He hides out in that bookshop like it's a cave with all those cats and only leaves for food, for wine, which he always does alone. Doesn't that seem like a lonely existence to you? Like he's given up.'

'So, he might not have a wife, a family then?'

Sebastiano gives me a funny look. 'I have no idea, but I haven't seen him with anyone at the trattoria before.'

Well, that flips the script. Maybe he needs me as much as I need him. I can forgive the man his surliness if he's suffering a broken heart, much like I am.

Chapter 10

Sebastiano suggests a walk through the sunny squares and we head towards the Rialto Bridge. When he slips his hand in mine, I'm still turning the meeting over in my mind so it takes me far too long to react. Then I overthink *this* instead.

I push Giancarlo out of my mind; it's all too messy and convoluted and needs processing when I'm alone. Instead, I concentrate on the moment with Sebastiano. He squeezes my hand as if to comfort me, sensing – I think – that my mind is still stuck in that musty old bookshop.

Shouldn't I know if I want to start something with this guy or not? My heart seems to be lost in action, and it's no help to me. Almost like it's put up a sign: *closed for repairs*. Yeah sure, Sebastiano is gorgeous, but so? Give me a man who has a way with words, a scruffy deep thinker who loses half a day in bed reading. A gentle soul who quietly does his bit and treads gently on this earth. There's a showiness to Sebastiano, but maybe he's just a theatrical kind of guy with a lot of layers I'm yet to uncover.

We come to a stop by *Corte Seconda del Milion* and Sebastiano points to a marble plaque on the stone wall. 'This was once Casa di Marco Polo. The writer and adventurer. This square here is believed to have been named after his travel memoir *Il Milione*. The palazzo itself is still very fine.'

'It's beautiful.' Stunning arched windows face the canal. The building itself isn't as ornate as others but it has an air of mystique about it, as though Marco Polo's ghost still walks those halls or something equally kooky.

'He went on an amazing journey to the east that spanned decades,' Sebastiano says, awe in his voice. 'That was no easy feat back then.'

I imagine Marco Polo planning his trip from these very rooms. 'Anyone who's up for adventure is good in my eyes. If I remember correctly, he went to learn about their customs, the culture and went to Court of the Khan, such an exotic undertaking when travel was so arduous.' Mom was big on teaching me the history of people and places around the world and Marco Polo was part of those studies. 'I haven't read any of his books.'

Sebastiano laughs. 'Why would you! He wrote them over seven hundred years ago, but they have been reprinted. Maybe you'll find some in the bookshop if you do go back?'

'Yes, I bet Giancarlo has some somewhere in that muddle. Half the fun will be searching for them. Who knows what I'll find in that labyrinth.' I intend to find as many books about Venice as I can while I'm here and then I can search out places mentioned in the books. While romance novels are my first love, a good memoir is second on the list. Who doesn't love going behind the curtain of other people's lives?

'Is it your love of books that has you so determined to work there?' Sebastiano shoots me a puzzled look.

'Something like that.' I smile up at him. Bookish places tend to be a magnet for those seeking something they can't quite name but will find in a novel, a sort of thirst that needs quenching. The bonus is meeting other readers there, people who've also been to Narnia and know the magic between the pages.

We walk slowly to *Piazza San Marco*. The square is full of people enjoying the early spring sunshine. Venice really is another world, surrounded by the sea, an island that makes it feel like anything goes. I can rediscover myself here. Reinvent myself. Find that missing link. The man who has lived purely in my imagination will come to life and indelibly change me. He wears his sadness like armour whereas I hide mine behind a smile.

'Is it too early for an Aperol spritz?' Sebastiano asks. He leads me into a bar. I get the feeling he knows I'm lost to a daydream. It's hard to focus directly on Sebastiano – it's almost like staring into the sun. The way he gazes at me is so intense. I haven't seen anything like it before. The sensible part of me sends a warning, an alert to go slowly.

I shake my head, no. 'Sparkling water for me. If I drink an Aperol spritz before lunch, there's a very good chance I'll fall asleep.' Already, I'm languorous from the sunshine, the promise of what might be here in the floating city. Possibility perfumes the air; I just need to be open to signs that point me the right way.

'Ah, it's why we have siestas.' He winks and rubs his palm over my hand. At the counter he orders us drinks and then we head back outside.

'Shall we sit in the gondola?'

I look to where he's pointing. The bar has three gondolas tied to the side of the canal. They've made seating areas with colourful cushions and old oars have been fashioned into makeshift tables. 'How adorable! Yes, let's sit in one of them.'

Sebastiano leads me to the far gondola that's empty of customers. He helps me on as the gondola shifts under my feet.

With his seductive accent, he has the Italian charm down a treat. The art of flirtation is almost another language unto itself here in Venice. It's a casual place and they offer a handful of freshly made meals meant to share as a snack, almost like a tapas bar. It seems Sebastiano has ordered one of everything as the waiter comes back with small plate after plate.

While I should be delighting in his attentions, my mind is elsewhere. 'I need to work out how to get that job. Any ideas?' I'd like to consult the tarot, but I don't have my cards with me and it's probably not the done thing in one of these little bars.

'I don't understand why you're so keen to work there. There's plenty of other places. I get the feeling Giancarlo won't budge, Luna. I'm sorry to say.'

There must be a way to convince him. If I don't get the job then I won't get very far in my quest to find out what kind of man Giancarlo is. I probably should give Sebastiano some kind of reason I'm so adamant about the job too. 'A few weeks ago, I stumbled onto a blog about the bookshop and I came to Venice in the hopes of getting work there. Silly, I know. But have you ever had such a strong feeling about a place and knew it was right for you?' He nods, but I can tell he thinks I'm crazy for making such a rash decision. 'Well that's how I feel about it. If I'd have known he was so strict about the visa, I'd have organised it. There's no point worrying about what I should have done; I'm here and I've got to make it happen.'

'OK. Well if you're determined, then I'd go back with a plan how to get Giancarlo more business. With all the closures and the recent flooding all businesses have suffered, especially the *La Libreria sul Canale* because a lot of stock was damaged by the rising tides. Maybe that could be a way in with him?'

'That's a great idea, Sebastiano.' I need to prove I'm not someone who just wandered in off the street, that I actually have skills that can help his little biz. I resolve to learn the Italian language, it can only help my cause.

We share our drinks and chat about Sebastiano's life in Venice. He tells me his family own the trattoria we dined in the evening before, and that he's all set to take it over from Nonna one day. The feisty little Italian woman rules the roost but he's her favourite. His family live in a sprawling apartment in one of the best areas of Venice but he plays it down, says it's been in the family for generations. I'm impressed by the way the family stick together. How settled they are. It's such an alien concept to me, but I can imagine it's comforting, going home to an apartment full of relatives. The sound of laughter, TVs, sizzling pans always on the go in the hub of the family home. They probably all take it for granted, have petty disputes over who ate the last piece of lasagne, or who used all the hot water, not knowing how lucky they are.

I've roamed all my life and I don't know anything else. But hearing Sebastiano talk openly about his family and the way their lives entwine, makes me a little heartsick. Will I ever fit, anywhere? I love my life, I remind myself. I love the freedom. I don't answer to anyone. But is that enough? Is this grief sneaking up on me, making me second-guess every little thing? Making me think that man is my father, for crying out loud! But then there's that niggle, every time I think of my mom and those letters. Those letters that almost hum when I hold them, as if alerting me there's a secret that needs uncovering. There's a reason I've been drawn to Venice but, right now, I'm not quite certain what it is.

After our break at the bar we continue walking through Venice. The day heats up so we find some shade in yet another sun-drenched piazza. Sebastiano holds my hand as we lean against the trunk of a tree. 'You're beautiful, Luna. I'm glad you came to Venice whatever the reason.'

Sebastiano's expression is so earnest it's hard not to get swept away by it. He leans closer to me, his lips a whisper away, and I know he's waiting for permission or some kind of sign to kiss me. I take a moment to decide what I want. It's his perfume, the passion in his gaze that gets to me. What if he's real? What if he means what he says?

If so, could I fall for a guy like him? Sometimes a kiss is all you need. Your body will react, your soul will know, if he's right or not. I tilt my face up to his and pull him tight against me. When we kiss, I'm taken by surprise by how soft and gentle he is.

I place a hand on his chest and feel the speed of his heart beating – does it beat that way for me? Or is it just the fact he's kissing a girl in this beautiful setting? Our kiss deepens and I give in to it completely, wanting to escape from my life, my mind for a while.

When we break apart, we're breathless. His eyes are glazed with want. 'I hope you're here for a long time,' he says and leans in to kiss me once more.

Back at the hostel, I find Gigi surrounded by women hanging over her shoulder, checking out her Instagram profile. 'This was us in the outback of Australia. That's a crocodile and lemon myrtle spring roll! Was delicious, tasted like chicken but sweeter. Ooh and this . . . this was in New Zealand – we had a traditional hangi. Like an earth oven, you know?' There are murmurs and nods. 'The flavours are earthy and rich and it's a foodie experience you have to try.'

'Hey,' I say. Gigi introduces me to the gathered women who have clearly forgiven her for her voluble wake-up. Better they get used to it. Gigi doesn't do quiet. If she's up, we're all up but she will make up for it by cooking for everyone.

'So how did it go? Actually, don't answer that.' She turns to face the gang. 'Pancakes for breakfast tomorrow, yeah? I'll bring the fruit.' They agree to pancakes and smoothies. Gigi has that way about her, breaking the ice so easily in new group situations. It's one of the things I love about her and it makes up for her often less than ideal moments. I know that she'll have convinced the women to clean up the dorm room already, and tidy their things away, but she'd have softened her need for order by making it fun and bribing them with some sort of sweet treat.

Gigi likes order in a disorderly world.

She takes my arm and we head to our room where I'm not surprised to find it immaculate, and I proceed to tell her everything that happened that day in minute detail with her only butting in every few minutes to ask questions.

'So, in a nutshell, your Giancarlo is a grumpy recluse, who sticks to the visa rules? I mean, it could be worse, right? Sticking to the rules shows he's got morals. And maybe he's a grumpy recluse because he never got over losing your mom. And that is a *love* story, not a horror story.'

'There's more though and I'm probably thinking crazy here but hear me out. Could he be my dad, do you think? Could Mom have run from him, and then made me promise not to run because she knows it was a huge mistake?'

'What? You think . . . ?'

I shrug. 'Why would they have communicated all that time?'

'But what about Thailand – Luna, the full moon baby?'

'I know, I know. And the thing she left behind in Venice. What was that? Him? The chance to live a proper family life? Something else?'

'There's no other clues in the letters?'

'No, but maybe I need to read them again with that firmly in mind.'

'You suspected all along, didn't you? That's why you wanted to come here so desperately?'

'Yeah, I did. I've always wanted to know my dad. It hurts to think there's a guy out there who might not even know I exist. But maybe he does know I exist, maybe it's Giancarlo; but he didn't react to hearing my name, didn't even flinch. Not a flicker of *anything*. Didn't do a double take on seeing me. Wouldn't a man recognise his own daughter?'

She taps her chin. 'Not if he's so lost inside himself that he's given up ever finding his first love and his darling bambino.'

'Yet, Giancarlo knew where to address the letters to. He mentions her writing back.' Not the actions of a woman who wanted to hide.

'The big question is, if your mom kept this big secret from you, why?'

I exhale a heavy breath. 'Yes, therein lies the tough one. What was so wrong with him? Was it just that she didn't want to be tied down here? That makes sense to me, but not enough sense that she'd make up this fiction about who he was to me my entire life.'

She shrugs. 'That's the weird part, Luna. If he wasn't a monster, and we don't think he is, since she communicated with him, then why all the secrecy surrounding your birth? Why say you were a gift from a full moon party?'

'None of it makes sense. He didn't even give me a chance to talk, let alone plead my case for the job, so I still don't know anything else about him. It's odd because I felt connected to the bookshop. It's strange though, I didn't feel connected to *him*. Do you think that's a sign?'

'As in knowing for sure he's your dad?'

'Yeah, I guess I expected to see myself in him. I expected this instant zap of recognition, and it didn't happen.' Perhaps the psychic part of me has switched itself off, shorted out, with the crackle of electricity as my mom left this planet? Nothing feels clear, my usual intuition is fuzzy, like there's a fuse that needs changing.

'It doesn't mean he's not your dad though.'

'No, it doesn't, but shouldn't I have felt *something*? Shouldn't *he* have felt something? Aren't we connected on some spiritual plane? Yet, it doesn't feel like that. It feels as though he's just another stranger in the crowd. I'm just another backpacker looking for work.'

'I know you look for signs, for symbolism, your tarot to guide the way, but maybe in this instance you're going to have to admit who you are. From what Sebastiano said, Giancarlo is not really a people person, so don't take it to heart there wasn't instant recognition and a welcoming party. It's going to take time to get to know each other, especially if you don't open up about the fact Ruby is your mom.'

'Yeah, but I need to tread carefully. He's so grumpy, I don't want to blow my chances of getting to know him first before I say anything. I want . . . I want to go slow with this.'

'So what's the plan?'

'Sebastiano's idea was that I should figure out a way of increasing revenue at the shop, proving my worth so Giancarlo will hire me on a seasonal working visa.'

'All good in theory, but how will you increase the revenue?'

'Well, firstly the place needs some kind of system. Languages and genres are mixed. There's no discernible order. Aside from that, there's no online presence, perhaps you, influencer extraordinaire, can give me some pointers about how to tackle that?'

'I'm only a budding little baby influencer but I'll take any compliments you swing my way, and I can definitely give you some pointers. We know the bookshop doesn't have any social media pages, or a website, right?'

I spent several evenings in Mom's tiny home searching the web for any clues about Giancarlo but there was no information about him. There were a few posts about the bookshop itself and pictures taken by travellers but none from any accounts linked to the bookshop. 'Nope, no social media pages for the bookshop and no website. What business in this day and age doesn't even have a website?'

'Maybe he's a luddite?'

'Could be. And that's understandable. I'd rather read all day too than post on social media, but it has to be done. It's not as though the bookshop is flush with customers. So, is that my way in? I can suggest I design a website, set up his social media but it doesn't feel like enough. I'm sure he's had plenty of people wander in and offer to do the same. Also, he has a coterie of cats lounging about the place. Perhaps, that could be a drawcard too. Who doesn't like reading with a cat purring away on their lap?'

'Bookshop cats, this I have to see.'

'Right? I need to wow him with an idea he hasn't heard before, something that grabs his attention long enough to pull him away from the pages of his book.'

'You're right – it has to be big! But what . . . ?'

'It has to be an idea that will generate a definite income, not just the *promise* of one.'

'I know what'll help!' she says, and rummages in her bag for something.

I cluck my tongue when I see it. 'Not the magic eight ball, Gigi. I've told you a million times that's not actually real.' I can't help but tease her. While I have my tarot, she has her magic eight ball. She uses it to make big life decisions, which freaks me out but I guess it's the same for her when I use the cards to guide my life. It's all about faith!

'It's real, and you know it!'

'You're *such* an Aries.'

'Thanks! Anyway, stop distracting me. Let's ask the magic eight ball, or as I call it the great prophetess. Will Luna get the job at the bookshop?' She shakes the very life out of the small black ball.

I peek over her shoulder. 'What does it say?'

'*Cannot predict now.*'

'Give me that!' It's too late, I'm invested. I shake the ball gently. '*Ask again later.* Well that's because we haven't come up with our grand plan yet! Of course the magic eight ball can't predict the answer until we come up with the solution!'

'Always so wise, my fair Luna.'

'My past lives have made me that way.' I'm only half joking. 'Eventually, I'll be on the right path once I work out which direction I'm supposed to be going in.'

'You don't think you are now?'

I ponder it. 'No, I haven't quite found my way, just yet. Maybe it's losing Mom – these feelings are heightened and I have these moments of panic, like life is passing me by and I still haven't figured out my place in the world. Not a destination exactly but where I *fit*.'

'It's going to take time, Luna. Losing your mom is a huge adjustment. You have to figure out where you see yourself in a world without her in it. Everything is going to feel off. I'm no expert but I think these feelings will settle in time. And if they don't, then you'll address them when it's not so raw.'

'Who's the wise one now?'

'It wasn't me, it was the magic eight ball.'

The mood lightens. 'Right, so what's our cunning plan for the bookshop?'

I flop back on the bed and stare up at the coils of the bunk above, lost in thought about it all. Before Mom died, I hadn't felt so lost, so adrift. Gigi is right: it's going to be a period of adjustment. And the best thing to do is try and figure out what led me here.

I picture the bookshop, all those English books lying in an unloved pile. So many forgotten gems, hidden away in the damp space. It's such a waste. Most people wander in and take pictures, but they don't stop to search for treasure. Why? Is it such a jumble they can't be bothered? Is it a time thing – they're off to see the next tourist attraction and can't be bothered rummaging through jumbled stacks. And all those haughty cats, slumbering in shafts of sunlight. An idea takes shape. Could it work?

'What?' Gigi asks. 'You've got that faraway look in your eyes, and that can only mean one thing.'

'I've got an idea, but I'm not sure if it would work.'

'Pray tell.'

I sit up. 'The bookshop is a mess, romcoms are mixed with crime and history. They aren't separated by languages. It's time-consuming to search through the many rooms to find the genre you want, *if* you can find it. But there are *so* many great books just waiting to be found.'

'Right, so say you're stopping by for a book about the history of Venice, there's no way to find it except to search every single pile and there's a chance you might not even find what you're looking for.'

I nod. 'Right? What if we offered a particular service whereby guests come by gondola to the bookshop? They can take all the pictures they want, while we curate a list of books for them to buy. It could be called "*The Venetian Book Concierge*". We give them a checklist to fill out, like what genre they like, which characters do they relate to, that kind of thing. While they're enjoying afternoon tea by the canal, I can find the perfect books for them. Instead of just taking selfies, they're treated to a bookish adventure they'll never forget.'

'Yes!' Gigi says. 'It could be an experience that tourists allocate actual time to before they flit off to the next thing.'

'Because that's the problem, right? Cashed-up travellers are trying to fit all the sights in and the bookshop holds no appeal aside from a quick selfie, if they have to spend hours searching for a book when they may only have one full day in Venice.' The many cruise ships that pull into port for an overnight stay spring to mind.

'Oh my God, Luna! I would pay to go to an event like that! You could collaborate with local eateries and have all that side of it catered so you could focus on the book side of things. The possibilities are endless. Do you think Giancarlo will go for it?'

'Hard to tell. He's so closed off and gruff, but if he wants to save his bookshop then he might just agree, especially if I say I'll run the service for him and that will include getting the bookshop in order so I can also find out what's there for the book concierge service. I'll go back tomorrow, wearing my most serious bookseller outfit.'

'Ooh, you'll need specs to make you look intelligent.'

'Thanks?'

'Welcome. You might need more than just a good bookseller outfit. You'll need a business proposal so he knows you're serious about this. *Committed*. I bet he's had all sorts of bookworms through that door with some grand plan or other.'

'Good idea. I'll borrow your iPad and make something that will knock his socks off, thus proving I'm not a regular bookworm, I'm the bookworm who is going to save his shop . . . and hope-fully find out exactly who he is into the bargain.'

'Yes! And you have to highlight the cats too. They'd make great subjects for social media posts. Now, on to my next question. How did it go with the smoking-hot Italian stall—'

I push my hand firmly over her mouth to shove whatever word was intent on escaping. 'Do *not* say stallion.'

Gigi muffles a reply.

'I'll only take my hand away if you agree not to call him anything cringey like that.'

She nods affirmatively and I remove my hand. 'But he *is* an Italian stallion! Don't make me pull out the magic eight ball for some bloody answers again!'

'Fine, *fine*. He loves Oscar Wilde! *The Picture of Dorian Gray* is "one of the best books ever written", not to mention he also enjoys the Brontës who were "literary geniuses". Don't you love a man who isn't bashful about reading them? Most men would scoff, or lie, or outright deny it.'

'Especially one who looks like *he* does.'

I flop back onto her neatly made bed again. I bet she's got hospital corners, it's so pristine. 'You sound like a throwback from the Eighties. Sebastiano is a gold medallist in flirting so does that counteract the book nerd in him? I'm not sure.'

'You can't hold that against him! All men flirt here – he's got to stand out from the crowd.'

'Hmm.'

'Oh God, I remember when you were obsessed with the Hot Men Reading hashtag on Instagram. I'm sure half of them had the book upside down.'

'Are you implying they were faking it?' I ask, outraged. Surely not!

She laughs. 'I'm insisting on it. Men can be cunning beasts, you know.'

'Yikes. Well, I wasn't obsessed with it, I checked it out to see what they were reading in case anything caught my eye and could be added to my TBR pile.' OK, I was a little obsessed. But they were hot men reading – hot in a bibliophile sense!

She raises a brow. 'Riiight.'

'So what's your point?'

'That you always get caught up on whether they read or not.'

'So?'

'So it can limit your dating pool, that's all.'

I roll my eyes. 'You were pushing Sebastiano on me not two minutes ago? Last night you were talking matrimony for crying out loud. And now because he reads you're saying the opposite? Which parallel universe have I stepped into this time?'

She shakes her head. 'I'm not saying that – he's gorgeous, delectable even. I'm just saying you should broaden your parameters. Great, he reads, but what if he didn't? Would you still date him?'

I drop my gaze to the floor.

'Oh my God, Luna! Really?'

I shrug. 'My dream man is one who goes to the bookshop and comes home with two of the very same book, so we can sit on the sofa together and read it at the same time.'

'Wild!'

'It doesn't end there!'

'There's more?!'

'The perfect man surprises me with ecofriendly bookmarks instead of flowers.'

'Whoa I didn't even know there was such a thing.'

'And best yet, date night is spent together in bed reading, only stopping every now and then to share illuminating metaphors or sip a glass of bubbles. He does not interrupt my reading ever if I have my concentrating face on, and I will of course return the favour.'

'Oh, *saucy*, and then one thing leads to another …'

My eyebrows pull together. 'Not while we're reading, Gigi, sheesh. That time is sacrosanct.'

She throws her hands in the air. 'This is why you're *resolutely* single, Luna. You're a goddess, a living breathing goddess, but you'd rather read than get any action. I despair, I really do.'

I laugh. 'Get any action? Italy has *changed* you.'

We fall about laughing. Once we're composed again, I say, 'If you must know, we kissed, so on the action front, I think that puts me well ahead.'

The pillows catapult off the bed by the force of Gigi jumping up and down on the floor beside me. 'Oh my God, I knew it! I sensed there was something special about that boy! You *never* kiss on the first date, so he must have done something right.'

'I got caught up in the romance of Venice!'

'Was it earth-shattering?'

'I will never understand that reference when the earth shattering is downright terrifying. In order to feel something, the earth must what . . . explode? It just doesn't make sense. If it did explode then how could I feel—'

She cuts me off. 'Can you focus for one minute, Luna! You're in the early stages of lovestruck. It's written all over you. You can't even answer the question without zooming off to lovestruck land and being all dreamy-eyed and babbling about whatever it is you're babbling about.'

'Look who's babbling now! Fine. The earth remained in one stable piece. There were the first flutterings of something, could be lust, could be the proximity of a man after a bit of a man drought due to no fault of my own but it didn't feel like love, nope.'

'A man drought due to the fact you only accept bookworms. That guy in New Zealand who trailed after you like a puppy dog with his tongue hanging out was definitely worth pursuing . . .'

I scoff. 'Not in a million years! He said romance books were smutty drivel!'

'Oh, yeah, that was a bit uncalled for. If you *did* read smutty drivel then I'd probably be more open to reading your books, just saying.'

I throw a pillow at her. She ducks and it sails onto another bunk. 'Put me out of my misery, was the stallion in the top three as far as first kisses go?'

'Top five, maybe.' Yeah sure the guy can kiss but it's still early days. My inner voice is telling me to think before I leap.

'I knew it!'

'The thing is Sebastiano's not really my type. He's too . . . snazzily dressed. I can picture it now, we'd go out and people would point and say, *Look at that odd couple!* Me in one of my four outfits, wrinkled tees and shorts. And him, whose clothes probably cost more than my flight here. Can I really go out with a guy who takes longer getting ready than I do?'

'Luna, everyone on planet earth takes longer to get ready than you do. So what?' Gigi sighs. 'You and your need for men who need a good rub-a-dub and a haircut sometime this century. Why you always go for those broody, long-haired messes is beyond me. It stems from your childhood. You're used to the sort who bathe in rivers. Plunge their hands into fertile soil and grow their own vegetables all while reading a bloody book. Rustic. Your man vibe is rustic.'

I give her a playful push. 'So?' She's right though. 'I prefer men who don't care about their aesthetic. Their cars. Their houses. Their pile of money sitting in a bank. I prefer men who talk about the magic of words, their shape, their melody when they're in a specific order. Men who question life and all its foibles. Men who are at one with the earth. And yeah, if they grow their own vegetables, it's definitely a plus.'

'That's all good on paper but what about reality?'

'What about it?'

'Maybe the reason you haven't found love is that you're going after men as flighty as you are. Men who hear the distant hum of a new adventure and take off – just like you do. What about a man like Sebastiano who seems enmeshed in Venetian life. He *could* be a steady sort.'

I frown. 'Since when am I looking for love? It's the very last thing on my mind right now.' Where is she going with this? And why the sudden pressure to give Sebastiano or any man a chance?

It's not like her to act this way, as if trying to convince me that I've met my soulmate when I'm certain that's just not the case.

There are times I catch her staring at me, as if she's worried my silence means I might break. I'm quieter than normal but that's to be expected. My mind isn't quiet though, it's buzzing in about a hundred different directions. This is a side to grieving I hadn't considered before – the people around you care so much that they try and find ways to fix your broken heart. That must be her plan, hoping that a love interest will distract me . . . 'Sebastiano is enmeshed here with his great big family and his roots that go back centuries. I always feel a little like an outsider around people like that. I don't have the same experience with that sort of thing.'

'Oh, Luna. But you *do*! You've been in communities your whole life. Yeah sure your family unit might be structured differently but it doesn't make it any less special. Any less real.'

'Yeah, I know. It's just . . . different.' When Sebastiano walked me back to the hostel he talked about their bickering, their joking, the silly things they argue over, the way they raid each other's wardrobes and steal coins from bedside tables for a loaf of fresh baked bread. That sort of closeness, you can only do with family. I can't imagine anyone ever doing that where I'm from. It's what real families can get away with, not found families.

'You think it's weird that I'm pushing for him. I know it's unusual, but I haven't seen a thunderclap like that before, Luna. Seriously, the man looked as though his dream girl appeared before his very eyes. In my thirty-four years on this planet, I've never witnessed such a thing. You're right, he might lay on the charm thick but isn't that just the way Italian men show their love – with great big theatrical gestures? Even the guy from the bakery flirts with me and he's about a hundred.'

'You don't think it's an act?' That's what holds me back – Sebastiano is a little *too* polished.

'There's the flirting and then there's the thunderbolt. Two different things.'

'I'll take it one day at a time.' I'm still not sure how I feel, but he's fun to be around and lifts my mood with his flirtatious banter.

'My BS detector didn't go off. And there were no "Down with the Patriarchy" T-shirts in sight.'

I laugh, thinking of Thailand. 'Oh, Gi, doesn't that seem like a different life?' The guy mansplaining to Gigi about women's rights. 'Things were so simple all those weeks ago.'

'Time sure flies when you're transforming.'

'It sure does. Soon I'll be a butterfly.' It slips out and I'm reminded of Giancarlo's letter to Mom. He called her his *farfalla* and I wonder if he meant that she flits from flower to flower or meant something deeper, a caterpillar who grows beautifully patterned wings, like a woman who discovers her own power and chooses independence and flies into the sun.

'Let's read tarot and see if the cards can provide any clarity . . .'

'*And* the magic eight ball.'

Chapter 11

I'm dressed in one of Gigi's ensembles. Mine are far too flower child to be taken seriously as a bookseller but I still wear my rose quartz crystal necklace, which links to my heart, the earth, and the whole cosmos. It has many healing properties and provides a sense of inner peace, which I'll need today.

In the kitchen the girls sit around while Gigi flips pancakes like a pro and stacks them high on a plate, like the Leaning Tower of Pisa.

'Luna, breakfast before you go? We have strawberries and Macey picked up some fresh cream from the local *cremeria*. It's like nothing you've ever tasted before. Thick and luscious, it's the stuff dreams are made of. In fact, I might just eat it with a spoon and forgo the pancakes.'

'Just a coffee would be great if you've got any made, thanks.' Too many nerves for a full pancake breakfast that may up and revolt when I least expect. I toy with the rose crystal around my neck, letting it calm the inner turmoil.

'*Il caffè!*' she says and pours me an instant coffee. Watching Gigi hold court is one of my favourite things, how seamlessly she fits into any new place. Socially, I'm quieter. Gigi hands me a piping-hot mug of coffee. 'Sadly we're still on the instant stuff for a bit but hey, it has caffeine, right? We need to buy a café press. Aside from job hunting, that will be my mission for today.'

'Job hunting?' Macey turns to Gigi. 'If you're looking for work, the *osteria* down the laneway needs a kitchenhand – not very glamorous, but they pay OK and they also give you a free meal every shift.'

'What is this place you speak of? You had me at free meal.'

Macey grins. 'It's called *La Cozza Arrabbiata*, which means the Angry Mussel.'

I shake my head at the name. It's so Gigi, she's sure to find work there and probably have a hand in restructuring the place while she does it. 'You should go and visit them today,' I say, as always thinking about funds and the lack thereof.

Work is usually easy to find in most places if you're happy with more menial-type jobs, and we're always happy to find anything that will boost the coffers and leave us some time to explore.

Menial is such a misnomer though. I've had the best experiences being a dishwasher or some other job deemed lowly, because of the people I worked alongside or the owners of the place. Singing, dancing and enjoying the time go by as I worked with some of the happiest humans I've ever encountered. Is any job menial if it provides a sense of purpose, happiness and puts food on the table? To me that's hitting the jackpot, if you get all three.

If Gigi gets a position at the *osteria*, I'll be able to breathe easier. At the back of my mind is the worry that I've dragged her to Venice without much thought about what we'd do if we ran into money trouble. The lump sum that Mom left for me paid for my flight to Italy and a few weeks at the hostel; aside from that it all comes down to finding paid work. My emergency account is depleted after paying Gigi back for the travel costs of leaving Thailand. She didn't want to accept the money, so I had to convince her that it meant a lot to me to be able to fund my own way home when my mom needed me. If we don't start stocking the coffers, I worry we'll be in a bind with nothing to fall back on.

If it doesn't go well at the bookshop today, I'm not going to give up, but I'll have to look for another job to keep myself in the style I've become accustomed to. A dorm room and instant noodles, that is. The glamorous life of a wanderer. Right now, that sounds like luxury compared to running out of money completely.

If all goes according to plan and we manage to stay for a while, then we'll conserve our cash and try and find an affordable apartment flat-share. There are times when I crave solitude and a bit of space to stretch out. And Gigi prefers a clean, tidy place. But it's a luxury and not the priority right now, and Venice is known for being an expensive city to live in.

I down the coffee fast and rinse my cup before saying my goodbyes. 'Wish me luck!'

Gigi gives me a lung-squashing squeeze and I'm on my way.

When I get to the entrance of the bookshop, I take a moment to compose myself. The display window is downright dusty in the light of day, and the books have a forlorn air as if they've been sunburnt and forgotten. I wonder if Giancarlo will be amenable to me sprucing the window up, making a fresh display that will catch the eye of passers-by, and give these poor old novels a break from the glaring sun.

My presentation is prepared, and I know it backwards. I'm wearing my serious bookseller outfit, which includes ridiculous spectacles that don't serve any purpose except to help allegedly disguise my true hippy persona. *How*, I'm still not quite sure, but Gigi insisted as if my inner bohemian was obvious with unadorned eyes. The job advertisement is no longer stuck to the glass. Has Giancarlo hired someone else? My heart sinks at the thought I might be too late. A black cat saunters into the display window and sits, surveying me with regal eyes as it licks its paw. Black cats are lucky, despite people thinking the opposite, so I take that as a good omen.

There's no point dilly-dallying. I push the door open and head inside. I don't think I'll ever tire of the scent of the bookshop, a dusty vanilla punctuated by salty canal water and an earthy under-current. Inside it's almost sepia-toned like an old photograph. There are no lights on above. The only brightness comes from the arched canal openings at the back of the bookshop, which cast a shimmery light on the books. And there Giancarlo sits, in the same position, legs crossed, book aloft. For a moment, I stare at him, hoping my aura will recognise his, that I'll feel a connec-tion that will prove I'm on the right track, but nothing happens.

The tarot warned me that the road ahead would not be linear but was worth pursuing, so I have faith in that. Once again, the cards didn't quite give me the detailed answers I usually find such solace in. It's probably that my own energy is off, and I'm not clear enough of mind to connect.

'*Buongiorno*,' I say, in a big bold voice, channelling my mother who spoke up when she needed to. Was brave when her knees knocked.

Giancarlo turns to me, his face more open than the day before. Until he recognises me, then it shuts hard like a shop door in the wind. Today a fluffy white cat sleeps on the armchair of the sofa beside him. 'The answer is still no.'

I make my way over to him. 'Totally understand. I wouldn't hire me either without the correct visa in place, but I can apply for one and I'm sure it won't take long. I've worked all over the world without any issues, it's only that this trip was undertaken very last minute.'

'That's not my problem.'

Aha an opening! 'No it's not. Your problem is that you have one of the most beautiful bookshops in the world, yet you don't have any customers. You need help and I have a plan.'

He graces me with a slight turn of the head, not quite his full attention but better than nothing. 'And how would you know such a thing?'

'Let's just say I've made enquiries about this place and leave it at that.' *Oh God, Luna, that sounds like a line from a detective novel.*

'Enquiries?' His brow wrinkles.

I wave the word away. 'It doesn't matter. I've heard it whispered that *La Libreria sul Canale*—' oh how I butcher the pronunciation! '—may not be around for future visits if your sales don't pick up. Is that true?'

He heaves a long sigh. 'All the businesses in Venice have financial woes. Like the rest of the world, we didn't have tourists for a long time, then we had major floods. We're *all* getting back on our feet.' There's an edge to his voice that suggests he doesn't like being talked about behind his back. Who does?

The wind of the canal blows in sideways, making me shiver. 'Exactly, so let this be a time of transformation. Like a caterpillar who turns into a butterfly.' Again, no reaction. Why did I expect that he'd react to a word he used once about a million years ago? 'Could I show you my idea?'

He doesn't say yes but he doesn't say no either. I take a spot next to him on the old sofa that wheezes as I sit in its embrace, making dust motes dance. A stripy orange feline jumps up and does loops on my lap before kneading my leg and purring. I hide a smile as I pat it. 'What's its name?' I ask.

'Dante.'

'Ah, for Dante's *Inferno*?'

Giancarlo lifts a brow. 'Yes. All the cats are named after books, authors or characters from novels.'

'I love that.' I make a mental note of that for future social media posts.

I swipe the iPad to life, cringing a little when the background music I used to accompany the presentation plays cornily in the background.

It takes forever for each slide to pass but I have Giancarlo's full attention. The glare from the iPad reflects on his face while I hold it in front of him, giving me time to take a good hard look at his features. I don't see myself in him. What I do see is a man who doesn't like small talk, doesn't suffer fools. Prefers the comfort of the written word and not idle chitchat. And that we have in common at least. He's watching the presentation, which leads me to believe he does have some fight left in him. He does love his bookshop, his cats, he's just lost his way.

There are laugh lines, tiny rivers sketching the planes of his face. It's his eyes that give me pause, deep pools of sadness like he's a lonely man determined to be left that way. I'm going to get to know him, whether he likes it or not. Sebastiano says Giancarlo always eats alone but that could mean anything. His wife and family could live on the other side of the island.

The presentation comes to a close and thankfully so does that god-awful music. I search his face for clues, but the man does not make it easy. He seems to have one expression – stony.

'So what did you think? First of all I'll set up social media for the bookshop, including designing a simple website that also promotes the book concierge side of things. We can even sell books on there if you want? Although I'm not sure about the intricacies and cost effectiveness of worldwide postage but I can investigate that and see if it's worth doing. The focus should be on monetising this experience.'

'I'd hate this place to be full of people who disturb the peace and quiet.'

'Sure, who wouldn't? Having a book concierge service will attract paying customers who will help pay the bills and will look upon the books they got here, curated especially for them, like a gift. I know I would. I'm sure the cats will love the extra atten-tion.' I pat Dante, who stretches backwards with full abandon as if inviting me to massage his little body.

'Dante usually hates people,' he muses, staring at me and then the ginger cat who lies sprawled in my lap.

'Really?' In response he lets out a long purr.

'Sì, I've never seen him go near anyone before.'

'Cats are good judges of character, highly attuned to the energy around them. I've always founds cats fascinating. They were

101

considered sacred in ancient Egyptian times and they've carried that air of haughtiness through the ages, as if humans are their servants and they're these tiny little fluffball gods who demand to be worshipped.'

Giancarlo stares at me for an age. 'I think so too.'

He closes the book on his lap and gazes mournfully out to the canal. This man needs a shake-up, no two ways about it. Holding a perpetual frown cannot be good for his chakras. There's a blockage of some sort. Probably the heart chakra. I'm no expert – I always called my mom for advice in these matters. My gift is tarot, but I don't see him being open to that somehow. Best to leave that for when he knows me a bit better.

'Look, I understand you've . . .'

I cut him off. When someone starts a sentence with 'Look', it's never good. 'OK, so I'll make a start on setting things up, yeah? Do you mind if I take some happy snaps of the place for social media? We can work out my salary later. Whatever you think is fair.'

'Luna, is it?'

'Yes, that's the name my mother gave me.' He doesn't take the bait.

'I don't see this being viable. I get so many itinerants in here, just like you with their bright eyes and eternal youth, suffering the same God complexes where you think some pretty pictures online will fix everything. Soon the shine will wear off Venice for you, and you'll catch the next water taxi out of here, and I'll have these bookings for a service I don't need. You may have noticed, I love books, I adore cats, people not so much.'

He's got a very valid point because he doesn't know my motivations yet. And truthfully, even if I was his daughter that doesn't mean I'm going to affix myself here forever either. I might visit from time to time if things go well, but I won't be taking root here – it's not my way.

'You're right, so let's make it an exclusive service for this summer only. It will probably entice people to book, knowing it's a limited-time opportunity. Is that a good compromise for you?'

He scrubs his face with a bear-sized hand. 'You're not going to let this go, are you?'

'No, I'm not. I live and breathe books. They've been there for me when I've been all alone and not sure of my place in the world.'

Giancarlo stays silent.

'But most importantly, we *need* bookshops. Magical disorderly places like this that can transport us to another world where the possibilities are endless. Places we know we can stumble into and find a friend, fictional or feline. Bookshops are more than just a place to exchange money for goods – they're where the lost go to find sanctuary. Where the lonely go to find their tribe. Where else can wanderlust be sated from the comfort of an armchair? Kids' imaginations are ignited in places like this. Adults' too. So many adventures to be had, between the pages of these forgotten tomes. But what use are they stacked in waterlogged piles? It's almost a crime. In fact, it *is* a crime. These books should be revered the way they deserve. So what if they're not perfect? What is? They may have a few battle scars, but don't we all? They should be held again. Loved, laughed with. Cried over, tears spilling onto the parchment, absorbing all those emotions we feel when we read second-hand books, who've had lives as great as our own. But they can't live again, not if they're stashed in some dark corner, squirreled away for all eternity awaiting a slow death by the elements.'

'Are you finished?'

'Depends.'

'On what?'

'Whether I have the job.'

'Fine. Start next week. Monday.'

'Why not tomorrow?'

'I have another person starting next week and I don't want to have to do this twice. Whoever shows the most promise will

103

stay. And that's my final word.' It sounds so fatherly. Like he's about to ground me for breaking curfew. I can't help but smile at the thought of it.

'Fine, may the best bookworm win.'

With that he picks up his book and creaks open the cover. It's my cue to leave and I dare not push my luck. I give Dante one last belly scratch and take my bag and head out into the light of the day, blinking against the glare. I let out a *whoop* and commit to a happy dance until I remember where I am. I can only get away with dance-offs when Gigi is around because she hoots and hollers and takes the attention away from me. I quickly compose myself but can't hide my triumphant grin. I didn't exactly have high hopes that Giancarlo would be amenable to my plan.

I don't know who my competitor is, but there's no chance in hell I'm going to lose this job to them. I race back to the hostel to tell Gigi my news.

'You got the job?' she screeches like a banshee from the balcony above. She's going to be the death of me, this girl!

'Sort of?' I explain about the other bookseller, all the while craning my neck to talk.

'It's in the bag! I bet whoever it is didn't do a presentation like yours!'

'I'm not sure, but I'd hazard a guess not! And what about you? How did it go at the Angry Mussel?'

'I got the job! I had lunch with the owner and talked his ear off. I'm sure he didn't understand a word of what I said. Anyway, I'm doing my first shift tonight. So you know what this means?'

'Celebratory pizza?'

'Why can't a man know me inside out like you do, Luna?'

'It's pretty simple, the answer is always food-related.'

'Yes, simple! So are you hungry?'

'Always! But let me call Aunt Loui first.'

* * *

'Wow, baby girl, there's no chance he'll hire someone over you – there's just no way. You know so much about literature, so just wow him with that so he's aware you know your stuff inside out.'

'Yes, and it'll just be familiarising myself with the stock. He mainly sells English books to tourists so I can be an asset to the shop. I bet there are some beauties in there that we just need to find the right homes for.'

'I love the book concierge idea, it's fabulous.'

I fill Aunt Loui in on all that's happened and the fuzzy idea that maybe Giancarlo is more than just Mom's former pen pal.

'You think he's your dad?' I detect worry in her voice.

'What do you think? Did Mom ever tell you anything about that?'

'I heard the same as you, baby girl. You were a gift from the full moon party, and came to her when she needed you most. It was never about the man, it was more sacred than that. It was always solely about you. What's with the sudden change of heart about this?'

'The letters. This place. I get the strangest sensation here, like there's a message, something I need to figure out. If it's not that, then what else could it be? I know I'm connected, I feel it, but I just can't quite translate how or why.'

'Probably wise to hold off for a bit telling him any of this,' she says. 'See the lay of the land before you share that with him.'

'Yeah. He's hard to read. I don't know how he'll react. When he finds out Mom has gone that might break him once more. I need to know more about him before I drop that particular bombshell.'

Aunt Loui exhales a long breath. 'I wish I was with you. It's so strange being here without Ruby. The days go on forever with no one annoying me like she used to. Calling me over to help with a crossword, or to play cards. She got obsessed with David Attenborough documentaries and made me watch every single one with her, which bored me to tears at the time, but now I'm so thankful for it. Although I won't miss hearing her crunch on sunflower seeds, used to drive me to distraction.'

I smile, welling up at the thought of their friendship and how lonely it must be for Aunt Loui without her bothersome neighbour a few steps away. What can I say to ease her pain? Grief is such a gnarly beast it's hard to find the right words. 'Can you come to Venice for a bit, Aunt Loui? I'd love to have you here . . .' My heart expands at such an idea. Being together as we navigate life without Mom.

'That's just the thing, baby girl. I opened Ruby's mail today. She owes the bank a bit of money for her tiny home. You know, things slowed up for her when she got sick and it looks like she got into a bit of a pickle money-wise and she's in arrears. I've been sick about calling you. I can help with a portion of it but I think we might need to rent out her tiny home. I can pack and . . .'

'No, Aunt Loui.' I pinch the bridge of my nose. 'I shouldn't have taken the money she left me. I could have put that on the mortgage. Why didn't I even *think* to call the bank?' Nothing practical had crossed my mind at that point. I'd been so set on solving the mystery of the letters.

'She wanted you to have that money, Luna. Don't you worry about that.'

Mom wasn't a numbers person. Money used to flow through her fingers, but she *always* put the mortgage of her tiny home first. It's strange she'd leave me money and risk the loan going into arrears. Mom was adamant about keeping it forever so we'd both have a base and some security, she made me promise no matter what happened I'd do my best to hang on to it. So why would she leave me money when the mortgage hadn't been paid? Unless . . . it wasn't her at all.

'That was your money, wasn't it, Aunt Loui?' There'd been just enough funds for me to get to Italy and pay a few weeks' hostel accommodation. 'Aunt Loui?' I prompt. Has she given away her rainy-day fund for me?

'It was from your *mom*.'

'You're a terrible liar.'

106

She lets out her infamous honking laugh. 'Doesn't matter where it came from. If your mom had had it, she would have left it for you, so let's leave it at that. You're on a quest to find out more about what your mom left behind, and what can be more important? We all share and that's my contribution in her name, and I was happy to be able to do it, after everything your mamma has done for me.'

I choke up, as memories of them flutter through my mind. They had the type of friendship movies are made about and nothing could come between them. Eventually I manage to compose myself. 'Thank you, Aunt Loui. It means the world to me that you'd do that. But I'm going to pay you back.'

'You're welcome, baby girl, and you can't pay it back when it's a gift. That would be rude.'

'Let's call it a loan.'

'Let's not. Let me do this one small thing.'

We debate back and forth for a bit until I give in. I'll make it up to her somehow.

'What should we do about the tiny home?' I ask. 'Renting it out seems like the only option but the thought of having someone move in there, when her perfume still lingers, well it hurts more than I can say.'

There's static down the line and Aunt Loui says, 'I know, I know. I thought the same. I wanted it to be left exactly how it is for your return home.'

'Yeah.' I let out a sad sigh. 'But it's only a *thing*, right?' Mom wouldn't want me being sentimental over it all, but she *would* like me to continue paying the mortgage so I have a home in the future. 'I don't think there's any other option. Whatever I make working if I get the job won't be enough to cover living costs here, the arrears and the monthly mortgage.'

Aunt Loui exhales a pent-up breath. 'I'll pack up her things then? I can store everything in the outbuilding. It's the last thing I wanted to do and I know Ruby would be telling me to stop blubbering like a baby and get it done. It's just . . . with her wind chimes blowing in the breeze and all her gnomes in the garden, it's easier to pretend she's still there some days. I look over and yell out that I'll be over in a minute for sweet tea and some days I'm sure I hear her holler back.' My big tough aunt starts to cry and it's all I can do not to wail with her.

'Should I come back, Aunt Loui? It's not right leaving all this on you.'

'No!' she says. 'No, absolutely *not*. It's a privilege to be able to do this. I want you to find what you're searching for, Luna. This is my journey and that's yours. I'll pack everything with the utmost care so it'll all be ready for you whenever you decide to come back. We'll find the right tenant for the tiny home and that will be that.'

'OK, if you're sure.'

'I'm sure. We've got each other, baby girl. Remember that. I need you just as much.'

'I love you.'

'Love you too. Now head up, OK. Don't be swept back into the doldrums – she wouldn't want that.'

The thought of someone sleeping in my mom's bed, sipping sweet tea on her porch is strange. Will they tend to her flowers, the wild roses that perfumed the balmy evenings? Whatever they do, I know it'll be that much harder for Aunt Loui who'll have to witness a newcomer walking in Mom's footsteps, and I only pray they tread gently where Ruby Tuesday once did.

Chapter 12

'What's this?' Sebastiano asks, as a notebook falls from my bag onto the grass. Before, I can snatch it back, he's flicking through it with a grin on his face. '*I am fearless. I am in control of my destiny. I am never alone and always supported by the universe.*'

With a groan I wrench the notebook from his grasp. 'You shouldn't have read any of that. But if you must know, it's my daily affirmations and gratitude journal. I write in it every day and repeat the affirmations that I need to hear to connect or centre myself, whatever the case may be.' I can't really blame him for his surprise – Gigi was the same when she first witnessed me reading them aloud to myself in the mirror. It helps though. It shores me up for the day and reminds me who I am and what I'm striving for.

'It's sweet,' he says and pushes a lock of my hair from my face. I lie back on the picnic rug. The park is busy with people and there are a few other couples like us who've spread out on the velvety green to while away a Saturday at a slower pace.

'Do you ever want to escape Venice for a bit?' I ask. There's nowhere you can go that's ever void of people completely and even though I'm used to big cities, the narrow laneways and busy thoroughfares often provoke a slight claustrophobia. The beauty of the city is worth the crowds, but I wonder how residents feel about it. There's never a pause for them to take a breath and be quiet here. As much as I love being lost among so many faces, I usually save my pennies and then go somewhere off the beaten track to rejuvenate, replenish body, mind and spirit – but do Venetians have the same luxury?

'Yeah, sometimes. Especially at the height of summer and working long shifts at the *trattoria*. But I have time off occasionally. The Dolomites are two and half hours' drive away so I go there in the winter to ski, or hike in the summer. You really have to see it, Luna. It's breathtaking. That time surrounded by nature allows me to forget about work for a while – we all need that right? Time away so we can appreciate what's right in front of us.'

'And what do you see?'

'I see a beautiful woman who has taken over my every thought. I can't sleep because you're on my mind, and when I finally do, my dreams are full of this girl who roams around the world, free like a bird. I've never met anyone like you, Luna. I didn't even know such an existence was possible. It makes me contemplate my own life, my future. Do I want to be living this very same life in twenty years? You'll probably be in Antarctica by then, saving some exotic species of penguin while I'm still serving plate after plate of gnocchi. You've opened my eyes up to a whole new world. And it's hard not to let myself fall completely in love with you.'

I blush at his exclamations. But talking about love so soon . . . Still, I'm a heart-on-sleeve type and just maybe he means every word. He might be a hopeless romantic, and who doesn't love that kind of person – the one who risks saying how they feel no matter what? The one who is open and honest and doesn't let the fear of rejection stand in their way. Yet, it gives me pause. My heart is still under maintenance, so I'm not quite sure if that's why I can't decide either way with Sebastiano. One moment I'm caught up in his charm, the next the warning lights flicker and I stand back.

'You have a way with words, Sebastiano. And I would love to save an exotic species of penguin but I don't think I could live somewhere that cold.' I take the easy way out and try and change the subject. It's too soon for declarations of love. It's just too soon!

He silences me with a kiss, and I try with all my might to let go and feel my feelings, discern whether this is worth pursuing, or whether it's time to put up an out-of-order sign on my forehead. When we break apart, that same numbness returns. Side by side on the picnic rug, we stare into each other's eyes. With a finger he traces my bottom lip. His touch is so sensual a small tingle races down my spine. 'You're not sure about me yet Luna. But I've never felt this strongly about a woman before. Never felt such strong emotion that I had to act on. It's such an intense feeling, sometimes I wonder if it's real.'

'We're so different though.' And really, we haven't got to know much about each other at all. We've stolen some kisses and chatted about life in Italy and that's about it. We've haven't delved deep into one another's heart, hopes and dreams. Or is that just the hippy in me, always wanting to get to know a person right down to their very soul?

'Does it matter? Just listen to your heart.'

If only my heart wasn't closed for repairs.

Chapter 13

Sunday rolls around and brings with it lots of time to explore Venice alone while Gigi does a shift at the *La Cozza Arrabbiata*. She's been working all hours. Apparently, staff have been hard to find recently, so they also offered a slightly higher salary than expected. It's helped ease the worry that we'd run out of funds, but I should have known better – Gigi is the queen when it comes to job interviews. Best of all, she loves the family who own the place and says they've welcomed her like she's one of their own.

While she's busy working, I plan to retrace my steps when Mom and I came here all those years ago. We stayed in a fancy hotel, fancy for us at any rate. Even that should have struck me as odd, but at the time I'd been oblivious. I'd put it down to Mom wanting to splurge, to spoil us one last time before she hung up her travelling boots for good.

After much searching, I find the San Marco bell tower and from there find the hotel we stayed at on *Calle Frezzaria*. If only I could go and quiz them, ask if they remember the woman who wore flowers in her hair and had flushed cheeks. Why were her cheeks so rosy? That visit had a different quality to it, in that it *felt* like a real holiday and I followed Mom's lead.

The more I go back in time, the more questions I'm left with. There's this overwhelming desire to walk where she walked, connect with her however I can. *I miss her.* I miss her laugh, her smile, the way she'd hold my hand as we walked as if I was still a child.

Did she and Giancarlo have secret meetings while I slept, the curtains blowing across my face, sweeping in the scent of the canal? Did she bring me here to introduce me to my father and then get cold feet? Perhaps she worried she might lose me because she'd kept this secret for so long and thought I'd never forgive the deception. It's hard to reconcile the fact I could have had a relationship with him and now I'll never get that time back. Mom knew I yearned to meet my dad and spent my life wondering about what kind of man he was. Did that scare her? Did she think I'd cut those ties that bound mother and daughter so tight? Surely she knew I wouldn't? Whatever her faults were, I loved her unconditionally.

The hotel looks much the same. The curtains still blow from open windows. I continue and find Harry's Bar, famous for its bellinis and its celebrity patrons, including Ernest Hemingway back in the late Forties. Again, it was out of character for Mom to choose such an extravagant restaurant, but she insisted it'd be fun to pretend we were part of the jet set. We sipped our peachy bellinis and ate fresh oysters. A splurge I'd put down to the frivolity of being in the floating city and the excitement of acting like we were the type of people who frequented such establishments all the time.

Mom had been joking, pretending she was a lady who lunched, and then she sort of deflated. The light went out in her eyes. Afterwards she begged off with a headache and went back to the hotel for a nap while I read a book on my bed, feet up at the window, the curtains swishing inside and out like they were waving.

Today I peek inside Harry's Bar. Well-dressed patrons sit at small tables, sharing long languorous Sunday lunches without a care in the world. Their famous bellinis cost the equivalent of one night's accommodation at the hostel, and I marvel at how different we all are in this big wide world. What one prioritises. For a moment, I drift to fantasyland. I put myself inside that fancy bar, wearing fancy clothes, expensive high heels that nip my ankles, as I summon the waiter for another drink, *hell make it a bottle of your finest champagne*, and then I laugh at the corniness of it – like a scene from a movie. I've never envied this kind of life but I envy the people who occupy its place in the world. Like they know exactly where they're going and where they're meant to be. While I'm trudging around, quite lost, quite alone. No mom, no dad, no siblings. A family unit of one. Do I even exist?

I continue my walk down memory lane, not paying much attention to what's in front of me as I'm resolutely lost in the past. I try to shake the fug away – there's no solving this puzzle right now.

Reading is where I go when I want to make the real world disappear so I head to Venice's most famous park – *Giardini Reali* near the *Palazzo Ducale*. As I walk through the colourful lush gardens, I come across an orchestra playing. I watch for a while and let the music slide straight into my heart. Music was so important to Mom and it feels like a sign somehow. To stop overthinking things. I take a book from my bag, a historical romance I found on the shelves at the hostel, and search for a place to sit.

The gardens are teeming with people, and a walking tour group stand next to me, so I wander further down to find a quieter spot to lose myself in my book. In the distance, I see a willowy figure walk towards me and for a moment my heart stops. From here, it looks just like my mom. Same dirty-blonde hair, same graceful gait. Same casual flick of the hair over a shoulder. I swear my soul leaves my body, while I blink and blink to make sure this is not a mirage, not a dream. As she gets closer, I see she's younger than Mom. She's only a few years older than me. It's my heart playing tricks on me again. I feel Mom here, close by. It's being alone with my thoughts, examining my feelings – bringing her to the fore again. While it hurts, it's necessary. I don't want to forget her mannerisms, the lyrical sound of her voice, her mellifluous laugh.

I find an empty bench and pull out my romance novel. Promise myself that next week will be better when my days are filled with dusty books and my mind occupied. I'd thought that being so far from Mom's tiny home and all her trinkets and possessions, would ease these early stages of grief. But she's everywhere. Now she's a stranger walking down the cobblestone path. Tomorrow she'll be a reflection on the lapping water. Is she trying to tell me something?

Chapter 14

Giancarlo glances at his watch a couple of times and grumbles in Italian. I'm learning quickly that for a voracious reader he's not big on using actual words to communicate. I'm guessing we're waiting for the other employee before we begin our training, but it's already half ten and there's no sign of them. A golden-haired cat sits atop the counter pawing at a ball made from scrunched-up notepaper. This little beauty wears a collar with a nameplate: Wilde.

'For Oscar Wilde?' I ask, knocking the ball out of his grasp so he can chase after it.

'*Sì*. When he first arrived at the bookshop he was quite wild. Wouldn't come in, would only wait for food at the entrance and then leave again. It took me months to coax him inside. And months more before I could pick him up. Eventually he trusted me enough to give him a good wash and treatments for his many maladies.'

'And look at him now? The exuberance of a kitten.'

'*Sì, sì*, now he knows he's safe.'

'Where do all the cats come from?'

He shrugs. 'They find their way here, or they are unceremoniously dumped by the door.' His face darkens. 'Some locals bring them to me, if they see them scrounging for food. They know I will never turn a cat away.'

'How many do you have here?'

'Fifteen or so. I try and find them forever homes but it's difficult. I never want to let them go, and I must make certain the home is a safe one. The ones who remain, I am too attached to now.'

'I can see that.' He always has a cat in his arms, around his ankles or on his lap. He's like the Pied Piper for cats.

Time slips by and still the other employee is nowhere to be found. Giancarlo won't let me begin my training until they arrive. I rock Wilde to sleep in my arms like a baby before setting him down on one of the plush reading sofas, placing a few cushions around him like a barricade so people see there's a cat snoozing away and don't sit on him.

'The new person is late on the first day?' I say as boredom sets in. There are so many things I could be doing, but Giancarlo's asked me to sit behind the counter and wait.

I'm rewarded with a grunt in response that I've come to learn is just his way of communicating.

I broach the subject again. 'While we wait I'm going to make a start on those social media pages, if that's OK with you?'

'Sure, sure,' he says distractedly, as he flicks through his mail, making two piles – only one of which he opens. The unopened pile appears to be more business-related by the look of the logos on the envelopes. Perhaps he needs help with that task too, sorting and filing invoices so he can keep track. I make a mental note to ask later once I have a better idea of what's expected of me and the best way to use my time.

The radio is on in the background, and he sings quietly to an upbeat Italian song.

Despite his gruff exterior Giancarlo seems softer today, and I wonder what's made him so. He's up and about, and even greets a few customers. Is it the thought he has two employees who might facilitate change, or something else entirely? Whatever it is, it's nice to see him up out of the well-worn sofa and behind the counter as if he's inspired again. The cats are more energetic, as if reflecting his mood as they traipse along after him in a conga line.

While we wait for the missing mysterious employee I wander around the bookshop, familiarising myself with each room that comes off the main area. I take photos of each space and stumble on some older cats who sunbake atop piles of books. They stare at me through half-lidded eyes, lazily watching my progress around the space. It's an Instagrammer's dream – using the canal as a backdrop. Posting pretty pictures on social media of these glorious nooks and crannies will be a drawcard. The bookshop is a rabbit warren of rooms and quirky displays. In one, there's a typewriter on a table made exclusively from encyclopaedias. I snap pictures from various angles, trying to catch the view of the water and a feline or two.

In another room I find a maze made from hardback books. An actual *maze*! Who designed this? Someone painstakingly built this book by book, layer by layer. Was it Giancarlo? Was he once so enthusiastic about the bookshop that he did this? It's hard to imagine him committing to such an arduous task, but maybe once upon a time, he was inspired here.

The maze is wide enough to walk through, but low enough I can see over the top. It's been built for children. I tentatively peek over to make sure there are no cats waiting to jump out and scare me before I head in, following the trails until I come out the other side. It needs a good dusting, and some minor repairs – some of the tomes have edged their way out like displaced bricks, but it's a marvel. I haven't seen anything like it before.

It could be a real highlight for the shop. What child wouldn't like to take up the challenge of entering a real-life book maze? I take some arty pics, trying to hide the elements that need fixing, and then step back and survey the rest of the space.

As expected, there's no order in this room; it's a mélange of books in every genre, every language. But it would be well suited as a children's room. If we filled the shelves with colourful young readers, paint the furniture pastel pink, yellow and blue, we could make a cosy hang-out for baby bibliophiles. Surely tourists would love their offspring to have their own kind of Alice in Wonderland adventure here? It strikes me as odd that Giancarlo would build this room with a children's maze; he doesn't exactly seem the sort to cater to children or their sense of fun when he's so dour himself. Perhaps the maze has been here since his own father's time.

My pulse thrums as I consider the endless possibilities that will add to the appeal of the canal bookshop. As I leave the room, I flick through the pictures I've captured. They're good, even if they're only from my ancient cell phone. I can use some filters to improve them, maybe some moody black and whites and some . . . *Ooof!* I run smack bang into the back of someone and my phone goes flying out of my hand. I do circus juggler hands as I try to catch it, but each time my fingers just manage to flip it into the air until eventually I miss, and it goes crashing to the floor with a crack.

'Who walks backwards like that?' I say to the guy standing there, who wears a passive expression as if he hasn't just caused me great harm. He has dark fiery eyes, but they remain muted, almost like they're shuttered against my protests, as if he too is caught up in the beauty of the bookshop and hasn't returned from dreamland just yet. His curls flop over one side of his face . . . He's the guy from the dock whose book had an unfortunate swimming accident. He's the guy who I saw at the bookshop that night! Is he here to replace *Into the Wild*?

Still, we have more pressing matters to deal with. While my phone might be as old as the hills it's sufficient for my needs and has been with me through every up and down. I bend to retrieve it, finding the screen is a spiderweb of cracks. I'm baffled by his silence and my usually Zen reserve jumps up and dashes out the open window. 'Well?' I say. They don't even *make* screens

119

for phones this antiquated anymore! I'm going to have to buy a new phone, an expense I can't afford right now.

'My apologies, I was walking backwards to get an overview of the bookshop from this angle.' He too holds a cell phone in his hand. I'm no expert but it looks a top-of-the-range, fancy-pants model, which manages to irk me. He's taking photos, which can only mean one thing – he's my competitor for the job! He's not here to replace a novel at all; he's here to steal the bookseller position!

'As you can see, you've shattered my screen because you weren't looking where you were going.'

'You weren't looking either, obviously,' he says, as I try and pinpoint his accent. It's British with perhaps a Spanish inflection. There's challenge in his eyes, as if he has also figured out that I'm his rival for the position. 'By the looks of it, that model should have been retired sometime back in the early Noughties.'

I fold my arms, and glare at him. I'm not usually the glaring type – that's more Gigi's speed – but this . . . this . . . unassuming guy wearing faded chinos, and a wrinkled tee, with his dark mussed bed hair that he hasn't even bothered to tame, has pushed me over the edge, not only by breaking my phone but worse, by judging it. How dare he!

'So just because it's old, means it should be relegated to the scrap heap even though five minutes ago it worked perfectly fine? Have you heard about climate change? About sustainability? I don't subscribe to the principles of a throwaway society, but you obviously do!'

'And you know that . . . how?'

'It's written all over you. From your . . .' well, he's not exactly wearing Sebastiano-style designer labels, not even close '. . . big fancy phone to your . . .' *help me, Jesus* '. . . big fancy . . . attitude.' I'm acting like a petulant child; I know it, I can't help it. It's the way he stares at me like he doesn't care one iota about the destruction he's just caused. I have so few belongings, I'm not a materialistic person, but that phone is my lifeline. It keeps me connected, especially to Aunt Loui who will worry if she can't get hold of me. And he couldn't give a damn.

'This fancy phone?' He points to the shiny monstrosity in his hand.

'Talk about a penis extension, someone is clearly making up for a lack.'

He grins, he *actually* grins. Doesn't he know I'm insulting his very manhood? 'Good quality photographs for social media are kind of important, don't you think?'

'Quality photographs come from a quality eye and not some fandangle piece of equipment.' Did I just use the word *fandangle*? Yikes, this guy has really rubbed me the wrong way, it must be his energy, his aura, something my subconscious is reacting to on a primal level. I'm wondering why the tarot cards gave me no warning about this set of spiky circumstances . . . I might be reduced to asking the magic eight ball at this rate.

He has the audacity to smile, and while the rest of him is a bedraggled mess, his teeth are of the white shiny variety. Another red flag. Toothpaste-commercial smiles are as fake as *Down with the Patriarchy* tees worn by non-feminist feminists.

'It seems to me that you're the one causing all the accidents around here. Weren't you the girl from the dock who almost knocked me into the canal with that monstrosity of a backpack, and killed my book in the process?'

'Again, you weren't looking where you were going! I'm all for reading but even I have limits!'

'You're right,' he concurs. I see his ploy a mile away. If he thinks he can be all agreeable while sneakily getting me on side to steal my role here, then two can play at that game.

'I often am. Look, we've got off on the wrong foot. I presume you're here for the work trial too?'

'Trial? No, I'm here as a full-time employee from Spain.' Damn it all to hell and back. If he's from Spain he doesn't even need a work visa. This doesn't bode well for me and, even worse, he says he's been actually given the job. Did Giancarlo only invite me to participate in this farce to stop my lengthy monologue the other day? Did he feel bad rejecting me, so decided this was the easiest way to let me down gently under the guise of best bookseller wins? My adversary continues, 'I plan to stay in Venice long term. I'm here to finish my first novel and what better place to do it than the city of love.'

A broody writer. Now his scruffy appearance makes sense. Probably up all hours clacking away at the keyboard, writing the next literary masterpiece. I don't have the energy for this today. 'It's a romance novel then?' He might just be redeemable if so.

A frown mars his face. 'A romance? Why would you think that?'

'You just implied the city of love would be the perfect place to finish your novel, so I don't think it's a leap to join those dots?'

He cocks his head as if I'm speaking in another language and he's trying his best to make sense of my garbled words. Why does he make me feel a little off balance? Like I'm the anomaly here, speaking in riddles.

'No, it's not a romance but it has romantic elements. Doesn't every story?'

'Pretty much.' At least he'll admit that. The number of heated conversations I've had with men about this subject is mind-bending. Romance is at the core of so many novels, even espionage, thrillers, action, but for some reason this is always scoffed at. Even frowned upon as if admitting that reading a book with a love story arc will somehow take away from it when it adds to it. It's bamboozling because aren't we as humans drawn to love in real life? Isn't it one of the fundamentals we strive for? Makes no sense that we can't admit to enjoying it just as much on the page whether it's a romance or a crime novel.

'Are you going to stand around all day talking to each other or are you here to work?' Giancarlo thunders from behind, making me jump in surprise. 'Neither of you will get the job if this is what you plan to do all day!'

I turn to Giancarlo who wears an expression of abject annoyance as if we're already testing his patience. 'Well I'm glad you asked. As you know *I* arrived on time today and was innocently taking photos of the space when . . . this *guy* here ran into me and managed to smash the screen on my phone.'

'Oscar,' the scruffy writer adds unhelpfully. 'She . . .'

'*Luna*,' I interject.

He gives me a nod. '*Luna* bumped into *me* and dropped it. I wouldn't exactly say I had any involvement in the smashing of her 1999 Nokia.'

I roll my eyes. He just can't help himself. 'It's a Samsung, I'll have you know, and it still had plenty of years left in it. It's fine. I'll replace it myself, but it shows what kind of person you are when you can't own up to your mistakes.' I shoot a long look at Giancarlo hoping he catches my meaning.

'You need to be able to work together, so sort it out.' And with that he hulks off. Well, no help there then.

'I'll need your phone,' I say, and hold my hand out.

'I don't think so, butterfingers.' Oscar smiles but all I see is a snake in the grass!

I don't react – that's what he wants. Instead I change tack. 'Oscar, we need to make the best of this, or neither of us will be here next week. You take the photos then and email them to me and I'll log into Giancarlo's computer and work from that.' I look to the boxy old thing and wonder if it's just a prop. I can't exactly complain about its age since I've just waxed lyrical about not subscribing to a throwaway society. But I haven't seen a computer that size since . . . ever.

'Fine. But I want the credit for the photos.'

'Who are you, Annie Leibovitz?'

'Who?'

He is the limit. I ignore him and stomp to the counter. Tomorrow I'll bring a smudge stick. This place has got some bad juju all of a sudden.

Chapter 15

A few days later, I've smudged the bookshop, garnering only a slight eyebrow raise from Giancarlo. Does he remember my mom being obsessed with smudging? If only he had a more readable face. Already, the atmosphere feels cleansed, fresh with promise.

Oscar arrives late again, so I feel duty-bound to report this to Giancarlo. 'Oh look at the time!' I make a show of looking at a watch on my wrist – that I don't wear. 'The afternoon shift is here!'

Oscar rolls his eyes and takes his jacket off, hanging it over the stool behind the counter. Dante meows and jumps into his arms. The traitor! So much for him being suspicious of every newcomer.

'He must like me!' Oscar grins and draws the attention of Giancarlo who throws a smile Oscar's way. The fact his cats seem to like Oscar gets his attention, and not that he's woefully late again. It looks like Giancarlo is playing favourites already!

'He's starved of affection, more likely,' I say.

'You think?' Dante basks under his touch. We're going to have words later, and I'll explain to Dante about learning the ability to spot fake friends. Another cat lopes lazily over and winds itself around Oscar's legs. '*Alighieri!* Hey little fella!' Oscar says.

'Cats are marvellous communicators and I think you'll find they're showing you who's boss and not vying for your attention.'

'Is that so?' Oscar says in a voice that implies I'm incorrect.

A third cat appears, as wide as it is long. Oscar bends, with Dante still in his arms, Alighieri at his feet and pats it. 'Moby!'

'Dick!' I finish.

'Excuse me?' Oscar says, frowning.

'The name is Moby *Dick*.'

'Right. Moby Dick, makes sense due to the sheer size, I guess. But I'm not into fat shaming; maybe he's just big-boned. Could be a thyroid issue. Perhaps he eats his feelings, and there's nothing wrong with that.' Oscar scratches Moby Dick's ears.

'Are you finished?' I ask. He thinks he's some kind of animal whisperer.

'Well . . .'

'Moby Dick is an old Italian cat who sneaks food from Giancarlo at every opportunity, so it's not a thyroid issue. It's a consumption issue that is well earned considering the life poor old Moby Dick had before Giancarlo rescued him.'

Oscar ignores me as more cats come running. 'It must be my pheromones.' He laughs as a few fickle felines approach him. I've never seen anything like it. Cats are great judges of character, so I try not to hold it against them. Oscar does seem to be the golden boy for some inexplicable reason. Perhaps they feel sorry for him, with his bedraggled appearance as if he fell straight out of bed and made his way here. Do they sense something about him?

'Yes,' I agree. 'You're like one of those hundred-year-old cat people.'

He snubs the jibe and says, 'Our Instagram post of Dostoyevsky cat blew up last night. It went semi viral.'

'What? Let me see!' Somehow Oscar managed to catch a picture of Dostoyevsky leaping from one bookshelf to the other, like some kind of bungee jumping adrenaline junkie with arms and legs splayed and the most wicked and wild smile on her face.

He pulls out his phone and brings up the post. 'Oh, wow, Oscar! Look at all those comments! We have to answer them all!'

'No!' Giancarlo thunders, startling us both. 'You're here to work, not try and become the next ViewTube sensation.'

'ViewTube?' Oscar says.

'I think he means YouTube,' I whisper and then turn to Giancarlo, rearranging my expression to match the Golden Boy's, who seems to get away with a lot more than I do. 'We're not trying to become the next ViewTube sensation, but we are trying to get the bookshop name out there, that's all. And a big part of social media is being social and interacting with fans. The cats are a hit and I think they can really draw a . . .'

'The answer is no. The cats aren't for sale.'

I give Oscar a quick elbow to the ribs, so he can take up the fight. 'For once, I do agree with Luna.'

I give him a gee thanks look.

He moves Dante to his other arm and says, 'We want the right kind of customer, don't we, Giancarlo? And cat lovers, well they're the best kind of humans, so we're already halfway there.'

The right kind of customers? He's not going to buy this baloney!

Giancarlo rubs his chin. 'OK, fine. Ten minutes to reply and that's all. I don't want you getting carried away with it.'

How did that work? Either way, it's a win. Oscar and I exchange victorious smiles and scuttle away before Giancarlo can change his mind.

In the piano room, we sit at the stool. 'Do you want to reply to them? The post was your idea.'

'Yeah, but it was your amazing photo that grabbed their attention.'

He shrugs. 'You do it.'

'You'd trust me with your phone?'

'If it ends up in the canal then I'll know you did it on purpose.'

I give him a half-smile.

* * *

126

Later that day I'm cleaning behind the counter with the pretence of sorting dusty stacks of paperwork that appear to be kept for no apparent purpose. Really, I'm looking for letters my mom wrote back to Giancarlo while also creating a space for future book orders. So far, I've found out nothing. It's not surprising though. Maybe they're bundled up and by his bedside? He strikes me as the kind of man who'd read her letters time and again. What do they say? Does she make excuses for her absence? Or make flighty promises she has no intention of keeping? Or I could be way off track and they're gone, never to be read again.

Giancarlo is a man of few words, and when he does speak it's more of a grunt, a head tilt, or a wave with his hand that could mean anything from 'it's over there', 'get the hell away from me', 'feed the cats', or 'go pick up my lunch order'. It's quite the skill to be able to decipher these interactions and I'm getting adept at it.

I'm hoping I can find his address, find out where he lives and get Gigi to do some reconnaissance while I know he's here at the bookshop. Does he have a wife, a family? Does he live in a dungeon, and use bookshop employees as human sacrifices? That kind of thing.

I heave bundles of paper onto the counter and sneeze. Bookshop dust is like not like regular dust. It leaves a thick layer on everything and there's no keeping up with it. As soon as you wipe down one section, it's danced off to the next. I bet that's why Giancarlo usually sits in one spot and doesn't move, so the dust can't catch him. He lets it settle around him and lives peacefully with it.

Speak of the devil. 'What are you doing?'

Busted. 'For a big guy you have very stealthy movements. Just how do you manage to creep up like that?' Ah, it's because of the dust. He glides instead of makes heavy movements.

'I asked you what you were doing?'

'Well.' I dust my hands on my jeans for the hundredth time that day. I'm not sure if an apron would work in this environment,

127

maybe I could make apron chic a thing? Giancarlo does his trademark glare. It doesn't worry me a jot, I'm so used to it now. 'I took it upon myself to sort these bundles of paperwork in the hopes of clearing up under the counter. That way we'd have room to hold orders from the new website that's coming soon, so they'd be ready for postage and . . .'

'You wouldn't make a very good spy.'

I pretend to be outraged. 'Excuse me?'

'What are you *looking* for, Luna?'

I feel colour race up my cheeks and I remind myself a spy definitely wouldn't blush. They wouldn't give the game away that easily. Is it some kind of breath work they do or . . . There's no time to research such a thing when the man monster is starting intently at me. This would probably be a good time to tell him I'm looking for answers! But nothing is certain with my job here and I don't want to show my hand just yet.

'I think *someone* has read too many espionage novels.'

He raises a bushy brow. 'Leave the paperwork, clean up the books.'

I bite back a retort. Originally, I couldn't wait to clean up the books and make some sort of sense of all the piles. But now, not so much. Dark burrows here now hold a certain disgust after finding so many mouldy damp novels and all sorts of detritus people leave behind when they can't be bothered finding a bin. There's a certain type of terrifying species of bookshop spider that particularly loves those little crevices too. It's downright nightmare-inducing.

'You're the boss!' I give him a salute. 'But can we agree to store this paperwork elsewhere then? I was hoping to . . .'

'No.'

'OK-K-K.' Hey, he's a man who knows his own mind. There's nothing wrong with that. He's doing things the wrong way but it's his business and I must respect that. I snatch a glance at the puddle near the front door, but wily old Giancarlo sees it. My spy skills need a lot of work but I'd love to ditch these reams of old invoices that he surely doesn't need anymore. Maybe Mom's letters are secreted here somewhere and that's why he's being so tetchy about it.

'Don't even think about it.'

'What?'

'Dumping all that paperwork into that convenient puddle you keep looking at so you can get rid of it all.'

I grin. 'It *would* be so convenient. Gah!'

I'm sure I detect the merest uplift of his lips. I'll count that as progress. Just as I'm about to ask Giancarlo some pressing questions to get me further ahead in my quest, Oscar bumbles over, covered head to foot in bookshop grime, like he's trying to prove the shadowy hidey-holes hold no fear. Well good for him! I personally need some sort of vaccination against whatever lurks there.

'Hey, guys. I made some headway with the Italian room. It's spic and span now, but I desperately need a shower as you can see. I don't know how you stay so *clean* in here, Luna. The water gets in everywhere and turns to sludge. All adds to the appeal though,' he puts in hastily.

'I wear multiple layers.'

He smiles. 'I could really use a hand tomorrow, Luna. It would be great to make a start on the children's maze.'

Please don't make me stick my hands into dingy crevices where spiders hide! 'Busy, tomorrow. Giancarlo wants me to finish the website and start planning the Venetian book concierge service.'

'It can wait one more day,' Giancarlo says, throwing me right under the bus with nary a care for my arachnophobia. He's tried to assure me the creepy things are actually tarantula wolf spiders (as if that helps!). Allegedly they're completely harmless and don't actually resemble the hairy, terrifying tarantulas of nightmares.

I'm not sure they're harmless because if I accidentally pick one up I *will* set fire to my arm to be free. My fear is completely irrational, but it comes from living in remote tropical places and coming far too close to these eight-eyed monsters. Now my skin prickles just thinking of it. Giancarlo says it's the change of weather and that soon they'll be gone from their little bookshop hidey-holes but what the hell, Venice! No one mentions this in any of the guidebooks, do they?

'I'm going home for the evening,' Giancarlo says. 'Can one of you lock up?'

I look to Oscar in the hopes he'll agree so I can duck off and follow Giancarlo. My last two attempts had been aborted when he spotted me and I had to shuffle off in the other direction.

'Sure, sure,' Oscar says. He's always so amenable in front of Giancarlo, which I'm sure is all an act. The model employee with his perfect smile and endless patience with customers. Giancarlo grabs his jacket and gives us a backwards wave as he shuffles out.

Thankful he didn't pick up on my nefarious reasons for asking him to lock up again, I momentarily soften towards Oscar. 'I promise I'll help you sort the book maze tomorrow.' I'll wear gloves. Gloves and an all-in-one plastic suit.

'Thanks, that would be great. Between us, I'm beat. Staying back late to clean up and hauling books from one side of the place to the other all day takes a lot more energy than I'd ever have imagined. I can see now why Giancarlo leaves it the way he does. No sooner have I put a book away, than someone picks it up and leaves it in another area. It makes you wonder if it's worth sorting out in the first place.'

I glance at the door. Just how far has Giancarlo got already? I don't have time, as much as I'd like to chat about this too. Working here has been a real eye-opener. English speaking customers ask the funniest questions and often exhibit strange behaviour. Earlier that day I'd watched a customer carry a stack of books around as she wandered through the shop, only to see her pile them on the damp floor and use them like a stepladder. In the end, she left with nothing and I had to rescue those beauties so they didn't get soggy. If the book concierge idea does take off, I do wonder how Giancarlo would deal with the extra bodies in here.

'Gotta run but let's talk about this tomorrow?'

Oscar's face falls, and the shutters come back down over his eyes. I've disappointed him again but it can't be helped. I vow to make amends with him tomorrow.

'Sorry, it's only that I've got someplace to be.' I snatch my cardigan off the back of the chair and dash out into the street, hoping to catch up to Giancarlo. Luckily for me he ambles at his regular pace. Everything he does is slow, measured and walking is no different. He waves to the owner of the *rosticceria* where he stops and chooses rotisserie chicken and potato salad that he takes with him. Then he stops into the *enoteca* where he buys a bottle of wine. Is he buying dinner and wine for the family? The crowds thin as we get further out from the district of San Polo. It makes it harder to hide, so in case he spots me I take my broken dead cell phone from my bag and hold it aloft as if I'm following directions and not Giancarlo himself.

At the end of the laneway, he pauses as if deciding which way to go. I duck behind an archway of a trattoria and wait. He goes into a *tavola calda* and orders a negroni, chatting in rapid Italian to the barman. These little places are dotted around Venice and translate to 'hot tables'. It's a tiny bar where patrons slug back a negroni or glass of wine at the end of a long day. Behind display cabinets are plates of ready-made food, like bruschetta or arancini. Most locals seem to enjoy imbibing a quick aperitif before going home for dinner, but I like to think it's about community, visiting a friendly barman and catching up on the day together, before they trudge home, their blood warmed by alcohol, hungry belly assuaged by a tasty little morsel or two.

Is this a way in with Giancarlo? Making his *tavola calda* my drop-in spot too? Maybe we can connect over a quick drink, his tongue loosened by Campari? Just as I'm about to step from behind the archway there's a tap on my shoulder. I jump so high I'm sure my soul leaves my body. *Follow the light, Luna.* Soon, I'm returned back to my human suit, my heart lodged somewhere up near my throat . . .

Chapter 16

'Why are you spying on Giancarlo?' Oscar whispers, pushing spectacles up the bridge of his nose. Spectacles I've never seen him wear. They give him an aloof lost writer quality. He reminds me of that cutie pie author Simon Van Booy, and for a moment I lose track of what I'm doing.

'Well?' he prompts.

Right. The spying. 'I'm not spying. I'm . . .' I glance back at Giancarlo, a lone figure standing at the bar, with a book that's materialised from somewhere. The waiter is busy making mushroom bruschetta. Does Giancarlo love reading that much or is it a way to close potential conversation? He's said his hellos and that's it? 'Look at him. Doesn't he seem like he's carrying the weight of the world on his shoulders?'

Oscar edges close behind me. 'Yes. He's lonely. It radiates off him.'

As much as we've clashed, Oscar seems to have good observational skills and an empathetic heart. Is that because he's a writer, or just the person he is? 'So is he lonely because he chooses to be so, or because it's been forced upon him?'

'How can loneliness be forced upon anyone? He's obviously made a choice at some point to seek solitude. Why? Who knows. There could be hundreds of reasons.'

'Loneliness can be forced on someone if they lose a loved one, or they go missing perhaps? Just spitballing.' I gulp and remind myself to be economical with details when it comes to Giancarlo. Oscar is too clever for his own good and being called a spy by both of them in the same day is concerning, even if they meant it in jest – which I'm still not sure they did since the accusations weren't accompanied by any *hardie-ha-has*.

Oscar gives me a nod that says he agrees with me. 'True, I hadn't thought of that. Now you mention it, he wears the mask of a man who's had his heart broken, doesn't he? Perhaps that's why he's so gruff, so impatient with people. He doesn't care anymore. Even his beautiful bookshop has lost its appeal, and that is a tragedy.'

I wish I could tell Oscar my story and ask for advice. As much as we clash, he is intuitive and has a surprisingly compassionate side when it comes to anyone other than me. But I can't risk it in case he uses the knowledge against me to get the job. When I study him, seeing the thoughtful way he gazes at this situation, I have the sudden sense I can trust him. Even if we're vying for the same job. There's an inherent goodness about the guy, and I don't sense that sort of thing very often.

Oscar stands back from the archway. 'Anyway, we'd better go. I don't think he'd like to stumble upon us here speculating about him like this.'

'You're right. He already thinks I'm some sort of spy.'

Oscar grunts, and motions with his head at Giancarlo. I blush.

'OK, yes, this might be classed as spying,' I say. 'But it's only because I care – it's not for any nefarious reasons.'

He narrows his eyes. 'It's not just that though, is it? It's the way you dart a glance over both shoulders every time you do something behind the counter. You act like you're about to rob the till. Then there's the way you sift through the paperwork like you're an agent of the Italian Revenue Agency or something.'

'Oh come on!' Sleuthing isn't my strong suit, I guess. I really need to work on that. 'It's only that he's so attached to everything, even paperwork that goes right back to when Italy still accepted lire as currency for crying out loud. He's obviously a clutter bug – you can tell by the books – but that's charming, all the rest of it is junk. I'm trying to make things more streamlined so if we do manage to increase revenue at the shop he's got a system in place to keep up with it.'

Oscar frowns. 'But the job description didn't mention doing any of that – so why push his buttons? And here you are following him. You couldn't get out of the bookshop fast enough. It appears that you're fascinated about Giancarlo, the question is – why? I'm not buying this *he's lonely* baloney.'

'That rhymes.'

He simply raises a brow. Damn writers and their ability to read people. 'I'm not fascinated. I'm . . .' What am I? 'I'm *concerned*. I'm simply the sympathetic sort and Giancarlo is crying out for a change in his life, but he's so stuck in a rut, so fixated on the past he can't see the future and *we* need to help him. Like he told me, staff have these grandiose ideas and then they up and leave. I know for sure I won't be here forever, so I'm hoping together we can design this for him for the long term. He needs help, Oscar, or the bookshop will close. It's only a matter of time. We have to join forces against him and his unwillingness to change, like we did with the social media thing, don't you agree?'

Oscar pushes me into the shadows of the archway and presses his body hard against mine. *What the hell!* I go to protest when I feel his breath against my ear. 'When I said join forces I didn't mean literally!'

'Shush! He's walking this way.'

I freeze. What's worse, being discovered spying, or found in a compromising situation as if we were so desperate to kiss we could only go a few steps before landing in a passionate embrace? Neither option is good. I close my eyes and hope we're hidden well enough that Giancarlo won't take a second glance at two lovers canoodling. It's Venice, the city of love – people are kissing all over the place!

Oscar smells just like the shop, as if its scent has permeated his skin. If only we could bottle such a fragrance. 'Sorry,' he mumbles into the warmth of my neck. 'I didn't mean to startle you.'

'It's fine,' I whisper as his unruly hair tickles my cheek. If only we weren't after the same job, I'd probably like to befriend Oscar.

'Can you see him?' he whispers. His breath against my neck makes my skin tingle.

I hold on to Oscar's shoulders and peep over the top. The laneway is dim with only soft shards of a sinking sun catching the tops of the buildings. 'No can't see him, can't see much at all.'

Oscar steps away, and blushes. 'Sorry again, Luna. I reacted, that's all. I need this job and I'd have hated for him to think we were following him.'

I wave him away. 'Me too. I really need this job, more than I can say.' Oscar already has the correct visa so I'm one step behind him.

Oscar sighs; in the shadowy twilight of the laneway his features are softer, like he's left his angst back at the bookshop. 'Then we're at an impasse. What do you suggest we do?'

I pull my cardigan tight as the air grows cool. 'What can we do?'

He shrugs. 'You don't have a work visa.'

'And how do you know that?'

'Excellent powers of deduction.'

'I'm in the process of obtaining a seasonal work visa, so . . . ?'

'So until then, really you shouldn't be the face of the business – he could get in trouble and then he'd have even more problems . . .'

'Don't try and guilt me. That's not fair.'

'It's true though.'

Damn it. 'Why can't you find another job? Yeah, you're a writer, but it's not like you're sitting there bashing away at the keyboard during the day.'

He shoves his hands in his pockets. 'It's inspiring. I feel like I'm absorbing the words that surround me. I haven't felt as alive as I do there. Sure, the place needs some TLC but its faults are what make it so beautiful. The fragility of those books, their stubbornness to survive when the elements are doing their best to ruin them.'

'You speak about them as if they're alive.' Why, why does Oscar have to mirror my own thinking? Why do I have to relate to him on so many levels? It's easier when we're enemies so I don't have to feel any which way about him, but he's got a way of getting under your skin. It's his *laissez-faire* approach to everything that softens people up.

'It feels like they're alive. Like they hum almost.' There's a look on his face that I can only describe as love, as if Oscar is mad for the bookshop in the way that only bookworms would understand. And dammit it all to hell and back, that's me. I feel the same way in there. Yeah, sure there's a lot that needs doing every single day, there are spiders, there are puddles, there's mould we have to sandpaper from the top of the books, and yet, it's the most magical place. Maybe it is something about being in a place among trillions of words that originated from twenty-six letters of the English alphabet. Or twenty-one letters in the Italian alphabet, depending on what language they're reading in.

'Oscar, there's more to it for me, but I'm still processing it all myself – so can I ask you to trust me when I say, I need that job far more than you do.'

He crosses his arms. 'Tell me why.'

'I can't. Not yet.' I'd love to be able to trust him, but I don't know him quite well enough.

'Then I don't believe you.'

'Fine. Then may the best bookseller win.' And win I will. If he won't listen to reason, there's not much I can do.

'Fine.'

'This is the part where you storm off.' I stare him down.

'I'm not much of a storm-off person.'

'Fine, I'll storm off then.'

'Be my guest.'

He's infuriatingly calm as he calls my bluff. Still, I make a show of stomping off only to see Giancarlo chatting to someone in a deli further along before he waves to them and heads back towards me. I spin on my heels and dart back into the shadows.

'Reconsidered already?' There's no time for talking. I launch into him and we land hard against the wall, our arms and legs a tangle.

Oscar lets out an *oomph*. I can hear Giancarlo's heavy steps close by. 'What are you *doing*, Luna? Trying to take my job by force? By breaking my legs. By . . .' There's nothing I can do to make the guy stop flapping his jaws, so I press my lips hard against his, caught up in the dramatic moment. I scrunch my eyes closed and give in to the kiss – hell, it's got to look believable if we're caught – and absolutely hate myself when I feel a sort of sensation, like falling. Like excitement. It's the adrenaline. It's the *subterfuge*. All I know is I don't feel like this when I kiss Sebastiano. Again, I remind myself, it's the situation. It's NOT REAL.

The footsteps continue, in that same heavy cadence until the sound fades. I step back. 'Sorry,' I say, double blinking as I search Oscar's stunned face. 'Giancarlo was there.'

He looks for all the world like he's been slapped in the face with a still-wet fish. Is my faux kissing *that* bad?

'And you thought kissing was the answer?'

Upon reflection I could have just said shush. But I panicked. And Oscar would have kept on, wanting an explanation and then we'd have been busted. 'It was the only way to stop your jabbering. I don't know if you know this, but you're a talker. You talk. A lot. And there was no time.'

An affronted expression moves across his face. 'I don't talk a lot.'

'You kind of do. And you have a lot of opinions. Your "best of" book list leaves a lot to be desired.'

'And that's a problem?'

'Far be it for me to say.'

'But you just said it.'

'You're putting words into my mouth.'

'Words that *you* said.' He throws his hands up, exasperated.

'If you say so.'

He shakes his head and mumbles in Spanish. He very rarely speaks in his other tongue, so I try hard not to get lost in the rhythm of another heady language.

'Goodbye, for real this time!'

He touches his lips as I go. Probably trying to wipe off the kiss and pretend it never happened. Urgh, there he goes back on his high horse. Oscar doesn't know it, but his bookshop days are probably numbered due to his inability to gauge social cues when it comes to customers. Yeah sure, he's a conscientious employee, but when he's asked for a book recommendation and he goes a hundred years back and works his way forward on the timeline, including orating passages from said tomes, customers' eye glaze over and they lose the will to live. Canny as he usually is, with this one thing, he's totally oblivious to it.

I'm lost in thought as I walk all the way back to the hostel and have to remind myself more than once that it was a pretend kiss and it didn't mean anything. Why then, did I feel my soul ignite? My heart chakra expand and pulse? I shake it off. This is a complication I do not need. My under-maintenance heart seems to be working just fine around him, which is strange in itself. Besides, Oscar appeared for all the world like I'd terrified him. He'll probably jump every time he sees me now, afraid that I'm either going to break his legs, or kiss him. Doesn't he know I'm a peace-loving pacifist?

Gigi is on the balcony, surrounded by other travellers. She notes my arrival and smiles. 'I'll be right down,' she says.

I fill her in on Oscar and all his faults, of which there are many. 'Oooh, Luna, you kissed him?! Are we in the midst of a love triangle?' Oh God, Sebastiano. I hadn't given him a second thought except to compare the two and their smooching skills. This is not me. I'm not that type of person, but then I remind myself it was an act – an act of espionage! I cannot be held responsible. There are always victims when it comes to the subtle art of spying and I'm still learning the ropes.

'Well?' Gigi snaps her fingers in front of my face. 'Earth to Luna. Love triangle, love hexagon, tell me what we're up against here!'

'Hexagon, please! It was a faux kiss with Oscar and the guy couldn't speak *English* after. I'm sure he was cursing me in Spanish and muttering. He wore a look of *abject* misery.'

She shakes her head. 'You poor little fool.'

'What? Why?'

'The thunderbolt. Again. Twice in one place. This really *is* the city of love.' She looks up at the starry sky. 'Maybe I need to get out more if Cupid is darting arrows around so abundantly.'

I roll my eyes so hard I get dizzy. 'Gigi, it wasn't a thunderbolt. Why you keep insisting every man is in love with me is a mystery.' I let out a frustrated sigh. Is she not *listening*? 'If anything, it was the opposite. He looked downright *traumatised*. Shocked to the core of his being. When I walked off I caught him touching his lips, as if he was trying to remove whatever mark I left. He probably thinks it's his pheromones again! What if he tells Giancarlo I made a move on him or something?' Urgh, it beggars belief that I've put myself in this position. 'I'll probably get fired for being too handsy! Oh my God, can you even imagine? Won't be able to put that on the old résumé, will I?'

'Luna, Luna, Luna. So pretty, so clever, yet so very naïve when it comes to matters of the heart. You never gauge their interest – it's like it bounces right off you. You're a beauty, inside and out, but you don't seem to have any idea. I love that about you, but at times like this I want to beat your hippy little head against the wall.'

'Fine, I'm drop-dead gorgeous. I'm the whole package. Beauty, brawns, brain. So what? I'm not looking for a guy, so who cares if their interest bounces right off me?'

'Brawn?'

'Gigi!'

'OK, sorry. Your sarcasm aside, I only bring it up because you don't see what others see. And I'm not just talking about men; I'm talking about everyone who tries to get to know you, tries to get close to you. You tend to keep people at arm's length. Have you not noticed?'

I double blink. 'So? What's wrong with boundaries?'

'Absolutely nothing. But you don't let anyone in, anyone besides me, and that's only because I was downright persistent about befriending you.'

'You practically stalked me.'

'Well, I could see through your façade, Luna.'

'What façade?' She's never mentioned this before, ever.

She tilts her head as if she's disappointed I won't admit to such a thing. 'The façade you show the whole world, Luna. Under that ever-smiling, keep-the-peace girl is a lost soul who is too afraid to open up to people completely. And now you're doing it with these two guys . . . Can't you see?'

'I'm not . . .' I try to process the words, understand how they relate to me, how she can see behind the curtain of such things. But I know she's right. I've learned to stay well back, observe because it's easier that way. Growing close to people always ends in goodbyes. And goodbyes are tough for me.

'To the world, you're this free spirit – this bird of paradise living the dream – but I see through that. And now here you are, with people wanting to get close to you, and you hold back or make excuses as to why they're not genuine. But what if they see the real you, Luna, and they want to be in your spotlight? Want the key to your heart? Would you give it to one of them?'

'One of them? Gigi, I get what you're saying but the thing tonight was a farce, a parody of a kiss. Seriously.'

Since losing Mom I've battled with this very thing. Part of me feels I can't keep people at a distance anymore, or I simply won't have any close connections, other than Gigi and the community in the town of tiny homes. And I need more, right? I need my own connections. I need people who love me for me, and not because my mom chose them for us. I guess Mom's passing has shown me that life is short, sometimes cruelly so. And maybe that means I do need to trust in people and not stand off to the side and wait. Because, really, what the hell am I waiting for? Shouldn't I be actively participating in my own life? Pursuing those special people and not overthinking possible goodbyes? Wouldn't it be better to openly love and damn the consequences?

'Are you sure it was a farce?'

It's still too muddled to make sense of, Oscar and me. It's . . . nothing. But there I go lying to myself again. I have to admit, I felt a spark. But it's too messy to even worry about. I cannot make a play for my competitor for the job. I just can't. And he didn't exactly appear very happy about locking lips; in fact it was the opposite. I change tack. 'What's with the dissection of my life? I've got bigger fish to fry than a psychological unpicking of my past.'

'OK, I'll park that line of thought for now because I can see you've had a bit of a shock to the system, but let me ask you this. Why was Oscar following *you*?'

Chapter 17

After he'd cancelled on me last minute three times, I finally meet up with Sebastiano. He tells me all about the history of the Biblioteca Nazionale Marciana as we wander along Piazzetta San Marco. 'There are over 750,000 books inside the library.'

We wander inside and I'm blown away by the palatial design and the frescos on the ceiling. So much ancient beauty. We find the famous bird's-eye-view map of Venice that was made by Andrea Palladio, which dates back to the 1500s. It puts the sheer size of Venice into perspective and its long history and the many changes it's been through over time.

Sebastiano takes my hand, and I try not to think about what Gigi said, and whether I purposely stay back from people, especially men. It's not like I need a man to make me whole, but that I stop people from getting close. All people. It makes goodbyes easier. It makes the decision to move on again easier too. But am I missing out by being so aloof?

The kiss with Oscar is on my mind. Pretend or not, I have to tell Sebastiano. Really, I feel lukewarm about Sebastiano, and I'm sure it's not because of what Gigi said, alluding to the fact I distance myself with people. It's not that, in this instance. It's that there's a distinct lack of chemistry between us. And I just get this weird vibe from Sebastiano – a sort of disingenuous aura about him. Again, Gigi would tell me I'm making excuses but it's not gelling between us. There's an element here that's off. Him cancelling on me time and again hasn't helped. He said he had to work, but I went past the trattoria on my way home from work and stopped in and he wasn't there. A small thing maybe, but it adds to my hesitancy. I wait until we're outside of the library to bring it into conversation.

'Sebastiano, I kissed Oscar from the bookshop the other night.' His eyebrows pull together and he scowls. 'But it was a fake kiss.' I explain about Giancarlo potentially catching us spying on him and what led up to the lip locking.

'I think he took advantage of you, Luna. Are you sure he didn't set that up on purpose?' A muscle in his jaw works.

'No, no, it was innocent, I promise. We're arch-rivals, actually. I just wanted you to know, transparency and all.'

'Thanks for telling me, but please be careful around him. I don't trust this guy at all.'

I laugh. 'He's fine. He's obsessed with books and doesn't really know how to make conversation other than that. He's bored the brains out of many a hapless customer.'

'Hmm.'

'What does that mean?'

'What's happening with us, Luna? We're still holding hands, like teenage sweethearts. Do you want to get serious with me? I can't help but feel this guy might snatch you away before we've even had a chance to begin.'

Shouldn't I be on fire with passion and longing? Sebastiano is gorgeous and I enjoy our jaunts around Venice, but I don't go back to the hostel and pine for him. I don't dream about him. 'I don't know what I want, Seb, truthfully. This is a time of change for me, figuring out who I am without my mom.'

'I can go as slow as you need.'

He kisses me once more with the cool Venetian breeze blowing through my hair and I wait to feel fireworks, but nothing comes except the fluttering of a few butterflies in my belly. I need to consult my tarot and see what the cards have to say about this predicament, but I can't wait that long. I have to do this now.

I gently pull back from him. 'I like being with you like this.' I motion to the library. 'Hanging out and laughing. Being friends.' As soon as the words leave my mouth, I feel a sense of relief. He's not the one for me.

'You don't want to be in a relationship with me? Is this because I kept cancelling? I had . . . to work.'

I don't call him out. 'Friends is all I can do right now, Sebastiano.'

He sighs. 'OK. I'll walk you back to the bookshop and we can continue this chat another time.'

I've been given the Sunday afternoon shift. It'll be just me and the cats today.

Sundays in the bookshop are deathly quiet. It's almost eerie being in here without Oscar and Giancarlo. Shouldn't Sundays be one of the busiest days for the little shop on the canal? I pen a few ideas about what we can do to drive more people here on their weekends. Perhaps we can get an author for an event? Or start a Sunday book club. So many ideas, it'll just be getting Giancarlo to agree to them. Dostoyevsky does her best to destroy my notebook as soon as my back is turned, so I have to pocket the pad every single time or the little minx shreds the paper before I know it. She's a cunning little varmint, her cheeky side making her irresistible, even though she adds to my workload when she leaves a path of destruction in her wake. It's a call for attention, because she knows I'll stop what I'm doing and pick her up and cuddle her.

The long day finally comes to a close. It's time to lock up the shop, so I double-check everything is secure, and give the cats one last belly rub before filling up their water and food bowls and heading out into the warm evening.

Back at the hostel I make a bowl of hot noodles and head to the dorm room to read some more of the love letters. They've become a comfort to me, to ease the long nights while Gigi is at the *osteria* and I'm alone in the room.

I finish my noodles and then reach for the letters. Shuffling through until I find where I'm up to in the stack. I settle against my pillow and read.

Dear Ruby,

Every day is interminable without you. I know you need space but think of our daughter. Think about what she needs. A loving family, a stable life with us all together under one roof. Won't you reconsider? For me, for her, for us?

I will love you forever,
Giancarlo

I hold the letter against my heart. Here it is! The proof. *Our daughter*. This is not a wild goose chase but a real and valid connection to my father and the life I might have had if Mom hadn't run away. Mom left these letters for this very reason, I'm sure of it. She might not have been able to face this head on, herself, but she left me this one last gift. The gift of finding my father. The gift of questions that will be answered. The only gift I ever wanted.

Chapter 18

Another week slips by, and somehow both Oscar and I are still gainfully employed at the bookshop. Either Giancarlo isn't ready to give me my marching orders or he's waiting until the heavy lifting of the post-winter clean-up has been done.

Quietly, I'm proud of how spick and span the place is looking while still keeping the chaotic atmosphere that makes it so alluring. We've tided and sorted books into sections, which has helped when it comes to directing customers. The cats seem to be multiplying, as if they've heard down some kind of cat grapevine that the place is clean and would make a cosy home. There's a new tortoiseshell puss that Oscar calls Harper Lee, who I swear I haven't seen in the bookshop before.

Oscar hasn't mentioned the kiss that wasn't a kiss and we've managed to studiously avoid each other, as much as we can in this place. It's not that I don't want to clear the air, it's just that I get the feeling he thinks I've overstepped the boundary and I don't want a lecture over it.

He can't even look me in the eye, so I have taken that as a sign that we're never going to become friends. Harper Lee hides under a stool behind the counter and swats at my ankles when she thinks I'm not looking.

The phone rings. '*Buongiorno, Libreria sul Canale*. This is Luna speaking.' Most of our customers speak English but I'm trying to hard to learn Italian and use a mix of both languages out of respect for the Venetians who do shop here.

'Do you have tantric sex?'

My eyebrows shoot up. Did I hear that right? '*Excuse me?*'

'Do you have tantric sex?'

'I don't see how that's any of your business!' I'm outraged.

'The *book*, do you have the book, *Tantric Sex*? Aren't you in the business of selling books?'

'Oh.' Golly, no greeting, no forewarning. 'Umm, no, I haven't, erm, come across it.' *Oh my God.*

'OK, thanks.' And with that they hang up, and I'm sure I'm as red as one of Aunt Loui's home-grown beetroots.

Eventually my pulse returns to normal, and I'm getting ready for our very first book concierge experience when Sebastiano comes in. He's been texting me all day and night on poor Gigi's number, telling me how much I mean to him, asking me to reconsider, which is driving both Gigi and I crazy. I really need to replace my phone and pronto. And have a word with him to stop this nonsense.

'Luna!' he says at full volume, striding over with a wide smile on his face. It's all a bit much in a work environment, so I give him the standard Italian greeting of a peck on each cheek and go back to the relative safety behind the counter.

'What's up?'

He surveys the bookshop as if he's looking for something. Or someone? My heart drops. He's not here to confront Oscar, is he? That would be such a Sebastiano thing to do – a big performance thus proving his everlasting love for me. I shudder at the thought.

'It's been a while since I've seen you.' He takes a hand from behind his back and produces a bunch of fresh flowers. 'Beautiful roses for a beautiful girl.'

I take the proffered flowers; red roses that have the perfume of the garden grown and not some hothouse that steals the scent from the delicate petals. 'Thank you, Sebastiano. They're beautiful.'

'They're from my nonna's garden, freshly picked this morning.'

I don't quite know what to say. I don't want to encourage Sebastiano, but he really is trying. Have I given up on him too easily, pulling away just like Gigi suggested I do when people try to get close? Still, I hold back. Outwardly Sebastiano is the whole package, but that's not enough for me. It's what's underneath that counts.

Sebastiano beams and it's hard to resist that smile when it lights up his face. But he's just that little bit too perfect, too polished, as if he's done this so many times. Or am I being a little harsh?

'This morning on Instagram I saw you have your very first book concierge guests. I expect you're a little nervous, so if you do get flustered you could look upon these and know I'm here for you.'

He's right to sense my nerves. So much rides on the book concierge service working, not just for me, but for Giancarlo. 'Thanks, Sebastiano. Once the first session is done, we'll know whether the idea is a viable one.'

'I'm off to the trattoria but I might see you later?'

Sebastiano leaves so quickly I don't even get a chance to retort. He's not going to give up easily and I'm confused by it. Why can't we just remain friends? Why is he pushing so hard for this when he cancelled on me so many times? I'm lost in thought and don't notice Giancarlo until he taps me on the shoulder while I'm absent-mindedly patting the one-eyed Tolkien who mewls in response. The man must think I never work! Whenever he appears I always seem to be stationary, leaning on a counter or against a wall, daydreaming.

'Be careful of Casanovas.' There's a dark look in Giancarlo's eyes.

'Are you implying that Sebastiano is a Casanova?'

Giancarlo lifts a palm. 'Be careful, Luna.' And with that he walks away, back to his spot on the sofa. It's not like I didn't have doubts about Sebastiano in the first place, but it's unlike Giancarlo to get involved in anything personal or to even notice what's going on around him. It feels very paternal somehow . . .

I go to text Gigi and ask her take on the matter but then remember I still have no phone, dammit. I need to sort a replacement now that I'm slightly ahead moneywise again with wages from the bookshop. My questions for Gigi will have to wait until I see her in person. As I'm searching for a vase – a fool's errand in this place – Oscar approaches with an empty milk bottle. 'You could use this for the flowers?' he says, with a warm smile.

'Thanks, it's perfect.'

I glance over to Giancarlo and see he's surveying us over the top of his novel. And another thought hits – does he mean *Oscar* is the Casanova? Did he see us faux kissing the other night and is trying to warn me off? Perhaps Oscar has a girlfriend and that's why he reacted so badly to me kissing him.

Now I'm really confused. But does it matter? I'm already on guard with Sebastiano and there's nothing there except the possibility of friendship. And Oscar . . . well who knows. My intuition is off, just like everything else in this new topsy-turvy world.

'Was that guy your boyfriend?' he asks.

'No, not really.'

'It's only . . .'

'What?'

Oscar's cheeks pink. What now? 'Nothing, it's nothing.'

The energy in the shop is downright gnarly today and I feel like I'm in the middle of it all. Warnings and unspoken words.

'First of all I need to sage this place, because whatever's lurking here is upsetting the balance.'

'You really believe in that stuff?'

'You don't?'

'I've never been exposed to it, I guess. But I have an open mind. What makes you think it works?'

'The result. Once I smudge, the negative energy will be removed, leaving us with a cleansed, neutral space.'

'It's like opening the door and shoving the bad juju out and then slamming it closed.'

I laugh at the description. 'Sort of, yes. While I've got you.' His eyes go wide. Does he think I'm about to jump on him again, or break those legs of his? 'I mean . . .' I cough into my hand. 'While we're together.' Yikes. 'In a platonic work environment as colleagues . . .'

He frowns. He has the ability to make me forget what I'm saying with his many disapproving facial expressions. There's nothing for it, except to push on. I *think* I've made myself quite clear, that's he's safe with me, but somehow his body language tells me he's not so sure. He folds his arms across his chest and shuffles a step back.

'Anyway, on a strictly professional level, I wanted to run something past you. Giancarlo clearly pushes back against every change we try to make, much to the detriment of the bookshop and the sales we so desperately need. So like I was trying to say that night in the alley before we were . . . indisposed, I figured perhaps we could join forces and that might help us get those ideas across the line. And secure us both jobs in the process. For example, this morning I asked if I could start a local book club. We've got hundreds of classics here but he refused. I get it, he doesn't want to run it once we're gone, but we could easily make a dossier for the next employees to follow. And it would move a bit of the old stock in the process.'

'Good idea. What else did you have in mind?'

'Well, your idea about adding another seating area near the canal was great. But he says he doesn't want people loafing about and falling asleep in here. We can reassure him we'll monitor it. Customers need another space to read or wait for whoever is book shopping, right? It's not like anyone chooses to sit next to Giancarlo when he shoots them that impossible glare of his.'

'Right. OK,' Oscar says. 'Let's make a list of things we want to action and plead our case. We might only get away with a few things but it's better than nothing.'

'Yes.' We lean over the front counter and scribble a list. Giancarlo narrows his eyes at us, but I'm sure he can't hear our plotting from here. A lock of my hair falls over the page, and Oscar takes a moment to tuck it behind my ear. We exchange an awkward glance before he mumbles something about checking on an order. We get so close to working well together and then he dashes off! Just what is his problem?

Chapter 19

After lunch Oscar finds me restacking books in the piano room. It astounds me that so many customers remove books and pile them in some random location, like right on the ivories themselves. I'm searching for a specific book for an online order and I know I've seen it in here, yet now it's nowhere to be found.

'What's up?' I ask, creaking myself upright. There's something about Oscar, the way he looks at me sometimes, that catches me off guard. Perhaps he's filing away details to make me one of the bad guys in his book. He's saved from answering for a moment when Dostoyevsky comes hurdling in, jumping piles of books like she's an Olympian. Soon Dante follows in her wake and they tumble over one another, hissing and meowing. It's hard to tell if they're playing or fighting, until Dante swats her once more before slinking from the room as if he's given her a telling-off and order has been restored.

I pick up Dostoevsky for a hug while I wait for Oscar to continue.

'I . . .' He averts his gaze.

Now he's got my attention. Oscar is never shy on using words, lots and lots of words to get his point across. And this is the second time today he's gone to tell me something and stopped short.

'Are you OK?' A blush creeps up his neck and he can't look me in the eye. 'What is it?'

'I'm not really sure if it's my place to tell you, Luna, but if roles were reversed I'd hope that you'd come to me.'

I move Dostoevsky to my hip. 'Sounds ominous, but OK.'

'It's about Sebastiano. You said he wasn't your boyfriend, so maybe it doesn't matter.'

'He's not my boyfriend.'

'OK, that's good. It's just that . . .' His voice peters off.

I think I know what's coming. I've always known, hence why I've been so guarded. 'It's OK – truly, Oscar. I'm not a delicate little flower.'

He gives me a sad smile. 'A couple of weeks ago I saw him with another girl, but I wasn't entirely sure what it meant. It could have been innocent even though they seemed too close, too wrapped up in each other. So I kept my mouth shut.'

'OK.'

'Last Tuesday night I saw him with a different girl by the Bridge of Sighs. I'm sorry, Luna. But this time I know for sure it wasn't innocent. They were quite . . . close and it left no doubt in my mind that I should speak up.' Poor Oscar, having to be the messenger of such news. He looks for all the world like he wishes the ground would swallow him up whole.

'Ah, I see.' I sit on a stack of hardbacks and exhale. Last Tuesday night Sebastiano cancelled on me an hour before I was set to meet him. 'Thanks for telling me. I had a feeling he might be a bit of a Casanova. Giancarlo picked up on it too.'

'Do you . . . love him?'

'No.' I laugh at the thought. 'It was super casual. It all feels a bit soon.' You can't replace grief with romance, but I don't say this out loud. 'I guess I got a bit swept up in the excitement of it; his charm, his theatrical nature, sort of took me by surprise. I told him I had to take things slow, but I guess that freed him up to pursue other people.'

'He's not worthy of you.'

I smile at the formality of his words. 'I get the feeling it's all a bit of a game to him. His family are pushing him to find a nice Italian girl and get married and settle down, so while he's still got his freedom he's going to enjoy it.' And I don't begrudge him that, but he could have been open about it. 'I told him about our fake kiss; maybe he took offence.'

Oscar raises a brow. 'Well you were honest with him and it was done under extenuating circumstances.'

'Yeah.' Still, it does sting a bit that Sebastiano had been declaring his love for me and probably a handful of other women at the same time. It's all a little much, the thought of his well-crafted act of passionate hot-blooded lothario. I'm so glad my inner voice told me to go slow, otherwise I might not be feeling so calm about it all.

'Anyway, we're probably ready to start the preparations for the book concierge guests if you're able to give me a hand?'

'Sure.' He gives a one-shoulder shrug. We're working better as a team but there's still that niggle of unfinished business. I need to clear the air between us so we can move forward without any awkwardness.

'There's lots to do but first, I want to acknowledge my lapse of judgement the other week. I'm sorry about the kiss and how . . .' kill me '. . . passionate it may have appeared. My thoughts were all over the place and it was simply a case of reacting in the moment. It was out of line and I'm sorry if I made you feel uncomfortable working with me afterwards.'

Absently he touches a finger to his bottom lip again. Did I bite him, leave a mark, or something? 'It's fine, Luna. So what do you need me to do?' Straight back to business. I suppose it's better we don't rehash every moment. We can put it firmly in the past and move on. But still, I'd thought Oscar being so . . . in touch with his emotions, he'd have more to say about the matter. Perhaps he's trying to save me the embarrassment. A good thing, I suppose.

The first book concierge experience is for an American mother and teenage daughter from a cruise ship that is docking for an overnight stay.

I find my folder with my to-do list. 'Right, we've got to set up the table by the canal entrance, dress it with linen cloth, candles, cutlery, napkins. We need to check in with the *pasticceria* and confirm that the afternoon tea will be delivered on time.'

'OK, I can do that. What else?'

'The gift bags need to be picked up at the printer but they only accept cash for some reason, so perhaps we can send Giancarlo out on that errand? He can take one of his long lunches while he's at it, so he's not a stony-faced statue when they arrive.'

Oscar laughs. 'So you too have noticed he's a little more amenable after a carafe of lunchtime wine?'

'A slightly buzzed Giancarlo is way easier to manage.'

We laugh conspiratorially. We've come a long way already in knowing how to handle the gruff bookseller. 'So how long until our guests arrive?'

I check my watch. 'Three hours. Do you want to go through the running sheet with me?'

'Sure.' We go over the order of the event and what's required of both of us. We're stepping outside of our comfort zones but I truly think it'll make it special for our very first guests.

'I'm not much of a public speaker.' He grimaces.

'Me either. And I'm terrified they won't like the book choices I make and leave a bad review. Giancarlo would never forgive me. But then I flip my way of thinking. We *love* books, Oscar. You and I could chat all day about our favourite reads and this is all we're doing, wrapped up in a fancy package, right?'

Oscar nods. 'I hadn't thought about it that way. You're right. We get to share our love of reading and our book choices and what could be better than that?'

'And some of our less than perfect but still magical volumes get saved in the process.'

Just as we're about to start actioning items off our list there's a commotion by the front door. I edge over to see what the ruckus is about, encouraging the few customers in the store to keep browsing. The couple speak in rapid-fire Italian so it's hard to tell what they're talking about, but already I've managed to pick up a bit of the language and I can gather what he's asking. I glance at Giancarlo for a sign I'm right. He smiles and gives me an almost imperceptible nod and goes back to his book.

When the man drops to one knee the woman shrieks so loud it feels like I briefly lose consciousness but it's a sight to behold. I quickly run for Oscar to tell him to catch the moment on video for the couple, but he's two steps ahead and is already filming them, a grin splitting his face. So he's a bit of a romantic at heart too? I glance around the bookshop as customers stand riveted to the spot, enjoying the proposal.

'*Sì, Sì!*' she says when he pops the question, which is even more romantic in Italian. The beautiful, mellifluous foreign words add an extra level of passion to it.

The man stands and slips a delicate gold band onto his new fiancée's finger. My heart expands at the sight of their lovestruck faces. It's like they're the only two people on the planet. They haven't even realised yet that they have a rapt audience. It strikes me I haven't felt a romantic love like that before, and for one brief second it saddens me. Will I ever find a man who looks at me like that while the rest of the world fades to black?

I glace at Oscar and find him staring at me. He quickly looks away but not before I see that his expression mirrors my own – he wears a look I can only describe as longing. Does he too want to find his soulmate? I shake away the strange sensation. We're caught up in this moment and it's only natural to pine for that kind of joy yourself. This is love personified and I'd hazard a guess each spectator has their version of this moment in mind. The ones who've experienced it and those who haven't. Like me.

I'm reminded of my conversation with Gigi about keeping people at arm's length. I guess I never really gave it much thought. It was more a just a way of being that's ingrained in me, not from my mother, but from my lifestyle. It's easier that way, when it comes time to pull up sticks and leave. Sure, I've got lots of friends, but not in the way my mom did where they were an extension of family.

Aside from Gigi, mine are all on the surface. Mom made the type that would lay down their life for her, and by default me too. I'm missing out by holding back. But being tangled in deep feelings would surely make it hard to keep living this way. I've seen Mom clutch friends and cry buckets, as if her heart has been ripped clean from her body – who wants that? Maybe it's some kind of no-father syndrome, where my walls are built high so that no one can ever leave me again.

Once again, I'm torn about just how I'm supposed to *be* in this world. Sometimes I wonder if I really know myself at all or if I'm just playing a part, just like Sebastiano, the theatrical Italian charmer. Am I just showing the world a free-spirited wanderer who flits across the globe with not a care in the world, when inside I'm lost and, without my mom, my mainstay, a little lonelier too.

I shake the confusion away. This is that wily beast grief sneaking up on me again. Making me think I don't know my path, because Mom isn't here anymore. That's what it is.

'Makes you believe in love, doesn't it?' Oscar says as the couple embrace. When the kissing starts and turns a few shades too passionate for lunchtime in a bookshop, the crowd soon disperses and I'm sure I flush scarlet. It went from PG to adults only very quickly.

'Erm, should we . . .' I'm lost for words, so I point.

'*Oh Dios mío!*' Oscar says, which even I know translates from Spanish to *Oh my God!* The pair are definitely *consciously* coupling while perhaps forgetting they're in a public place. 'There are children here!' Oscar is scandalised and I'm not far behind.

There's nothing to do except . . . 'Excuse me, hi!' They continue kissing, and his hands go a-wandering beneath the more delicate fabrics. '*MI SCUSI!*' I bellow and they pull apart, startled. 'We have a video of your proposal. If you'd be so kind as to share your email with us, we can send it to you. But I can see you're in erm . . . celebration mode, so take this.' I pull a business card from my pocket. 'And call us later, yes?' Even the cats sit together perched on a high shelf and manage to convey their displeasure by giving the newly engaged couple the kind of supercilious look only cats can master.

'*Sì, sì, grazie.*' The guy pulls the girl by the hand and off they go into the sweet Venetian day.

'Talk about living *la dolce vita*, eh?' Oscar says and slaps a palm to his face.

I let out a nervous giggle. 'What were they thinking? You're going to have to crop that part out of the video.'

He shakes his head. 'No way! That's on them.'

'Only in Venice . . .'

'Only in *La Libreria sul Canale* . . .' The little bookshop in Venice where anything can happen and usually does.

Laughter bubbles up and out and before long we're doubled over, clutching our bellies because it's true. This place is a marvel and full to the brim of weird and wonderful people. Who'd have thought working in a bookshop would expose a person to such things?

I lean on tiptoes to whisper in Oscar's ear. 'No wonder Giancarlo took to his sofa with a book and never left! Who wants to be the one to step into that kind of thing!'

'I feel like doing the same! Let them run wild and pretend they're not there!'

I tell him about the phone call asking if I had tantric sex.

We laugh again. It feels good to share this with Oscar. I can go to the hostel and debrief with Gigi but it's not quite the same as sharing the kooky things that happen here with someone else who's experienced them.

'Right. Let's get ready for our first book concierge guests and make it an experience they'll remember forever.'

It's a good thing I'm busy because it doesn't leave me much time to ruminate. As I get back to what I'm doing I spot the book I'm looking for, stashed upside down on a shelf. That takes care of one problem.

Chapter 20

I'm running around sorting loose ends, in a bit of a flap for someone usually less flappable. We've had word from the gondolier that our book concierge guests – Mary and Bella – are en route. The table is dressed to perfection with a beautiful Italian lace cloth. Fresh flowers from the local market perfume the air. Candles flicker around the space, adding a warm ambience. We've set the table off to the side of the archway at the back of the shop, so they'll have a full view of the canal while they relax. I have to keep shooing the cats away, who think the freshly washed seat cushions are new beds for them. The little rascals duck and dive and slink back as soon as I've turned away. Let's hope our guests are cat people!

Soon enough they arrive by gondola, the gondolier singing operatically as he slowly pulls up to the entrance. The charming gondolier helps them step from boat to bookshop. We welcome them in. I hand them some fresh orange juice and introduce myself. They're all smiles as they gaze around the bookshop. Their eyes light up and they marvel aloud about the prettiness of the place. My shoulders that I'd been wearing as high as earrings drop and I relax into the afternoon with them. 'And who is this cutie pie?' Mary asks.

'This is Madame Bovary, but don't be fooled by her innocent expressions. She will steal a cannoli from your plate before you've noticed she's there.'

'I don't believe a word of it! Aren't you darling?' She grins as Madame Bovary leaps to the seat I've not long nudged her from.

'May we take a photo?' I ask as Moby Dick waddles over and rubs her head against Bella's ankle.

'Aww, yes please.' They gently pick up their charges and we take a few happy snaps with the canal as a backdrop. The cats lavish up all the attention, purring and kneading at our guests.

'Take a seat whenever you're ready.'

The women sit with a cat each in their laps.

While Oscar does a speech about the history of the bookshop, I slip off to the side and make sure the catering is presented well on a high tea platter. The Italian cakes and pastries are like little works of art and the smell alone is enough to make my mouth water. Everything is ready to go so I head back to the table.

Once Oscar wraps up he gives me the signal so I return with their questionnaires handwritten in flowery calligraphy in the hopes they'll take them as a keepsake afterwards. 'We hope you enjoyed hearing about the history of the bookshop. Our belief is that all books deserve to live a long and happy life, whether they're a little rough around the edges or still as pristine as the day they were printed. What matters most is the words they hold inside and how they have the ability to change your life or open your heart.'

Bella, the teenager says, 'I hadn't thought about books being overlooked because they're a little world-weary. It makes me want to adopt all those novels that are left behind because the cover is a bit shabby, or the pages loose.'

I give her a wide smile – she gets it! 'I like the idea of adoption,' I say and make a mental note about a possible ad campaign in the future. *Adopt a book, save a story!* 'A heroine like you, Bella, who sweeps in and saves those novels that need a little love.' She blooms under the praise and I think Bella and her mom Mary might just have taken the trophy for my favourite customers yet. I hand them clipboards for their questionnaires. 'We've created a set of questions for you so that we can curate a selection of books that are perfect for your tastes. We'd love for you to take your time and enjoy remembering novels you've read that swept you away as you share afternoon tea from the *pasticceria*. Think of the types of stories that you remember years after reading, the ones whose characters still live inside your mind. We can use that information to find books of the same ilk, books that you'll treasure forever, that will always conjure this special time at *La Libreria sul Canale*.'

'Ooh this is going to be so fun!' Mary says. 'You know the proudest moment for me as a mother was when Bella used to spend all her pocket money on books. I knew then I'd done my job well enough. If a child loves reading, they'll never be alone. Even when the hard times come – and they always come – they'll have a tonic for it. They'll have a place to escape. And now here we are together in Venice, in the loveliest little canal bookshop, about to be spoiled for choice with our first love – reading.'

Her words bring tears to my eyes and my mom is there just off in the distance, a ghostly spectre only I can see. It's not real of course, but how I wish it was. Mom and I shared a love of books like Mary and Bella. It was our one constant in an inconstant world. 'And you'll always have each other to share your books with.'

'Yes, our little book club of two.'

I swallow a lump in my throat and say, 'Well, bookworms, I'll leave that with you for a while but do let me know if you have any questions.' Oscar brings out their afternoon tea platter and refills their juice glasses.

They thank me and I rush off back to the counter, all the while fighting tears that won't stem. What has gotten into me? I hadn't expected our first guests would open up the floodgates, remind me of what I've lost, what I'm missing. And while it's sad, it's also beautiful that this mother and daughter are so close. They share an unbreakable bond that's strengthened by books and their love of them.

I'm a sniffling hot mess when Oscar pulls me into one of the back rooms. 'Stop, stop,' he says as I give him a fake smile, my eyes still bright with unshed tears, an excuse already formed on my lips. But he already knows. How does he always sense these things? 'Be honest and tell me what's wrong? Don't even try to say you're fine.'

I run a fingertip under my eyes, my heart galloping at the sense of loss and having to share it with Oscar. Dante pads over to me, staring up as if he can sense my sadness. I scoop him up and bury my face in his soft stripy fur. It takes me a moment to compose myself and trust in my ability to speak. Normally, I'd lie. I'd say I was fine, just having a moment, but why do I feel the need to pretend everything is fine, when it clearly isn't? For someone so attuned I'm letting myself down by bottling up my emotions. Perhaps this is why the tarot isn't playing nice. Because I'm not looking after my own mind, body and soul.

I peek out to make sure no customers are waiting. A few loiter but they seem content enough. Oscar hands me a tissue.

'I lost my mom recently to cancer and . . . Mary and Bella reminded me of that loss. It's hard to imagine that I'll never see Mom again, let alone sit down and talk about books, about anything, ever again. Forever is such a long time and it hit me anew today, that's all.'

'That's all? Losing a parent is one of life's biggest traumas. Really, it is.'

'You sound like you have some experience with this.'

He drops his gaze for a moment. 'I lost my father when I was seventeen. It was tough. I rebelled, and that rebellion for me was going to the library way past curfew.'

Despite it all I laugh. 'Wow, what a devil.'

He grins. 'Right? But I still have my mom and we're closer than ever. My dad was British, so after his death Mom wanted to move from Kent back to Spain, to be closer to her family. I understand now of course, but I didn't really at the time. I felt we were moving on, forgetting about him. Still to this day, I miss him and wonder what my life would have been like if he was around. It's hard. What about you, is your dad in your life?'

I freeze and hope my expression doesn't give anything away. Oscar's eyebrows pull together at my hesitation. I scramble to think of an answer. 'No, I don't know who he is.' If in doubt go with the truth. I haven't exactly confirmed it with Giancarlo, have I?

'Oh, Luna, so you've had this great loss and no family to share it with? Siblings?'

'No, no siblings. A big extended honorary family though, so I'm not completely alone. And I've got my best friend Gigi. The only person I want though is my mom.'

He gives me a sad smile. 'And you always will. That's the power of love.'

'Thanks, Oscar. I bet your book is going to sell millions of copies. You seem to understand deep down to the heart of things.' It's not just that though, it's that he always knows what to say and when to say it. He puts our differences aside when he sees me struggling and jumps in to help. I'm not usually the damsel in distress type. I'm usually capable of reining in my emotions well, but things have changed and maybe for the better. Why do I feel the need to survive alone? Keep my emotions bound up tight? Intuitively I know that if I tried to push these feelings down it would only be a short-term solution and soon they'd rise in a rage and demand to be felt.

I lost the person I loved most. It's always going to hurt. But perhaps I need to face it head on, and talk about it openly, instead of pretending I'm dealing with it just fine. I'm not even honest when Gigi asks me about how I'm coping. That protective instinct is hard to ignore: survive at all costs and put on that brave face, the one that I now associate with grieving.

'Are you going to be OK to curate the list? I can do it if you need some more time?'

I wipe my face on a sleeve. 'I'm good. I'll freshen up so I don't frighten them though.' I give Dante one last kiss and deposit him down.

'You look pretty when you cry.' Oscar holds up a hand. 'Wait, that didn't come out right. What I meant was, well . . .' He blushes and fumbles. 'The phrase "ugly cry" caught on for a reason, yet you have delicate pretty tears . . . Oh look a customer.'

I don't see a customer. As Oscar jogs off, I think about what he said, and what he's been through. I sense I can trust him, and maybe share the real reason I'm in Venice, with him. Open up to people, truly, like I keep promising myself I will. Might he have an idea on how to tackle this whole paternity thing with Giancarlo . . .

My computer beeps with an email: *Buongiorno, Luna. Can you sneak away today? There's something I want to show you at the Bridge of Sighs. Sebastiano xx*

Is he for real? The same place he took his mystery date? Is he that predictable that he doesn't even change locations? And now he's communicating on my work email?

There's no time to do anything other than tell him I know.

Hey Seb, Like I already told you I'm not ready for a relation-ship, casual or not. Looks like you've found a replacement or two. Please don't email me at work, as everyone uses this and I'd prefer to keep my private life private.

I let it go. There are always going to be Sebastianos in this world and I dodged a bullet there.

166

Chapter 21

An hour later, with their questionnaires in hand, I focus on curating Mary and Bella's book list. Their tastes are varied and eclectic, which makes the choosing so much easier. I can take a few more risks, knowing that they're open-minded when it comes to reading, especially Mary, who's read a wide range of literary styles.

I chose *A Bend in the River* by V.S. Naipaul for Mary, and also *To the Lighthouse* by Virginia Woolf. Both very different styles but ones I think she'll enjoy. I look for a lighter read, and stumble on Nora Ephron's *Heartburn*. Who doesn't love a good Nora book? The romcom queen herself!

For Bella, I think hard. She's sixteen years old and can handle heavier fiction, but I want to find something that sparks her imagination. I find a rather well-read copy of Maya Angelou's *I Know Why the Caged Bird Sings*, which is the perfect book for someone Bella's age. When I spy a copy of *The Joy Luck Club* by Amy Tan, I grab that too. It will be one mother and daughter can read and discuss. And when I spot *The Geography of You and Me*, by Jennifer E. Smith, I add that to the pile, remembering myself enjoying that sweet romance.

I take the books to the counter and give them a quick dust-down and make sure they're as presentable as can be. Oscar approaches with the gift bags. 'Did you want to make your presentation first and then we'll wrap them in tissue paper for their long journey home?'

'Isn't it funny?' I say running a palm over the cover. 'It's like saying goodbye to a good friend, when you curate books like this.'

'It's very special,' he agrees. 'And you've chosen well. Some great books there.'

'Thanks,' I say. 'OK, let's see what they think.'

We present the books and I do a little spiel on each of them so they know why I chose these particular novels and I double-check they haven't read them before.

'These are just delightful!' Mary says. 'I wish we could pull up that sofa over there and while away the day reading them.' Her face shines with the happiness you can only get with the prospect of a new book to read. And even Giancarlo rewards her with a smile from that very sofa.

'I've always wanted to read a Maya Angelou book but never got around to it, so I can't wait. That will be top of the pile for me,' says Bella.

'I'm so thrilled you liked the selection. Did you enjoy your afternoon tea?'

'It was beautiful, the best experience to date. Now, just how are we supposed to choose books for ourselves when we go home after being spoiled like this?' Mary laughs.

We chat for a bit longer about our shared love of reading, and the beautiful bookshops they've seen around the world on their travels, before it's time for them to head off to their next adventure. Dinner and the opera at the opulent *Teatro La Fenice*. Before they go we take lots of photos. Almost every bookshop cat glides over for their turn to be cuddled and captured on camera. Mary chats to Giancarlo about Venice and how delightful it must be to own such a shop before he goes back to his book.

They leave us with warm hugs and big smiles. Once they're gone, I catch Giancarlo staring at us. 'You both did well,' he says.

Oscar and I face each other. 'Was that a compliment from our fierce leader?'

'Wonders will never cease,' I say, unable to hide my grin. This book concierge service might just work after all.

As we're packing up the bookshop for the evening the old boxy computer pings in its unique, ancient way. I go to check the notification and see it's a Google review from Mary and Bella.

My daughter and I are on a month's holiday after we lost my husband a year ago. It's a way to regroup and learn to live in this big wide world without the man who was our North Star. To be honest, our trip has been a little rocky because we realised that distance doesn't make grief any easier to deal with.

I'd begun to wonder if I'd made things worse for my daughter, drawing out this time, pretending we were happy in these exotic locations, when really, we yearned for the comfort of home, for routine. For him.

We decided we'd go on a cruise to Venice and if nothing changed, we'd cancel our trip and return home. My daughter stumbled on a post on Instagram about a book concierge experience at a second-hand bookshop by the San Polo canal in Venice. We didn't have high expectations, both us of had mentally checked out and we were just going through the motions. We arrived at La Libreria sul Canale by gondola, canal water spraying our faces as our gondolier sang operatically as if we were the only two people left in the world. I tell you, I had tears in my eyes – the man could sing, all right! It was the first time in a long time I saw my daughter smile. How could you not, when the man was using every breath in his lungs to serenade us?

When we stepped from the gondola into the little bookshop it was like stepping into another world. Filmy light landed on piles of books; it was like going back in time. And for a moment I could breathe again, I felt inspired in only the way you can be when you're surrounded by books. But not just any books. Books that are swollen with canal water. Books that have been discarded because their covers are bent or ripped. Books that have been left behind. Just like me and my daughter Bella. We both felt an affinity with those lost and damaged novels. Then there's the motley crew of bookshop cats, who were almost impossible to leave.

Topping off the experience were Luna and Oscar. Their love of the bookshop and its history was evident and their adoration of reading and their claims of how it mends even the most broken heart, well, it was just what us two sad souls needed to hear. They lifted our mood. It was like their words lifted one of the layers of grief away, and the world became that little bit brighter.

Luna chose perfect books for us, books that will carry us through the next stage of our travels because we've decided to keep going. Life is what you make it, and what we learned today in that magical little canal bookshop is that books are there for you when you need comfort, and they'll always be there. Their pages might be yellowed with age, dog-eared, with notes in the margins, or a birthday scrawl in the front, but that's what makes them special.

Like us, real life has indelibly marked them but that just shows they've lived, like we must live. And those words trapped inside, well they have the ability to transport me from grief to hope. From sadness to happiness. Those words remind me that there's still so much living to do. And I get to do that with my daughter by my side. If you only have time for one experience in Venice, let it be the glorious book concierge service, and you might just find your way too . . .

'Oscar!' I yell, my pulse thundering. I didn't know, I didn't sense their grief. How small this world really is, and how many people are fighting a battle we know nothing about. There I'd been, so struck by them, their relationship, and they were feeling the very same sadness as me. I wish I'd known so I could have hugged them that little bit tighter when they left.

'What?' he says breathless, rushing to my side.

'Read this.'

He dons those specs that make him downright cute and reads. After a moment he looks at me, his eyes wide. 'You just never know what people are dealing with. It was meant to be.'

'Right?'

'I get the feeling that review is going to change things.'

'What do you mean?'

'We're going to get really busy, really fast.'

'Why?'

'Because the experience renewed them, it gave them hope. Everyone wants that.'

And they have no idea that review has done the same for me. It's made me feel like my trip to Venice matters, that I've been part of something bigger than me. More important.

Without thinking I take Oscar's face and kiss him quickly, smack my lips against his.

'Sorry,' I say. 'But that was worth a celebratory peck.' Before I can gauge how he's feeling, I dash off but not before I see Madame Bovary who I'm sure gives me a nod of approval. What has gotten into me!

Chapter 22

The next morning Gigi insists we go for a walk to debrief about Sebastiano. I've told her that it's totally fine, but she won't hear of it. She has very strict rules when it comes to matters of the heart – and walking it out is one of them. Our work schedules have been hectic and it feels like we've barely seen each other, so it's nice to have a free day together to catch up.

We cross Pont di Rialto that sits above the Grand Canal. It's known as the lovers' bridge, and as far as bridges go, it's a little swoon-worthy, I must admit, with its renaissance architecture. 'Isn't it breathtaking?'

'Yeah,' Gigi agrees. 'Ooh, look is that a marriage proposal?'

An elderly man is down on one knee, delicate velvet box in hand, and his paramour has a hand on her heart. I lean into Gigi. 'Love isn't dead! Look at those sweethearts. How old do you think they are?'

'Seventy-five or so?'

My romance reader brain goes haywire. 'Second-chance love, you think?' I concoct a backstory for the lovers. 'They were high school sweethearts until her family moved away and they lost contact.'

'They both married and had children, but they never forgot their first love.'

'And then one day they bumped into each other at the airport. They recognised each other after all these years. And it was as if no time had passed, yet a lifetime had.'

'And they decided there was no time to waste and they ripped their clothes off and . . .'

'Gigi! No! Oh my God.'

'What?' she says innocently.

'You're sex-mad.'

'Yeah.'

I shake my head at her antics. 'Venice is full of people in love. It's everywhere you look. I don't remember being in a city where I've seen such overt affection.'

And with that Gigi launches into her post-break-up spiel. 'You were too good for him.'

I give her a small smile. 'I'm relieved it's fizzled out before it even started. Something was always stopping me from taking it further. And isn't that more concerning – that I feel relieved? What if I remain numb like this my whole life? I don't even know if I'm numb – I'm just . . . nothing. The only time I get mad is when I think of the other lovestruck women who have no idea what he's up to. From what Oscar told me, they looked smitten with him. I mean, maybe he genuinely feels something for them, but you can't assume he's being honest and admitting they're not his only love interest. Right?'

'Do we believe Oscar? I mean, what's to say he's not making it up to get closer to you?'

'Oscar is one of the good guys. Can talk the hind leg off a donkey and is the sort who'll right wrongs because it's in his nature, even if it makes him uncomfortable. I believe that he saw Sebastiano with those other women. And Oscar's not interested in me the way you're thinking. Anything but. I tried to talk to him about the faux kiss and he slammed that door shut and got on with the business of the bookshop. Like he didn't want to hear one more word about it. That speaks volumes, to me. Seeing love

173

bloom all around, it does make me wonder if it'll ever happen for me. Maybe some people *don't* have soulmates. Have you ever thought of that?'

Oscar's floppy-haired smiley face pops into my mind again. He really is a sweet guy. And the cats all love him, even Dante, which says a lot. Cats always know!

'I promised myself I'd stop holding everyone back, but the thing is, it's really hard to be open about these things. Truthfully, Oscar is a sweetheart and if things were different I might have told him so, but I'm not in the right frame of mind. Sebastiano proved that. So maybe it's best if I just focus on myself for a bit.'

Gigi takes my arm as we head into the Rialto markets: it's total chaos. Locals shop for groceries and fresh seafood, and the stench of fish is heavy in the air. These markets have been trading for over seven hundred years and, despite Venice being a tourist mecca, they've managed to hold on to this tradition. Today, we pretend we're locals and hunt for mushrooms for pasta that Gigi plans to make for our lunch. We find our fresh earthy funghi and make sure we don't pick them up ourselves, even though temptation is great. No one wants to be blacklisted! The vendor gives us the biggest ones, dirt still clinging to them.

We thank him and find our secret hidden gem, a tiny little shop by the hostel that sells homemade pasta by the handful. As we peruse the glass cabinets for fresh handmade pasta we watch the women knead dough and roll gnocchi with expert fingers as they chatter and laugh. The only problem with coming here is trying to whittle our pasta choice down. There's so many varieties of ravioli filled with all sorts of deliciousness, from cheese to mushrooms. There's tortellini, gnocchi, pappardelle. We're trying to make our way through the selection each visit. We decide on agnolotti stuffed with walnuts and gorgonzola, which should pair nicely with our fresh mushroom bounty.

Outside, Gigi continues her pep talk. 'Luna, don't become bitter and twisted like me. I might have a cold, steely heart, but you don't. You're dealing with the loss of your mom so you're bound to feel a little numb when it comes to love. All you have to do is believe and let the universe provide. Perhaps now isn't the time for love but that doesn't mean you need to swear off it forever. And I feel bad because I pushed that Sebastiano onto you. I just thought . . . it would help while you were so sad. Take your mind off it for a bit. But now I see that was totally wrong.'

'For a moment, it was nice to forget everything else and be wooed. What I liked most of all was his stories about his family life. I liked the *idea* of him, not actually him.'

'Still, I can't believe my BS detector didn't wail its alarm.'

'Maybe it's a little rusty. My tarot hasn't exactly been providing answers either. Could be that we have to let nature take its course, and for me, that means finding out about my past. I haven't had the courage to ask Giancarlo, or even any idea how to go about it. I've fallen in love, that's for sure . . .'

'What?' Gigi gasps.

I nod. 'With the bookshop. Fallen hard. It's an amazing place and I feel whole when I'm there and isn't that crazy? It's a place, not a person.'

'Well, maybe it's that your father *is* there, and you know it could be the start of a new chapter in your life.'

'Yes, that's probably what it is.'

It's more. It's everything. It's Oscar. But I don't dare say the words out loud. And Oscar has made it abundantly clear by his actions that he's not on the same page. I miss my tarot cards guiding me; I miss having faith that I can read them and know my path. But I guess some journeys are meant to be taken alone.

Chapter 23

It's a little hard for me to part with money to buy a new-to-me phone, but I'm sure Gigi is tired of lending me hers every time we cross paths. Money-wise I'm ahead again so I can spare some funds for the ability to communicate once more.

The guy in the electronics shop frowns when I ask for the same Samsung model I had before and switches to English. 'We don't carry stock that old. Are you sure you don't want a newer handset?'

'I'm sure,' I say. 'I'll take your cheapest phone.' It blows my mind how much people spend on phones, as if it's more a status symbol than anything. I will never understand it. If I can communicate and snap a few pics, pixelated or not, that's enough for me.

'If money is an issue we have monthly payment plans. I can sign you up if you have enough ID.'

'No thanks. Just a cheapie is fine.'

The man offers me a slightly later model Samsung and gives me a hefty discount. 'I'll probably die with this phone, so I don't mind knocking the price down a bit.' He gives me a funny look as if he can't quite work out why a millennial would not have the latest smartphone.

'*Grazie!* I'll be sure and buy my next phone here, in ten years or so.'

His laughter follows me outside. Once I insert my SIM card I call Aunt Loui who left me a message on Gigi's phone to call her ASAP.

'Baby girl! How's Venice treating you?'

I find a spot in the shade and tell her everything that's happened since we last spoke, including the success of the first guests at the book concierge service. 'I'm so proud of you. Your mom would be too. I always thought you'd end up working with literature in some form or other. Always had your nose in a book, while the world kept spinning around you.'

'It's a dream come true, honestly. Even though we have to fight against Giancarlo to make any changes. It's almost like he doesn't want his peace disturbed, but he knows things need a shake-up if he wants to keep the doors open. He's giving in more quickly these days so either he's coming around or he's losing the energy to fight back.' I laugh thinking of the stony-faced bookseller when we come to him with yet another audacious plan. 'He has a huge amount of stock, so it's been great fun digging through all the books. I found all his romances boxed up and packed away. I guess he didn't want them on offer when his heart was broken and I found that sort of beautiful.'

'Did you restore them to the shelves?'

'Of course – after much debating with him on the merits of such novels. And they're selling better than any other genre. Goes to show, eh? He still packs them away when I'm not looking; I find them and display them again. It's a battle of wills and sometimes I get the sense he's enjoying the fun of it all.'

'It sounds like things are going well at that level, but are you any further along with the Giancarlo mystery itself?'

I exhale a deep sigh. 'Not yet. I haven't managed to find out anything about the guy. He doesn't say much, although he's slowly opening up to both of us but not about anything personal. Most days all I get is an occasional glance over the cover of his book as he turns the page and a wave of his hand that means go pick up his lunch.'

'Your mamma always did like the quiet ones.'

'Yeah, he's quiet all right. My next idea was to confide in Oscar and see what he makes of it. Oscar is really thoughtful, quite a deep thinker. He sees the underbelly of things, not just the surface level.'

'That's a great plan, Luna. He might have some suggestions you haven't thought of. But aren't you two vying for the same job?'

'It never comes up with Giancarlo anymore, so I'm not going to bring it up!'

'OK, but be careful. I'd hate to see him do an about-face and leave you with no job.'

'I'll be careful. If that does happen Gigi has said there's plenty of shifts available at the *osteria*.' I don't tell Aunt Loui that I'd be heartbroken if I had to leave the bookshop and work elsewhere. There's something special about that place – it gets under your skin. It's the history, the chaotic beauty, even the oddball customers that make it such a wild and wacky place to work, but it's more than that. It feels like for once in my life that I'm part of something, one of many building blocks, that make it what it is. And having a hand in helping it grow into the next stage of its illustrious life is kind of a marvel. Sure, I could get work elsewhere but it would feel hollow after this.

'You don't even need my advice. You're all over this new life, and I'm thrilled for you, baby girl. I really am. While you might not have solved the mystery yet, there's music in your voice and it's really lovely to hear.'

I consider it. I am happy here. Surprisingly so. But what's made it that way? Being busy, being around good people? The bookshop itself, healing me from the inside out? 'Oh I almost forget to tell you! We had a marriage proposal in store that turned . . . racy.' When I recount the story to Aunt Loui, she hoots and hollers.

'What on earth . . . ?!'

'I had to yell at the top of my lungs to get their attention. It was one of the more eye-opening incidents that's happened so far.'

178

'You need to write a book about this! The stories you collect deserve to be shared. *The Little Venice Bookshop*, by Luna Hart . . .'

I laugh at the thought. 'Would anyone believe such a thing? This proves that truth *is* stranger than fiction. There's the lady who comes in every day searching for her husband. Giancarlo said he left her at the altar fifty years ago, but like clockwork she stomps in bellowing for him. Then there's the old man who wears a suit and tie, sits at the piano that desperately needs tuning and plays Vivaldi for hours. Even with the dodgy tuning, it's the most beautiful part of my day. We don't know what his story is because Giancarlo has never once approached the man and, in a way, the not knowing adds to the joy of it. It's not muddied by questioning him; he must feel welcome, so he plays the piano and then he leaves without a word ever spoken.'

'Film it for me, next time, if you don't think he'd mind.'

'I will. Everyone films him. He has his own little fan club who drop past when they hear the notes of the piano float outside. This place is such a contradiction at times. One minute I'm welling up at the beauty of the piano player and the next I'm being berated by a customer because they say I talk too fast and they can't decipher my English. I've learned to throw my hands up and let it go. Tourists really are hard work! But we have the bookshop cats to snuggle with and that makes everything OK.'

'How did Giancarlo cope before you and Oscar arrived?'

'It was quieter. The social media side of things has really increased the foot traffic. The shop is hard to find, so even just posting maps has made a difference. Giancarlo had a revolving door of staff. From what I gathered from sorting the paperwork, most staff only lasted a month, at most. He tends to hire back-packers, so they only really stay for a season before heading off to the next place. If this book concierge service takes off, then I hope Giancarlo will have enough funds to hire us both, full-time, because the bookshop really needs at least two of us, maybe three, but at the moment the money isn't there.'

'I'm sure your plan will work, Luna. Your first session went so well.'

I don't tell Aunt Loui how sad the mother and daughter duo made me. It was more bittersweet than anything. Watching them have so much fun and bond over books brought it all to the fore, and then learning about their story was a full-circle moment. I feel steadier now. After my talk with Oscar, I've let myself feel those moments of pure anguish that pop up. I let myself cry, as the reel of memories play like a movie and then I sleep, usually. Sleep has been my safety blanket. Even in the noisy dorm room, I have deep dreamless sleeps that shore me up for the next day, help me cope with whatever comes my way.

'I hope it works. It's rewarding to see those books be cherished and live another life. Anyway, enough about work! How is the realtor going with finding a tenant for the tiny home?'

'So far so good. She's organised a viewing this weekend and has a few potentials that seem suitable because they've lived off-grid before. Everyone's in a tizzy about new people joining us.' She lets out her throaty Janis Joplin laugh. 'I can just see the viewing now – they'll certainly have an audience of nosy parkers.'

I laugh imagining them all pretending to have something to do right in front of Mom's tiny home. There will be a lot of fake gardening happening, that's for sure. 'I hope they're not too put out that we couldn't keep it vacant.' The last thing I want is some interloper coming in and upsetting the tight-knit community they've worked so hard to build.

'No, everyone understands. It's not the first time, baby girl, and it won't be the last. Remember we lost Georgie a couple of months ago and her van went to a lovely young couple who've really lifted the energy around here. Change is inevitable; we all know that. We'll find the right people, don't you worry. And if not, we have our ways of removing them.'

A memory forms of another couple moving in when Mom

first arrived there. 'Oh my God, that naked prayer circle and the outdoor séances weren't real, were they?'

'Of course not! Do we *look* like witches? Besides, we weren't *totally* naked but like I told Gigi, to get attention around here you have to shake things up, so we decided half naked would do the trick. And it worked. That couple couldn't pack their things fast enough.'

I let out a deep belly laugh, remembering it. They'd moved into the shack behind Mom's and straight away their complaints started. The guy ruled the roost, which made the community bristle, and then he tried to change things in the community and that would never be accepted.

'It was your mom's idea, you know. She was mad as a cut snake when the fellow told us that midnight yoga was disrupting his sleep! And the litany of complaints escalated from there. He took exception to the beehives – too buzzy apparently. And Jillian's peace doves pooped all over his solar panels. But birds are meant to be free; there was no way she was caging them. So Ruby waged this campaign against him and it worked. I'll never forget the sight of a hundred women, bazookas out to the moon, pretending we were summoning the apocalypse or something.'

'She never did like being told what to do.' I smile at Mom being behind the prank in the best interests of the town of tiny homes.

'Especially by a man who ought to know better, moving into a place like ours. Rest assured, baby girl, we sure learned our lesson about vetting new people.'

'I love it, you cunning little vixens.'

'I'll take it.'

'How is the tiny home packing going? I still feel bad I'm not there to help you.'

'What did I tell you? Don't waste your time worrying about me. It's all done. That's why I left you a message with Gigi to call me ASAP. I found a bunch of photos of you. You guys must've lived in Venice for a bit before she took off to Thailand. There's a whole heap of baby pictures of you all rugged up by the canal. It's hard to see your squidgy little face with the number of layers you were swaddled you in – I'm guessing Venice is quite cold in the winter, being surrounded by all that water. There's some of you as a toddler, sitting in a highchair at a café, and then some when you must've been about four or five years old and still had your baby teeth. God, you were an adorable little muffin.'

'In Venice?'

'Looks like it. There's the Bridge of Sighs in the background, and St Marco's Square in another. I'm no expert but even I recognise those landmarks.'

My breath leaves in a whoosh. 'But wait . . . we weren't in Venice when I was four or five. At least I don't *think* we were. I was born in Thailand, and we stayed there for a handful of years. I remember starting in the kindergarten homeschool groups at the commune when I was about that age.' Or am I remembering wrong? Unless . . . I wasn't really born in Thailand like Mom told me. Is this the missing link I'm looking for? Maybe Thailand came much later once she'd left Venice!

Aunt Loui clucks her tongue. 'Well this is confusing. She must've gone back and forth from Thailand to Venice, because you're all different ages in these pictures. But the oldest one I'm guessing you were four or five, but maybe I'm wrong. Maybe you're only three.'

Did I live in Venice those first few years? Did they try and make it work for my sake? 'You'd think I'd remember such a thing.'

'Not if you were only a toddler. I'm no good at all this kid stuff. You'll have to have a look yourself and see if you can guess what age you were.'

'OK. Is Giancarlo in the pictures?'

'There's a man in a few of them, a tall fellow. How about I take phone camera photos of them and send them over? Or I could go to the library and scan them properly. I only found them this morning. There's boxes and boxes of them.'

'Phone camera photos will do for now, Aunt Loui. Where were the boxes?' Gigi and I went through all the cupboards and drawers when we were looking at options for the photo montage.

'In the storage compartment behind the loft bed. It goes deep down actually. I only found it when I took down all Ruby's dream catchers. I had a hell of a time dragging the boxes out. In the end I had to get Jillian to help reach the ones below on account of her being so waiflike. I was worried I'd be stuck in there, half in half out for all eternity.'

I smile at the idea but my mind is racing. If I spent a few years in Venice that means she did try to make it work with Giancarlo early on. Perhaps I did spend some time with my dad, even if I don't remember it. It feels special, like we can work on that early bond that was made.

'OK, let me send them now.'

'Thanks, Aunt Loui!'

We hang up and my phone pings with photos. It takes an age to load but eventually they all appear. I search each image for clues as to where we were, who we were with. Aunt Loui is right: in the baby pictures I'm so bundled up, it's hard to make out my features. Venice winters must be freezing, with the cold wind blowing off the canals. As the pictures progress so does my age. And then I'm a chubby little toddler, holding a stuffed rabbit. Then I'm a little older and Giancarlo is there. It's definitely him, only younger and more robust. Mom isn't in any of the photos. Why?

Then I notice the difference. The child in the photos has fair hair.

The child isn't me.

Why would Mom keep photos of this child?

I phone Aunt Loui, my heart galloping in my chest. 'The child isn't me!'

'What?' Her voice is a shriek.

'The girl in the photos isn't me! And Mom isn't in any of them.'

'Let me get my glasses and have a look.' There's static down the line as she searches for her specs. 'Damn, I didn't look that close before. If it's not you then who is it? And why does she have boxfuls of photos of this girl?'

'This girl *and* Giancarlo.'

'It's definitely him?'

'There's no doubt. Giancarlo is still that same hulking presence; he's sort of hard to miss.'

'Then who is she, if she's not you?'

I rack my brain for an explanation. 'His daughter? He must have been married afterwards.'

'Could be, but then why send Ruby the photos? They might have remained pen pals, but he was clearly still in love with your mom. Why would he then send pictures of his daughter? One or two, I can understand, but not boxfuls.'

'Yeah, it's weird.'

'So where is she?' Aunt Loui asks. 'He hasn't mentioned her?'

'He hasn't mentioned anyone in his life. But that's not to say he doesn't have a wife and family at home. I need to find out for sure. And I need to find the letters Mom wrote to him to find out what she felt about him, why she left in such a hurry. Maybe they'll shed some light on this.'

'Have you searched the bookshop for them?'

'Most of it.'

'Most likely they're in his home. Forget about the letters for now, since we don't even know if they exist anymore. You need to get yourself invited over for dinner so you can see if he's married with children. See if he's got any pictures on the walls, that kind of thing.'

'How do I get myself invited to his house for dinner when he's not exactly big on social interactions?'

'Think of an excuse.'

What will he believe? What will make him care enough? Maybe I can appeal to his softer side . . .

'What if I say it's my birthday and I've got not a single soul to celebrate with and I'm missing the comfort of a homecooked meal with family.'

'Yes!'

'Maybe I should invite Oscar too? I've been considering confiding in him about the whole father-finding mission and then it can be touted as a bookshop birthday celebration? Or would Gigi be a better fit?'

'No, you can't mention Gigi or then you wouldn't be all alone! Pretend for the moment Gigi doesn't exist. He knows you and Oscar are new to Venice but it's your birthday and you're desperately alone in a foreign country and they're the closest you've got to family. You're going to have to really ham it up.'

I shake my head and laugh. 'Right. What could go wrong?'

Once we say our goodbyes the excitement wears off and I'm left feeling edgy. Did Mom know this child? Was Giancarlo *married* when Mom came along? Mom was always so pro-women I'd hate to think she had some torrid affair while his faithful wife remained oblivious. It would mean everything she stood for was a lie – but I'm beginning to learn there's a lot about Mom that she didn't share with me. Was that her right? Is it OK if she learned from her mistakes even if she didn't practise what she preached? The air cools and I sit there for an age, turning it over in my mind. I wish she was here so I could ask her.

I wish she was here.

Chapter 24

Giancarlo waves us goodbye as he heads out into the inky night, leaving us to close the bookshop. I wait a few minutes, duster in hand, before I approach Oscar who is sorting phone orders for pick-up the following day. We've done our best to learn enough Italian words for our social media posts so we can also appeal to book-loving locals, and so far so good. We've only made a few errors with our translations and the locals have been largely forgiving.

But I still haven't got anywhere with my mission and if anything, the busier the bookshop gets with our new incentives, the more Giancarlo pulls away. As if he's distancing himself even more. It just doesn't make sense. Doesn't he *want* to save this place?

I tap Oscar on the shoulder and he jumps as if I've scared the living daylights out of him. It's almost as though he can't handle being near me. Is it still the faux kiss worrying him? If only I could turn back time. The man acts erratic when I'm nearby.

'Can I chat you to for a moment about something?'

He wipes his hands on his jeans, leaving a grey smudge of bookshop dust. 'Sure, Luna. Is everything OK?'

'Well . . . let's take a seat on Giancarlo's sofa, eh?'

We head over there and it feels audacious somehow, when I sit in the space Giancarlo has made his own. Oscar sits beside me, but there's a depression and we roll into one another, and manage to crash heads.

'Ouch,' I say.

'Sorry!' He moves back but we roll again and this time reach for each other to steady ourselves. It's so silly and breaks the seriousness of the moment, as if we're trying to balance on a waterbed or something.

My heart beats fast and I will myself to focus. Oscar is a good guy and I know he'll steer me well in this confusion I feel. About Giancarlo. Venice. All of it.

'So, I need some advice and I think you're the best person to ask since you've worked alongside me and Giancarlo for a while now. But you have to promise me, you won't breathe a word of it to anyone.'

His eyes are deep pools of sincerity. 'I promise.'

I tell him the convoluted story of my past, and how I came to Venice to find my father. He doesn't interrupt once but pays his full attention to me as if every word is significant. 'As you can see I'm in a bit of a bind on how to move forward. It's fear, really, that stops me outright asking him. I don't want to be rejected by the man without finding out any answers and I don't want to lose my job here either.'

Oscar takes a deep breath and weighs up what I've said. I love that he doesn't rush any reply, doesn't offer up a solution immediately. He senses that this has to be handled delicately. I go on to tell him Aunt Loui's birthday party plan and ask what he makes of it.

'Well, it's one way to go about it. This glaring problem I see with it is that Giancarlo will never fall for it. He's not the sociable sort, Luna. He's just not.'

'Isn't he though? Because when I look at him, I see a man who is so lost in his loneliness he doesn't have any idea how to change it.'

'Exactly. And you think this will pull him out of his funk?'

187

'I don't know. But I have to try.'

'What will you do once you're there? Tell him?'

'I'll have to. What other choice do I have?'

He scrubs his face. 'This explains why you creep around the store like you're about to rob the place. What were you looking for?'

'Letters from my mother to Giancarlo.'

'And did you find them?'

'No.'

'This is like something from a book; it doesn't seem real. The communes, the roaming, the full moon party, you losing your anchor to this world. You've been through a lot, Luna, yet you still strive to find these answers. A lesser person wouldn't have had the courage – you know that right?'

'I don't know if it's courage, Oscar, or a deep abiding wish to know where I came from and who will love me now that my mom is gone.'

'You feel alone?'

I consider it. 'I have Aunt Loui. Gigi. The community in the town of tiny homes. But I need more, I need answers. I want . . .' It's hard to explain the emotions that float inside me. 'I want my mom back and since I can't make that happen, then my dad is the next best thing. I've always wanted to be part of a regular family, and I'm not taking away from how I grew up – it was amazing. It's just that this one time, I want to be normal. I want my father to call me up and tell me not to be late for dinner. I want him to remember my birthday and wake me up singing happy birthday. I want to argue about who ate the last slice of cold pizza. I want to steal those coins from his bedside for a loaf of bread just like Sebastiano and his siblings do to one another, things only a real family can get away with. Regular normal family life stuff. Is that too much to ask for?'

He gives me a sad smile. 'No, Luna, it's really not too much to ask for. And I'll help you however I can.'

I lean back into the sofa as we lapse into silence, watching the canal water slap against the stone. As Oscar shifts I sink deeper into the sofa sideways, so it makes sense to rest my head against his shoulder when the opportunity presents itself. There's something special about Oscar. He doesn't offer platitudes and he actively listens to me as if every word I say is valid. It's only going to make matters messy if I admit I feel these first inklings of something for him, and he's grown into a friend I can count on in Venice, so the steadfast, practical side of me tells me to leave it at that.

I can be very risk-averse at times, especially when it comes to matters of the heart, and if my brief foray into romance in Venice has shown me anything, it's that some things are better left unsaid. Oscar is a good guy and I'd hate to make things awkward at work, when we make a good team here.

189

Chapter 25

A few days later, I'm dusting the shelves near the sofa where Giancarlo sits. For the first time ever, I'm grateful for the dust because it gets in my face and helps me sniffle and sneeze and make a show of being sad. I dart a glance over my shoulder but his head is still bent over his book. It would take an earthquake to get his attention. I exhale an exaggerated breath.

Still nothing. Is he made of stone?

I will my fake tears to come, and I turn to him.

'What is it?' he says. 'Are you allergic to something?'

I have a momentary wobble at having to perform like this, but Giancarlo isn't likely to buy it otherwise. I remind myself of the pictures of the child. The desperate longing to find out for sure if he's my dad. That's it not too late for us. But lying about my birth date – will that confuse him more when I do admit who I am? I'll have to come clean about all of it whenever I do fess up. 'Oh . . . no . . . it's only that it's my birthday this weekend. I'm not usually big on celebrations and all that attention, but being alone in Venice I suddenly feel a bit lost, a bit lonely. Like another year is going to slip right past and I have no one to share it with. I don't know why it's bothering me so much . . .'

'What about that guy with the flowers?'

'He fell out of a gondola and I haven't seen him since.'

'Right.'

I continue moving the dust around. 'Celebrating a birthday in a foreign country is just plain sad. I thought I'd have made a ton of friends already but I'm always working so there hasn't been time to make any connections. All I want is a nice home-cooked meal around a proper Italian table, the company of a couple of friends . . .'

He narrows his eyes, so I sniff again.

'. . . A simple dinner. Nothing fancy.' I think back to Giancarlo's usual haunts. 'A rotisserie chicken and potato salad, even. A bottle of wine. Maybe a small cake.'

'Are you asking *me* to host your birthday?'

'If you insist.'

He narrows his eyes, but he doesn't say no.

'Oscar!' I say loud enough for my voice to carry. 'It's my birthday on Saturday, and Giancarlo has invited us to dinner at his home. I hope you can make it. Don't go to any trouble with gifts – your presence is my present.'

As discussed earlier he throws a fist into the air as if all his dreams have come true. 'I'd love to celebrate your birthday, Luna!'

'Isn't he lovely?'

Giancarlo's face is a thundercloud.

'Would eight p.m. suit everyone?' I ask. 'That gives Giancarlo enough time to prepare after we close the bookshop.'

'Fine by me,' Oscar says while Giancarlo grunts.

Aunt Loui told me to give up on finding the letters but part of me just can't. There's one place left to search in the bookshop and if I don't find them there then I will admit defeat. It's a small office behind the counter, which has become a dumping ground for damaged books. Buried under said books is a desk that hasn't seen the light of day in quite some time by the looks of it.

I investigate the tomes to see if they're salvageable. While they might have a cracked spine, or mouldy parchment I believe they can be saved. Some have beautiful gold embossing on the covers, and there are some that may be first editions. There's a potential here to make some serious money for Giancarlo if we research what we have. I've heard of book doctors who can fix damage such as this, which would be worth doing if they were worth a bit of money.

I make a couple of piles and pull out my phone to see what I can find on the titles. That done, I rake through the drawers, finding all sorts of odds and ends. There's a baby photo. It's the same blonde-haired girl. I dig a bit further and find more. It gives me an idea.

'Giancarlo.' I make a show of dusting my jeans so he knows I've been working and not snooping. 'I found some amazing books in the room behind the counter. Some of them might be first editions. We should look into it.'

'Yes, there are some. But they're damaged, and not worth anything like that.'

'I found a book doctor in Rome. We can send them away to be repaired.'

He waves his hand, which either means he can't be bothered undertaking such a thing, or go away, or both – it's hard to tell. 'OK, well, leave it with me. I'll take some photos of the damaged books and get some repair quotes before we research what they potentially sell for.'

'Mhmm.'

'Also, I found these photographs in the drawer. They seem special so I didn't want to throw them out. Who is this cute little girl? Your daughter?'

He grunts. 'Yes, my daughter.'

My eyes widen. Confirmed, Giancarlo has another daughter! 'She doesn't want to work with you here?'

'Does any child want to be shackled to the family business?' I recall his letters to Mom saying the same thing. He wanted

192

freedom but couldn't leave because of his family obligations. Now it makes more sense. He had a daughter to support. Maybe a whole gaggle of children.

'No, I can imagine it's a bit of a ball and chain at times, especially if you want to travel or meet up with . . . friends around the world, that sort of thing.'

'Give the photos to me.'

I hand them over. He stares at them, a smile lighting up his face. It might just be the first proper smile I've seen him wear. 'Is she in Venice? I'd love to meet her.'

'Why?'

'Why not? I don't know many people here yet.'

'I don't think so, Luna. She's a little . . . distant. We don't see each other often.'

'Oh?'

'Yes, oh.'

'Why? Did you have a falling-out?'

'Not that it's any of your business, Luna, but yes. Our relationship is strained. Why? Because it just is. Now I don't want to discuss this anymore.'

'Can she come to my birthday party?'

He waves me away. 'No.'

'OK, so it'll just be me, Oscar and your wife.'

'There's no wife.'

'Are you telling me you're single? Not a man like you with your jovial personality and penchant for witty repartee.'

'Very funny.'

'Is her mom still in Venice?'

'No. I understand your interest, Luna. Oscar told me you'd recently lost your mother. I'm sorry.'

I'm shocked silent. It takes an age for me to compose myself. He told him! 'Well, yes, it's been really hard. Impossible actually, to exist without her.'

'And you thought Venice would be the answer?'

'I did.'

'I hope you find some solace here.'

I so badly want to tell him, but what if a customer interrupts and the moment is ruined? I'll do it on my birthday. We'll be away from the bookshop, in the quiet of his home. I can't draw this out forever because Giancarlo isn't the chatty kind. I want to find out about his daughter. Did she find out he had an affair with my mom? Did he lose his wife over the matter? She is the key to this mystery. I need to find her.

'Thanks, I hope so too. What's your daughter's name?'

'*Sole*, why?' He pronounces it like Sole-lei.

'No reason.'

Chapter 26

Gigi and I make time to catch up between my workday ending and hers starting as we walk through the sunny streets of Venice, which get busier by the day as the temperature heats up.

'How's it going at the Angry Mussel? Your Instagram is benefiting from so many delicious Italian meals.'

'Who can resist all those woodfired pizzas!' Suddenly I notice that her cheeks are flushed and she's got a radiant glow about her that can only mean one thing!

'Oh my God, we've been so busy and working opposite shifts I didn't even notice! You've met someone!'

She shrieks and breaks into a dance. Only Gigi would do such a thing in a crowded market. I pull her away from the stalls and hope to avoid any more noisy outbursts. Gigi in love is loud, even louder than normal. When we first met, she'd been in a relationship for a year, but it came to an end when he broke up with her because 'their values didn't align' (translation: he didn't want to be exclusive). Since then, she's stayed well away from any men, but I know that relationship hurt her, and it's taken her this long to jump back into dating.

'I'm sorry, Luna! I was going to tell you but we kept missing each other, and then you told me about Idiotface and I thought it best to keep quiet in case you were nursing a broken heart.'

'Don't be sorry! I'll always celebrate with you, no matter what. So who is the mystery man? Let me guess . . .' I try to intuit who he could be. But we haven't crossed paths enough for me to know who she's been hanging out with except for the girls in the hostel. Her work has taken up most of her evenings. Ah. *Work*.

'Someone from the *osteria*!'

She grins. 'Yes! Enzo, the owner's son. He's a complete clown, and I mean that in the nicest possible way. He's the funniest person I've ever met. My cheeks still hurt from laughing during last night's shift. The feelings sort of snuck up on me. At first I only considered him a friend, a work pal, but the more time we spent together the more I rushed to work early to see him. And when has *that* ever happened?' She lets out an excited giggle, like a teenager in love for the first time. It's so nice to see Gigi radiant.

It strikes me, I've never heard her gush quite like this over a guy like before. 'Oh, Gi, he sounds wonderful. I can't wait to meet him.'

'He's got a brother, you know.' She waggles her brow.

'Being set up, not my thing.'

'I get it. So how's it going at the bookshop? The father-finding mission seems to have stalled, or you haven't told me the latest.'

I tell her all about my upcoming birthday and the photos Aunt Loui and I found at the tiny home and bookshop.

'What? He has another daughter?'

'He wasn't exactly forthcoming about her. All I know is her name is Sole and they're estranged but he wouldn't say why.'

She stops dead in her tracks, and stares at me. Her face pales.

'What?' I ask, alarmed that her lovestruck glow has dissolved so quickly.

'Sole?'

'Yes?'

'You don't see it?'

196

'See what?'

She slaps a hand to her forehead as if she's got a sudden head-ache. 'Sole and Luna . . . the sun and the moon!'

I feel the moment my heart constricts. It stops. 'No, Gigi. No. It must be a coincidence. It can't be . . .'

'No, Luna, it's not! Only Ruby would give her daughters names like that.'

'What are you suggesting?' The ground shifts. Rumbles a warning. 'Mom wouldn't have left her own daughter in Venice! Wouldn't have kept her a secret. She *wouldn't*, Gigi. She was many things, but she wasn't that.' A sinking sensation settles over me. I feel it deep in my soul. It's why Mom took to her bedroom sometimes and didn't come out again. It's why she was distant at times, closed off. Why she was so furtive. Inexplicably, I'm reminded of the watercolour painting in Mom's tiny home. The blurry girl in side profile who I thought was me, that my hair was made blonde by the sun glinting off the canal. But was it this other child, now a grown woman: Sole? No, surely not.

'She's *their* daughter?' I ask, mind racing to join the dots.

'Could be.'

I close my eyes against the knowing. The hurt. 'Did Mom leave Sole with Giancarlo? I remember one of the first letters I read: *'I woke to the sound of crying.'* That must have been the baby Sole crying. He woke up and Mom was gone and their child was in need of attention. He talked about what she left behind, namely them.'

The more I think about it, the more it makes sense. I've always looked at my mother through rose-coloured glasses. I've always forgiven her trespasses of which there have been many. Excused her mistakes. She was high on that pedestal and could do no wrong. But why would she do this? What reason would she have to abandon her own child?

'It's clearly very complex, Luna. You can't jump to conclusions until you know the full story. That wouldn't be fair to any of you – especially to Ruby who can't tell you the truth now.'

She's right. And we might be totally off base. But then I think of the timeline and know it makes sense. 'Mom must've left Venice when she was pregnant with me. We were in Thailand from when I was a baby onwards. My first memories are of Thailand and stumbling around the jungle with the other toddlers, earth mothers trailing behind us.'

'Maybe, but it's all still a bit of a mystery, don't you think? I want you to be careful about pinning all your hopes on this guy, Luna. I don't want to rain on your parade or anything, but be wary that things might not be what they seem.' Gigi rubs my arm to soften the blow.

I turn to her, unsure why she expects me to be so cautious when it's obvious to me what the truth is. 'Mom wouldn't have left those letters if she didn't want me to find them. I think she did it on purpose, leaving a trail, sensing I'd delve into this, knowing how much I'd want to find my dad. Don't forget that phone call in Thailand. There was something pressing she wanted to confide, and now I wonder if it was about this and not her illness like I first suspected.'

'I guess we won't ever know for sure what her intentions were, and all I'm saying is to keep an open mind.'

I exhale a heavy breath. 'I have to ask Giancarlo at the birthday party. It's time to find out the truth once and for all.'

'Look on the bright side . . . you might just have a sister! A ready-made family.'

'But like this? I don't know. I might have two ready-made enemies. They might dislike me because of what happened. Or worse, what if Mom never told them about me? What if she only found out she was pregnant with me once she left? That would probably hurt more.'

'Well either way, you can't leave it there; you have to drag it, kicking and screaming into the present. You can do this, Luna. And you know what? You'll finally have those answers you've been searching for your *whole* life.'

I smile through sudden tears. 'Is this one of those careful-what-you-wish-for moments?' I have a father and a sister! I've been roaming the globe completely unaware that there's two people in this big wide world who might also have been wondering just where I am.

Later that evening I meet Oscar at a *tavola calda*. He rushes in, as if it's an emergency. I suppose my text might have come across a little urgent.

'Are you OK, Luna? Your text . . . it was littered with emojis and I couldn't quite get the gist of it.'

'Right, sorry. I tend to overuse emojis when I'm fraught.'

'I'll forgive you this one time.' He grins.

'You're too kind.' Are we flirting when I've got a disaster on my hands? I shake the stupid thought away. 'I was out with my friend Gigi, and I told her all about finding the photos of Giancarlo's daughter Sole. Sole and Luna, the sun and the moon. Did my mother have a child with Giancarlo before me? Did she leave Venice when she was pregnant with me? Why would my mother leave Sole? Did they try for a family life and then Mom wanted to be free again? Why would she do such a thing? Tear a family apart and never mention it to us? Real blood family? She knew I wanted to find my dad; I asked her so many times. And now to find out I have a sister too. I don't know what to think!'

Oscar's eyes are wide as he orders us two negronis. 'Wow, that is a lot to process, Luna. That is a lot of questions. There must be a very valid reason that your mother did such a thing.' He toys with the glass. 'I can't think of one though, can you? Yeah sure, Giancarlo's not the most cheerful man in the world, but he's not a bad guy. In fact, I think he's a really decent human being who likes to keep to himself. It has to be something else. Even with the desire to travel, you wouldn't leave one child behind, and take the other.'

'If she was pregnant with me at the time, it's not like she had a choice. I couldn't be left behind.' The thought of such a thing pains me deep into my soul. The idea that we might not have been wanted! It doesn't ring true, not of the Mom I knew and loved. 'Maybe Sole is from another relationship? Maybe she was already there, or she came after? But then why would Mom have all those photos?'

'You have to ask him,' Oscar says. 'It's the only way.'

My heart gallops at the thought. No matter what I find out, it's going to hurt. And I will have to tell Giancarlo that Mom has transitioned to the next place. When I think of having to voice all these truth bombs I feel a sense of trepidation, but I can't run away from hard things. I must face these things head on and hopefully find the answers I've been searching for, for so long.

Saturday lunch rolls around ahead of the next book concierge guests. This time we have a group who are visiting Venice for the wedding of one of their friends. Oscar and I prepare everything, including bottles of champagne as requested.

'Where are the guests from?' I ask Oscar, reading through their booking sheet, which remains largely blank. All I have are their names: Eva, Diego, Joaquin, Ignacio and Manuel.

'They're from Spain.' He grins. 'So they'll clearly have great taste in literature.'

'Clearly.' I shake my head. 'Is it the same though? Are classics just as popular? What if they're a bunch of guys on a bachelor's night or something? How will I find the correct books for them?'

'They'll fill in the questionnaire and you'll be guided by that. Don't doubt your ability, Luna.'

We get a call that the gondola is on the way, so we get busy checking everything is ready. When they arrive I'm surprised to see they're young, maybe fifteen or so. A trio of spotty-faced youths, who wear suits and sheepish smiles. I think of the order of champagne and frown. When I see another gondola just behind them I relax. A couple of adults step from the swaying boat as Oscar gives them his hand to help them alight. They are a family of two adults and their three teenagers, which should make the event fun when it comes to choosing novels to suit them all.

They're dressed formally as if they're about to go to the wedding itself. I love that they've made so much effort for the experience.

We welcome them in and Oscar tells them all about the history of the bookshop, speaking Spanish. He must make a joke about me because they all turn to gawp and I blush under their scrutiny. We leave them to fill out their questionnaires and imbibe champagne, of which they pour the teenagers a small glass.

'Turn a blind eye,' Oscar says, noting my shocked expression. 'It's normal for them.'

'What did you say about me?'

'I told them this was all your idea and you're amazingly brilliant *and* beautiful.'

'Oh, stop. You did not.'

'OK, I didn't.'

I give him a shove for good measure but one of the teens approaches us, and asks where the famous cats of the bookshop are. They've become celebrities in their own right, the bookshop cats, and posts about them online always get the most likes. As if on cue, one-eyed Tolkien materialises and jumps on the table upending a glass of champagne. The guests squeal with delight as if he's just performed a magic trick and not spilled their expensive bubbles all over the place.

'If it isn't Tolkien the wonder cat!' Eva squeals picking him up. Tolkien purrs and flirts in the way only cats can. 'He's my favourite! The cheeky one, and he's just proved it.'

'He sure is. He probably knocked the champagne glass over on purpose.' I laugh. 'It keeps him amused.' I can't count the times I've managed to catch him pushing a coffee mug off the counter and watching it smash. We've caught him in the act and posted the videos to social media so he's become well known for his crimes.

Moby Dick appears, popping only his head over a stack of books. 'There's Moby Dick.'

Diego, the dad, picks him up and holds him like a baby, tickling his great belly. 'Isn't he so much bigger in real life!' Moby Dick takes offence and swats at the hand that pats him.

Soon, they all appear, including Madame Bovary, who saunters in regally as if she's the queen, and she sort of is. The other cats make way for her as if she's a model strutting the runway. Our presentation is forgotten as the group cuddle each cat in turn, except Dante who sits high on a bookshelf that no one can reach and looks down upon us as if such attentions are distasteful to him.

A few hours later we wrap the evening up. They're thrilled with their books and the many cat selfies they've taken.

We wave them goodbye and I turn to Oscar. 'They were just here for the felines, right?'

He gives me a nod. 'Who would've thought the cats would go viral and not the first edition of a slightly waterlogged F. Scott Fitzgerald?'

'Right?'

'And now we get to close up and celebrate your birthday!'

My pulse speeds up at the thought. 'Meet you back here in an hour?' I will have just enough time to walk back and fight my way into the hostel shower and hope there's still some hot water left. Saturday nights are hectic in the dorm, as everyone is usually getting ready to go out for the evening.

'Sure.'

Chapter 27

Just over an hour later we meet back at the bookshop and walk to Giancarlo's apartment together. My stomach is doing somersaults, which I manage to hide behind inane chatter. 'How far is it?' I ask.

Oscar pulls out his phone and checks the maps. 'About five more minutes. Not far.'

'OK, good.'

'Have you heard from that donkey Sebastiano yet?'

I shake my head. 'No. And I highly doubt I will. What's to say? He'll be hoping my visit is over soon enough so he doesn't have to face me. There's a lot of men like that in the world. I'm usually more savvy at knowing.'

'Don't blame yourself, Luna. It's men like him who give the rest of us a bad name.'

'Yeah, I'm just not myself at the moment, and I'm not sure why I thought a summer romance would help.'

'So you wouldn't consider a relationship right now?' His face is open and honest, as though he really cares about how I'm feeling.

'No, I've got bigger things to worry about.' I don't tell him that after the Sebastiano debacle I am a little jittery about opening my heart to Oscar himself. The poor guy would invent the 'customer is waiting' excuse and run away again.

'I understand. You've got a lot going on, and let's just hope tonight brings those answers you want.' He turns away but not before I catch a look of sadness in his eyes. Is it because he knows how much tonight means to me? As far as my intuition goes it seems to have left the building. It must be all the angst, all the secrets from the past.

'Ooh, we're here.' Oscar points to an unassuming apartment block. 'He's on the fifth floor.'

We go up and ring the bell. My nerves ratchet up. I wish I had Aunt Loui here for moral support or to take over if my voice shakes and the words won't come out. But I know she's with me in spirit, so I paste on a smile as the door swings open.

'*Buona sera, buona sera,*' Giancarlo says, his hulking frame blocking out the light so it's hard to see behind him. 'Come in.' He takes a tea towel from his shoulder and motions for us to enter.

Inside, there's a fusty scent, as if the apartment hasn't been opened for a while. When we go further inside garlic permeates the air and, despite my nerves, my stomach rumbles. 'The birthday girl is hungry; that's a good sign.'

Oscar and I exchange a glance. This is the happiest I've ever seen Giancarlo. If I didn't know better I'd say he's being downright jovial. It's so out of character. Maybe he just really likes birthdays? But somehow I don't see that being the case. Is it simply that he has people over for dinner and it's eased his loneliness? Whatever it is, it gives me pause.

Am I really going to detonate a grenade and blow this happy domestic scene up? I take a deep breath as panic sets in. How do I even bring such a thing naturally into conversation? And when? Before dinner? After? During? When's the best time to announce, *Hey I'm your long-lost daughter – returned! SURPRISE! And don't fire me, because I really need that job to be able to stay here and get to know the sister I didn't know I had.* I wish I'd talked to Oscar about this on the way here. Instead I give him a terrified look to let him know I'm internally freaking out.

And then I remember: I will also have to tell Giancarlo about Mom not being earthside anymore. I can't do it. Now the time is here, I don't have the courage to tell him that the woman he loved more than anything is gone forever. Why did I ever think any of this was a good idea? Maybe running *is* the best practice?

'Are you OK, Luna?' Oscar whispers, with a hand on the small of my back. 'Your eyes look a little . . . glazed.'

It's what fear must look like.

'I'm fine. Fine. Wine would be good.' Oh yeah, good plan, knock those drinks back and see how alcohol helps these heightened emotions.

'Would you like red or white?' Giancarlo asks.

I'm still lost in fairyland and say distractedly, 'Yes they sound great.'

The atmosphere in the room grows heavy. Why are they staring at me like that? A sweat breaks out on my brow. 'Is it hot in here, or is it just me?' I pull the neck of my tee.

'Ah, let me open some windows.' Giancarlo steps away.

Oscar peers at my face. 'What is going on with you, Luna? You look unhinged! Is everything OK?' He's so close I can smell minty toothpaste on his breath.

'Those pearly whites have to stay white. Amiright?'

'What? Have you been drinking?'

That snaps me back to the present. 'What? No, of course not. But I *think* I'm about to have a panic attack. And I really don't want Giancarlo to witness it.'

Oscar glances quickly over his shoulder at Giancarlo who is lifting the heavy sash windows in the living room.

'Bathroom, now.' Oscar grabs my hand and manages to find the bathroom down a small hallway. 'Sit on the edge of the tub and put your head between your legs. Focus on your breathing, in and out, nice and slow. I'll be back in a moment.'

I do as he says and try to erase the panic that's taken over my entire body, making it impossible to catch my breath. I ignore the shake in my hands and the erratic beat of my heart. I'm sure I'm going to die. I'm going to die alone in a tiny Seventies-style brown bathroom without telling my father that he's my father!

Stop, Luna, stop!

I recall the mediations I've done over the years and focus on my breath. I clear everything from my mind and sink my head lower. After a few minutes I regain control. Slowly, I sit up. The room spins as the blood rushes from my head.

'Are you feeling better?' Oscar kneels at my feet.

'Yes.' I inhale long and slow just to make sure. We sit silently for a while, as though Oscar knows I need more time to gather my wits.

'I told Giancarlo you were washing up before dinner. He's assembling an antipasto platter so you've got a bit more time if you need it.'

I give him a shaky smile. 'Thanks, Oscar. That's never happened to me before. I didn't handle it very well.'

He rubs my knee and I can't help feel a jolt at his touch. I am losing my mind! 'You handled it just fine. I used to have panic attacks all the time; I know how terrifying they can be.'

Oscar seems far too composed to be the sort to have panic attacks, but I suppose it's not a choice. 'What caused them?'

'The usual, people not liking my book recommendations.'

I laugh at his joke and the mood lightens once more. My breathing returns to normal. 'Those beasts!'

He grins back. How had I never noticed how his features all work so well together? Probably disarmed by the bright white of his perfect choppers.

'Right? I had a spell of panic attacks after my dad died. The smallest things would set me off with no rhyme or reason. It wasn't until much later that I learned it was a part of my grieving process and all the changes that were happening. Eventually, I learned to read the warning signs and became more prepared for them.'

We're both in the club no one wants to join. Losing a parent.

But now I've got the chance to find another and I'm sitting on the side of a bathtub instead.

'What about you, Luna?' He lowers his voice. 'I'm guessing it was the thought of confiding in Giancarlo tonight that's brought this on?'

'Yeah. Like just when exactly am I supposed to drop this into conversation? He was all smiles and actually seemed happy to see us . . . It dawned on me that this news might be really hard for him to hear.'

'It's not going to be easy, either way, but it's for the best. For both of you. Now come on, let's go before he sends a search party.'

I take his hand and he leads me back to the kitchen-dining room. We take a stool and watch Giancarlo's steady hands assemble a platter. He's gone to so much trouble but there's no way I can eat. Not with my belly doing flips.

'This looks amazing,' I say.

Giancarlo smiles. 'It's actually nice to do this sort of thing again. I can't remember the last time I had guests.'

Why is he being so nice? It makes it so much harder to tell him the truth and potentially wipe that smile off his face. What if he's still waiting for Mom to return? And I have to be the bearer of such terrible news . . .

'I have a gift for you too. It's over there.' He points with his elbow to a small sideboard where a gift-wrapped box sits.

'But I said . . .'

'Everyone needs a gift on their birthday, Luna. Don't make a thing of it.'

Duly told, I smile. 'OK, you're right. Who doesn't love gifts? Can I open it now?'

'Sure.'

I take the box and unwrap the delicate paper. I pull out what looks like a tee and unfold it. On the front in rainbow-coloured writing it says: *Don't worry, be Hippy*. I let out a peal of laughter. 'Thank you, it's perfect.'

'You're welcome.'

'I have a small gift too,' Oscar says and hands me a tiny box. Oops, had I forgot to mention to Oscar that it wasn't really my birthday, or is he just keeping up with the charade?

'Ooh, I am very spoiled!' I open the box and pull out a heavy-duty phone cover. 'Nice one!'

He laughs. 'It's bulletproof. Your new-to-you 1999 handset will last centuries with that thing.'

'It's early 2000s, I'll have you know. They don't build them like that anymore.'

'I know, I know. Been there, got the postcard.'

I throw some wrapping paper at him. So, he's been on the end of me moaning about old versus new a fair bit, but it's true. The older phones are more durable. 'There's a lot to be said for phones that will . . .'

'*Survive an apocalypse*,' Oscar and Giancarlo say in unison.

We fall about laughing. 'Thank you, I'm touched. Now where was that wine?'

Giancarlo pushes two glasses towards me. 'Red and white, as requested.'

'O-K-K.'

We eat companionably, talking about the bookshop and its share of erratic customers and absurd queries until we run out of conversation. That's my cue.

But I falter. Beside me Oscar gives me a nod of encouragement. I picture my pretty mom and wonder what advice she'd give me. Something like: *Blurt it out, baby girl, and stop all this fussing.*

'Thank you both for making tonight so special. I haven't laughed this hard in ages. But I have a few things to confess and they might not be easy to hear.'

Giancarlo frowns, his shoulders stiffen, and I hate to be the cause of him losing that jovial smile. Does he know? Has he sensed it? I can't seem to tell anymore; it's as if the perceptive part of me has been switched off these last few weeks. Sometimes

I get the sense Giancarlo and I are nothing alike. He's so tall and solid and I'm small and thin like my mom – but it's more than physicality; it's deeper than that.

'It's not really my birthday.'

Giancarlo's shoulders relax.

I grit my teeth and get on with it. 'I came to Venice because of some love letters I found, which I never knew anything about until my mother died recently.'

Giancarlo's face pales. Has he made the connection that Ruby is my mom and she's no longer here? I hurry on so I don't lose my nerve. 'The letters are from you, Giancarlo, to my mom Ruby.' I take them from my bag and hand them to him. His eyes fill as he flicks through them.

His features turn white. 'Ruby died? Sorry, Luna. I knew that your mother died but I didn't know that woman was Ruby. God, I can't believe it. A world without Ruby.' His face collapses in on itself and I'm not quite sure what to do. This is a big shock for him.

I nod, my own tears spilling, and I say gently, 'I know you loved her with your whole heart. I know she had some troubles. But what I didn't know was that I had a sister. Sole and Luna. The sun and the moon.'

'That's so Ruby.'

'Right?' I smile, feeling hopeful for the first time in ages.

'I didn't know, Luna. I didn't know who you were. Why didn't you say so earlier?'

'I wasn't sure how you'd take it. I wasn't sure exactly who you were or why she left. And then I found out about Sole and I knew I had to act. Never in my wildest dreams would I have imagined I had a sister as well.'

Giancarlo is lost in thought and mumbles, 'Half-sister.'

'Half-sister?' What? Oscar takes my hand under the table and gives it a squeeze.

Giancarlo glances up at me, reading the confusion on my face. Something must click for him but it doesn't for me. Not yet.

Half-sisters? What does he mean by that? So my mother is *not* Sole's mother. My mother didn't leave Sole then? Or . . .

'Oh, Luna, I'm sorry. I'm so so sorry. I only have one child, my daughter, Sole. *Ruby's* daughter Sole. Did you think . . . ?'

Wait. So I've lost him too?

I swallow a lump in my throat that's so big I'm sure another panic attack is imminent. 'You're not? But then . . .' The full moon story was real? My father is still some faceless, nameless man? 'You're not my dad after all?' My heart breaks all over again. I've come to love Giancarlo and his gruff ways. I imagined all the ways we'd grow close as father and daughter and make up for all those lost years. And here I am, still fatherless with no chance now of finding out where I came from. My theory that Mom left Venice pregnant with me is just that – a theory. But I've always known, haven't I? As soon as I saw Giancarlo and didn't feel that instant zap of knowing . . . I just chose to pretend that this would all work out like a fairy tale. I switched off my intuition because it was telling me things I didn't want to hear.

'No, I only have one child – Sole.' Giancarlo runs his fingers through his thick hair. 'I'm sorry, Luna. I can see this is a big shock for you.' It's devastating and I don't quite know what to do. I held him in my heart for so long, and he isn't my dad? In retrospect, I see all the ways in which we're different. I had those inklings early on that something didn't quite add up.

I need confirmation though. 'Sole is my mother's child? My mother's *first* child?'

Giancarlo nods sadly because he can see how upset I am. It turns out the truth does hurt.

Through tears, I say, 'Can you tell me what happened? How this all came to be?' Oscar fills up our wine glasses, and when we exchange a glance, I can see my sadness reflected in his eyes. I'm glad he's here with me. Tomorrow when I forget everything because of this pain, he can remind me what was said. He can bear witness for me. He must sense what I'm thinking because he says, 'I'm here for you, Luna. Today, tomorrow and every day. Let's hear their story and see if you can get some answers.'

Giancarlo takes a sip of wine. His eyes are still wet with tears too. 'Let me tell you about Ruby . . . We met when she was only twenty years old and she stumbled into the bookshop looking for work. She'd escaped from America and had adventure wired deep into her soul. I'd never met anyone like her before, so carefree, so alive with the promise of what might be. For her, the world was infinite and she planned to explore every inch of it. We fell in love, hard. At first, we made all these grand plans. I'd travel with her. What could be better than being young and in love? The world around us blurred.

'My parents didn't approve. They didn't like this wandering star who'd dropped into my universe and shaken it up. They thought she was a bad influence. I didn't listen; I didn't care. What do parents know about real love? My father decided then that I'd take over the bookshop; you know, I never really forgave him for that. I'm sure he did it to put a wedge between us. And it did. Now it was expected I'd run the family business so there would be no gallivanting beside the lady I loved with my whole heart. I couldn't go against my parents' plan for me; it just wasn't done back in those days. I convinced Ruby to stay. That's when the bickering started. She accused me of being a doormat, and I accused her of being too wild. That's when we found out we were expecting.'

He blinks back tears at the recollection. 'I begged her to marry me, to stay here and make a life for our little family. But she wouldn't hear of it. She agreed to stay until the baby was born, and not a moment longer. I expected she'd take the baby with her and that pained me more than anything. But I set out to convince her to stay. During that time, we continued working at the bookshop, and things were great between us. So great, I stopped asking about her plans, believing that she'd changed her mind. Why rock the boat?

'When Sole was born, I figured Ruby'd fall in love with this tiny human we'd made. We would set up a home and tend to our child, our business, and live happily ever after. Isn't Venice the place dreams are made? Who wouldn't want this life? But I soon learned that kind of fairy tale only happens in books. Baby Sole didn't settle, didn't seem to ever sleep. We were run ragged caring for her. I had to call my mother to help. Every day, Ruby pulled away that little bit more. I was running on empty, rushing back and forth from the bookshop, looking after Sole, rocking her to sleep, making bottles, meals for us, cleaning the house. I thought if I did all of it, if I made it as easy as possible on Ruby, she'd stay. She wouldn't take Sole from me. I couldn't live without my daughter.

'It was the most gruelling time, but I kept a smile on my face, and I didn't question her absences. Didn't ask where she'd been, why she left the baby with my mother more and more every day.'

My heart hurts imagining Giancarlo trying everything he could to make her stay. Why couldn't she stay? Whatever the reason, it followed my mom for the rest of her life. Regret? I squeeze Oscar's hand under the table, once more so grateful he's here with me for this. He squeezes mine back.

'Eventually, she told me she had this idea – she'd just leave for a few weeks and come back. I agreed. I thought that the distance would be good for her, that she'd miss us. One day, I came home to a note. And I just knew it wouldn't be the few weeks she had suggested by what she wrote. And unfortunately, I was right. Would you like to read that letter, Luna?'

The energy in the room changes, and I sense my mother here, just behind me. What will I think of her after reading this letter?

He shuffles to the small sideboard and takes a bundle of letters from the drawer. He finds the one he's searching for and passes it to me; his hands have a slight tremor in them and I know that by sharing his story he's opening old wounds too.

Dearest G,

I'm sorry to have to leave you and Sole. I love you both as big as the world, but I can't be this person. I'm stagnant here. I'm flailing in this life. As cruel as it must seem, I need to leave. I can't breathe. I spent eighteen years under my parents' roof, an unwitting participant of their mistreatment. It's left scars I didn't know I had until recently. I don't want that for us. For Sole. I want her to have a happy home life, and she will with you. With your family. I'm too messed up. Maybe you'll marry a nice local girl and add to your brood so that Sole will have brothers and sisters and you can pretend I don't exist.

I thought I'd take to motherhood, that I'd be a natural, but it hasn't worked out that way. I'm ashamed that I can't bond with her, soothe her. Only you and your mom have the magic touch and that leads me to believe that this was never meant to be, for me. She is a gift from the universe for you. She is your sun, stars and moon. And I'm happy to be able to have given you that, at least. I'll check in from time to time, and send you my forwarding address, but if you don't want that, I'll understand. You do what's best for you and Sole.

I'll always love you. But I can't be the person you need, the person you deserve.

I hope one day, you'll find forgiveness in your heart.

All my love,
Ruby

By the time I finish the letter, tears are streaming down my cheeks. What a loss for Sole. For Giancarlo. And for my mother. I see her more clearly through the lens of time. Something in her had been broken from her own childhood and she doubted herself as a new mother. So much so that she chose to run away, thinking it was the best choice for her child. Only someone truly suffering would do such a thing. Did anyone see her through her façade and see the pain?

'She had postnatal depression?' I ask or tell. I'm not sure which. Back then there wasn't education around such matters, but I sense it in her descriptions. Her feeling of lacking as a mother. Unable to settle her baby, soothe her. She felt that it was her fault. And it followed her forever. It's why she took to her bed for long stretches of time. Turned inward. Shut out the light. Felt regret. The ground shifts. The rumble of unfinished business.

'I guess so. If only we'd known such a thing existed. Back then my mother said Ruby had the baby blues. It was expected she'd improve once Sole got into a routine. But of course, I know now it was much more than that. Just like that she was gone, but I still thought she'd come back eventually. That after a while she'd miss us. I wrote almost every day but she always remained steadfast that we'd be better off without her, no matter what I said to convince her otherwise.'

I try to process it all from my mother's point of view. Did she really think her own flesh and blood would be better off without her? I sense the tremendous amount of pain she must've felt, leaving them both behind. Not the actions of a person sound in mind. 'Did she communicate with Sole?'

'No.' He shakes his head sadly. 'When Sole was old enough, I told her all about her mother Ruby. I showed her all her letters. And I let her make the decision. Sole chose not to contact her and your mother respected that.'

Did she though? 'We came to Venice once.'

He nods. 'Ruby wanted to see her, even if Sole refused. She just wanted to see her face once. So I told her where she worked. They looked so alike that I figured Sole would know her on sight and I'd let her decide what to do. Ruby was adamant and I only hoped that it would go well for both their sakes.'

'Did Sole work at Harry's Bar?'

His eyebrows pull together as if he wonders how I know. 'Yes.'

'We went there for lunch. But we left in a hurry.'

His shoulders slump as if the memory is a heavy one. 'Sole recognised Ruby and got another waiter to take a note to her asking her to leave.'

How awful. Both their hopes dashed. I don't recall noticing such a thing, but I wasn't looking for it, so how would I. 'She wasn't the same after that. We left Venice early. Is that why you and Sole are estranged – because you told Ruby where Sole worked?'

He shakes his head. 'It's more complicated than that. Sole never coped with her mother leaving. As she grew older she became more bitter about it, and quite rightfully so. There's those feelings of abandonment and she thinks she wasn't good enough to keep her mother here.'

So many layers of hurt. 'I can imagine. Will it be made worse if she finds out about me?' The daughter her mother then went on to raise? Who could forgive such a thing?'

'The one thing I've learned throughout this is that we can only be truthful. Trying to hide the truth never helps, even if you're doing it for the right reasons. During Sole's childhood, I told her that her mother was on a trip. Sole was too young to understand but always asked why she didn't have a mother like the other children at school. So I'd tell her these tall tales about this butterfly who had to travel the globe, having all these exciting adventures. It sparked her imagination, and we'd pull out the maps and she'd point to all these exotic places. Her mother became this mythical creature, like something out of one of her story books.

'It was only when she was older she demanded to know why Ruby wasn't here, wasn't present for her growing up. I had to explain. I showed her the letters from her mother but it was too late. The damage was done. Sole couldn't imagine why I hadn't been honest from the beginning. But how can you tell a five-year-old? And then, six, seven, eight-year-old the truth that you just don't know why she left and if she'd ever come back . . . ? Ruby wrote every single week. Sole was never far from her thoughts. To me, that shows how much she loved her but I understand Sole

215

doesn't see it that way. And then Sole made her choice about Ruby and there was nothing I could do to change her mind.'

'Is Sole still in Venice?'

'Yes, she's the manager of a ristorante just out of San Polo. Doing well for herself. I walk past after work to catch a glimpse of her, check she's still there.' I think of the night we followed him, how he went back and forth as if vacillating. Was he checking on his daughter then? 'Every day, I hope will be the day she calls, visits the bookshop, but she never comes. Sole has a lot of hurt in her heart. And here you are, Luna. Blowing into Venice wearing the same smile as Ruby. Maybe you'll be the glue that binds us all together again.'

If only it could be so simple. If only he was my biological dad. 'My mother never mentioned me, at all?' She acted like I never existed. She had this whole other family, and I didn't rate a mention to them? No wonder Giancarlo didn't react when he first heard my name in the bookshop and saw my face. He had no idea Mom had another child.

Giancarlo shakes his head sadly. 'It might seem odd to you but I presume she didn't want to upset Sole further. If Sole knew about you, well, perhaps it would open those old wounds once more. Ruby knew that I'd give all her letters to Sole one day, and she didn't want to upset that delicate balance by mentioning another child who *was* on these great big adventures with her. She knew Sole was hurt; she knew there was little hope for them to form a relationship. Nothing Ruby did was malicious. It was misguided at times but she did the best she knew how.'

'You still love her.'

His eyes well up and he averts his gaze. 'And I always will.'

I take a deep breath and try to unpack it all. There's a lot to consider. There's layers of love and pain that go back in time. I don't pretend to know what it feels like for Sole, but I can imagine. For me, my father was also mythical, but for her she had pictures; she could put a name to the face, and yet still her mother didn't come.

216

And Giancarlo. He raised his daughter the best way he knew how and hoped his true love would return and make them a family once more.

And me, I had Ruby all to myself, but not really. Mom was always half here, too. Those times when she clammed up, cried for days in her room. Those tears, that pain was for this family, for the choices she'd made that changed all of our lives.

I exhale a shaky breath. 'Mom was complicated – there's no question – but she had so much love in her heart. I only wish she'd shared this with me so I could have helped. Could have understood. There didn't need to be so many secrets.'

'Luna.' Giancarlo pats my hand like a dad would do. It's all I can do not to bawl. I feel so robbed that he's not going to be that person for me. 'She couldn't risk you being hurt like Sole. I'm sure she did what she thought best to protect you and keep you close.'

'Yeah I know but there will always be the *if onlys*.'

Poor Oscar sits next to me just as shell-shocked. 'Families are complicated,' he says. 'But there's still time to mend these bridges.'

Can they be mended though? 'So what now? Do we tell Sole about me, or leave her be?' Will it be one final betrayal or will she see it as a positive? I can only think it would be the former.

Giancarlo leans back in his chair. 'We have to tell her the truth. She deserves to know and, from experience, when you stick to the facts it hurts less in the long run.'

'Right. It'll be awful it if she automatically hates me because I'm Ruby's daughter though. I expected to come to Venice to find my dad; to leave without one and instead a half-sister who despises me would really shatter the old heartstrings. I don't think I can cope with that on top of everything else.' But I'm being selfish. This is about all of us, not just me.

'Let *me* talk to her,' Oscar says. 'Why don't I try and explain for you both? Sometimes having an outsider step in can make these things a bit easier.'

Giancarlo and I exchange a glance. 'I don't know,' Giancarlo says. 'It seems again like we're running away when we should be facing this head on.'

I agree, but will Sole hear us out before she slams the door in our faces? 'Perhaps Oscar is right. We want her to take a moment and really listen. A neutral third party might facilitate that better than we could. At least to get her to the point where she can decide what she wants to do.'

Giancarlo scrubs his face. 'OK. Maybe you could take a selection of the letters Ruby wrote. She's never wanted to read them before but maybe she will now and she'll see how devoted her mother was to her. Her love for Sole is evident in every letter.'

Mom's letters. The ones she wrote every week, without fail. That's not someone who forgot a child to me, that's someone who tried to give what she could at the time, tried to show her love the only way she knew how.

'Unless you want to read them first, Luna?'

I've been desperate to know what they contained, but now I'm not so sure. They're not mine to read. They're private correspondence, words that mattered to Giancarlo, to Sole. Maybe there'll come a time where Sole will share them with me, if she wants me in her life. Maybe she won't. And I'll have to respect her decision. 'No, that's OK. They're for you and Sole. But would it help to give Sole your letters too? I have them all here.' I take the precious bundle from my bag and slide them to Giancarlo.

He smiles as he picks them up and flicks through. 'She kept them. Somehow I never thought she'd be the sentimental type. She was never a hopeless romantic, not like me. Did she ever find love with another man?' he asks. His voice quavers ever so slightly.

'No, she never did. She found love among her women friends, deep abiding friendships that mattered most to her. Maybe she left her heart with you, Giancarlo. Did you ever think of that?'

His eyes glaze. 'No, I never did.'

Mom might have had flings here and there when she was

younger; I don't really recall, but she never loved a man, not in the true sense of the word. Which leads me to think Giancarlo was her soulmate, the man who made her a mother first and accepted it when she had to leave. Accepted that she had to walk a different path. Isn't that what true love is? Letting go, no matter how hard it is?

'Well, Luna. I know I'm not who you wanted me to be, but that doesn't mean to say I can't be a father figure to you. You're as much part of me as Sole is, because you're Ruby's daughter too.'

'Now you're just trying to make me *ugly* cry.'

I stand up and hug Giancarlo, give him a big old cuddle like I've just found home. And maybe I have. Maybe home finds you, and not the other way around. Is this my place in the world – is this what I've been searching for? We've got a way to go before we find out if I belong . . .

I'm home safe and sound. It's late but Aunt Loui will want to know I'm OK.

She texts back:

And?

Where to start? *I'll call you tomorrow and explain. Love you x*

I'm too emotionally wrecked to go through it all. I do some deep breathing exercises and try to find my inner calm. My inner self. I know it's time to connect spiritually again and find out just where I'm supposed to go from here.

I inch up the rickety ladder to my bunk bed and let the feelings come, just like Mom used to tell me to do. Hard, sad, heartbreaking, whatever they are, I have to acknowledge them before I can make sense of it all. The first most poignant one is: Giancarlo is not my biological father and while that cuts me deep, I get the distinct impression that the biology part of that doesn't matter much.

He said it himself, that he'll be there for me, as Ruby's daughter, no matter what. I didn't expect that. I didn't expect to come to Venice and find someone who'd step into the role of father, because of the love he shared with my mom all those years ago. He senses I need that. I need someone to be there for me, someone I can count on. Perhaps I can be that person for him too. When I really dig deep into it all, it feels real. Genuine. As if some families aren't made, they're found. Just like in the town of tiny homes.

Before, I felt like I had a piece missing, and now I see that it wasn't knowing who my biological father was, it was finding where I fit into the tapestry of the world myself, under my own steam. There are plenty of people who have opened their arms wide and asked me to step in, promised me unconditional love. From Aunt Loui, to Gigi and now Giancarlo. And this was Mom's doing. Teaching me that sometimes family is what you make it. And aren't I the lucky one that those who are part of my life are exceptional people?

I don't have to settle for a family who don't care for me, like Mom had. Her childhood remains a mystery, but I know it was full of emotional abuse. And that's why she escaped. And she taught me never to settle for second best. I guess I'm only just figuring out half the lessons she showed me by living life as a roamer and finding people who'd be her people. Those special ones, the ones she left behind for me.

Chapter 28

After a long call with Aunt Loui, whose head is spinning as much as mine on the retelling, I get ready for work with a spring in my step. As emotionally draining as the non-birthday birthday was, I got some answers. Mom's motivations and mysteries are clearer.

When I arrive, Giancarlo is in his usual position: nose pressed in a book. But instead of a gruff grunt, he gives me a smile. 'Don't forget to pick up my breakfast,' he says.

'Of course.' I've been picking up his orders since I arrived. The man likes to eat.

'I took the liberty of ordering you some too. We can eat together.'

We do, and it's the best part of the day. Over bacon wraps and strong coffee we discuss his favourite books, and he tells me more about the history of the bookshop. 'So you built the maze for Sole?'

He nods. 'The little scamp was always here, before and after school. During school holidays, I had to keep her amused somehow. A child can only read for so many hours . . . I made that maze a hundred different ways; I was always changing it for her. Until one day, just like that, the phase wore off and so it stayed just as it is now.' He shakes his head, lost in thought as he looks out to the canal, the water reflecting white light on his features. He appears younger today, or more energised. Maybe he needed his answers about Ruby as much as I did.

'Time really does fly, Luna. Those first few years with Sole, after Ruby left, were long and hard as I learned the ropes and how to do and be everything I needed to for her. But after that, the years whizzed by like the speed of light. And here we are. If I have one regret, it's that I didn't push harder for Sole to meet with Ruby. Meet her and see why she was so special that we could forgive her anything. But what use are regrets?'

We still have a long way to go to find peace, but we've made a start. And now I only hope Sole will agree to meet me so she can too.

After breakfast I get back to work, checking the clock every few minutes, wondering how Oscar is going on his mission to see Sole and try and get the information across before the door gets slammed in his face.

Out of the corner of my eye, I see a figure, and turn only to find Sebastiano there, looking sheepish.

'What are you doing here?'

He lifts his palms up as if in surrender. 'I needed to see you, Luna. I wanted to apologise.'

'For what exactly?' I fold my arms across myself defensively.

He gives me a sad smile. 'For ruining what we had.'

Do I care, really? But then I think of all the women this guy probably has on the hook, the way he plays the same game, using the same lines, the same locations. For the sake of innocent women who get caught up in his spell and are then discarded for the next, I have to speak up.

'What you do, that whole act – the thunderbolt, the charm, the never-ending text messages – it's not cool, you know.' What attracted me to him in the first place? I don't usually go for the polished metrosexual, the ones who can talk the talk. And then I remember – the book nerd. Brontës. Hemingway. Wilde. Was that a lie too?

'I'm sorry, Luna. I really am. You're different to all the others, and I want another chance. You're right, I do have an act that I used on women new to Venice. Why not? It's something to pass the time. But then I met you. And I will change, if you'll have me. When you said you wanted to go slow, I thought that you'd cooled towards me, that's all.'

'Where is *A Moveable Feast* set?'

'What?'

'Your favourite book, remember? Where is it set?'

'I read it a long time ago.' He has the grace to blush.

I roll my eyes. He knew I was desperate to work in a bookshop, he put two and two together and figured that was a way in? Is he *that* calculating?

'Sebastiano, there was never anything between us and there never will be. But preying on a girl who is grieving is a really low act. Lying about books – that's almost unforgivable! But if we want to salvage any sort of friendship here, after all Venice is a small place, can you promise me you'll think of the women you're hurting before you act like this again? Can you think of the fact you're using women, leading them to believe there's a chance at real love, with your constant barrages of texts and calls that proclaim so much, when it's all built on lies? What if one of those women believed you and decided to cancel the rest of their travels and move here for you? Have you ever thought of that? That you'd break someone's heart by playing this Casanova-like game?'

'I love women; there's nothing wrong with that.'

'So be honest about what you want . . . be honest for their sake. You're a great-looking guy, Sebastiano, and when you get serious and stop playing a part, you're also a really nice guy. Why not be yourself? You might just find you enjoy life more that way.'

He shoves his hands into the pockets of his jeans. 'I've been doing this for so long, I don't even know who that person is anymore.'

'Well start there. Start figuring out who you are first.'

'I'm on a ticking time bomb. Every day my mother pushes for me to settle down, find a nice girl to marry. I have this desire to be with as many women as possible because once I'm married then that's it. I'll be married, babies will come, and I'll take over the trattoria. My life will be one long workday, forever and ever.'

Oh how people make these cages for themselves!

'You only get one life, Sebastiano. And it's what you make it. You can say no to your mom, you know. You can take the reins and do it your way.'

'You say that but you haven't met my mother.'

I laugh. 'Well, she will forgive you eventually, and maybe by being yourself you'll find someone special, and then who knows what kind of life you'll want.'

'You're special. And I want that with you.'

At that moment Oscar walks in, his fiery eyes ablaze when he sees Sebastiano. I hold up a hand to let him know all is well and he goes to the office behind the counter.

'You don't really mean that, Sebastiano. You only think you want me because I haven't fallen under your spell.'

His shoulders slump and he nods. 'You're probably right. But I'll always think of you as the one who got away.'

Giancarlo wanders over, thunder face at the ready, and I have to smother a grin. It's such a fatherly like stomp he's got going on.

Sebastiano clocks him and says hurriedly, 'I hope we can remain friends. Ciao, Luna.'

'We can. Ciao.'

'What did that fool want?' Giancarlo mutters.

I wave him away. 'Nothing I can't handle. How did you know he was a Casanova type?' I ask.

He grunts. 'I always see him with a different woman on his arm. He's got a reputation in Venice, and it's not flattering. His nonna is always lamenting about the fact he won't settle down.'

'Let's hope he can turn that around.'

'It's too late for him.'

'Oh, Giancarlo, it's never too late! But I hope, for his sake, he finds what he's looking for, because to me, that's one shallow way of living and I don't think it brings him any joy. He's so used to being charming and acting like this man about town that he's forgotten who he really is, and what he wants. Like any good antagonist, surely he's redeemable?'

'You and your book talk. That's only in fiction, Luna.' A smile plays at the corner of his mouth.

'You know it isn't; you just want to be right!'

'Yes I do!' he thunders and walks away muttering to himself. Ah. The father figure come to life. I quite like it, I surely do.

I find Oscar in the office, sorting paperwork I've already sorted. 'Eavesdropping?' I ask, with a smile.

'Never!' He grins back. 'You're a woman of the world, Luna. I know you don't need saving, don't need the swashbuckling hero to rescue you, but just in case, I stayed close. Mainly because I really wanted to sock that guy at least *once* in the jaw, but I see there was no need.'

Why is he so angry with Sebastiano? Is it on my account or is there something more?

'Why thanks. But didn't your mother ever teach you violence is never the answer?'

'Yeah, and what a shame that is.'

'Why do you hate him so much?'

He sighs. 'Because you told him all about your mom, and what losing her meant to you, and he took that vulnerability and used it against you. Who does that? It brings out my protective instincts, and I didn't even know I had those!'

We laugh at the messiness of the situation. What a few days it's been! 'Well, I'm OK, and I said my piece to him. I only hope he'll think about it and try not to break any future hearts.'

'Did he break yours?'

225

I laugh. 'Oh hell no! It was already broken and there was no room left for anyone else.'

'Right.' And with that he's back to the paperwork, shuffling and sorting.

'How did it go with Sole?'

'It went . . . quick. Let's find Giancarlo, eh?'

We assemble on the sofa. Oscar begins. 'Sole was at the ristorante this morning, setting up for the day. I introduced myself and gave her the letters.'

'And how did she take it?' I ask.

'Not very well. I don't know Italian swear words, but I can guess that's what she lobbed at me.'

Giancarlo smiles. 'That's Sole.'

'Mom was the same. Worst potty mouth ever. Maybe they're more alike than she knows.' The idea warms my heart – that she could be so like Mom without ever knowing her. What other similarities do they share?

Oscar shakes his head. There's a possibility our messenger might just be reluctant to go back again. 'As we planned, I handed her the letters, from Ruby and you, Giancarlo. She wanted to know who I was and how I was involved. I said I worked at the bookshop and was passing them on for her dad. Then she asked how we came to have Giancarlo's letters. She presumed Ruby was in Venice and told me that she wouldn't see her. I wasn't sure what to say to that.'

I slap my forehead. 'We didn't consider that. What did you tell her?'

'I said no she wasn't but that her dad really, really needed to see her.' Oscar goes quiet. Too quiet. It's as though he's trying to contain his own emotions and I realise this is a lot, for all of us in one way or another. 'I'm fairly sure she knew what it meant. There was a moment when I could almost see the cogs ticking in her brain. Like she knew it must have meant Ruby was . . . gone. It was brutal actually; the light left her eyes and she froze.'

'I should have gone to her,' Giancarlo says, his voice heavy with regret.

'She might not have taken the letters then,' I say, trying to ease his worry. 'No matter how we did it, it was always going to hurt.'

'Sì, sì,' he says, holding his face in his hands.

'And then what happened?'

'Sole gave me a nod and took the letters from the table and walked away. I called after her that I'd come back in a few days but she didn't respond. For what it's worth, she cradled those letters against her heart. It made me hopeful that those words will help. But I don't know for sure.'

'So now we wait . . .' I say, worrying a thread on my denim jeans. As I do I'm reminded of the girl I saw in the Giardini Reali gardens that day when I had Mom on my mind. The girl with the same gait, the same hair flick as Mom's. The girl I thought *was* Mom, for one brief moment of time.

'Giancarlo, do you have a photo of what Sole looks like now?'

'You can look up the ristorante website. There's a picture of her on there.'

I hurriedly take out my phone and search for it. I go to the 'About Us' tab and click it. And there she is. My breath leaves my body in a whoosh. It is the girl I saw that day, and she is the spitting image of my mother, right down to the dimple on one cheek.

I glance at Giancarlo. 'They're the same. Like carbon copies.' The ache in my heart grows lighter. I don't know why, maybe it's because there's someone in this world who will always remind me of my mother, someone who could fill that void she left behind, if only she's willing. Perhaps I can help her too? 'I saw her in Venice – I thought I was imagining it. That my broken heart was trying to conjure my mom, so I looked back to my book when she walked past.'

Oscar's eyes go wide. 'Probably a good thing. Imagine if you'd stopped her that day and announced that she looked like your mother. At that point you didn't even know about Sole.'

I shake my head. As always fate does its thing when it's supposed to. It's why I haven't been able to read the tarot; this had to happen naturally in this particular order.

'I only hope she has a forgiving heart . . .' I say, because more than anything I want Sole in my life. And then it hits me. '*She's* the missing link. She's what I've been searching for – I just didn't know it.'

Chapter 29

We sit on a roof top terrace as Enzo regales us with a story about his childhood. Gigi's right, he's hilarious. His self-deprecating sense of humour is contagious and it's nice to laugh so hard I'm literally grabbing my sides and telling him to stop, my stomach muscles can't handle it.

Gigi's taken to life in Venice like a pro. And I have a sense that she's wanting to talk to me about something important. I have that feeling again, that something big is coming and that she's struggling with how to broach it with me. I'm sure that's what tonight is all about. This dinner is so they can break the news, whatever it is. She's radiantly happy, a softer Gigi and how can I begrudge her anything? If she's happy, then I'm happy for her. Every now and then I catch her smile drop; it's the worry over whatever it is. I want her to enjoy the rest of the balmy Venetian evening, on this fancy terrace where we eat fresh seafood and course after course keeps arriving, so much so that I'll be in a stupor if I eat any more.

I always knew our journey together would have an end point. When you live the way I do, it's only a matter of time. But like the women from the commune days and the town of tiny homes have proven, just because we might not travel together anymore doesn't mean our friendship is over. It's only just beginning. But I wait for Gigi to tell me, even though I know.

'So I've filled you both in on the latest in my life,' I begin, toying with my napkin. 'And it's a weight off my shoulders, sharing all of that with my very best friend – the only person other than Aunt Loui who knows everything there is to know about me.'

Gigi swallows hard. *What is it?*

'So now it's your turn,' I prompt, giving her a reassuring smile. We can get through anything. We're friends for life and even if that means she's about to announce she's moving to Antarctica we can make it work.

'Well, I know we had plans to get a flat-share once you got the tiny home tenanted and we saved a bit from our jobs.'

'Right.' Aunt Loui found the most perfect tenants. A couple of pescatarians who have circled the globe a few times and now want to enjoy the twilight of their lives in the town of tiny homes. Aunt Loui calls them Thelma and Louise and says they're strong, capable hippies who are also a bit glamorous and bring a little glitz to the place. If anyone has to take over Mom's home, I'm glad it's them. We've talked on the phone a couple of times, and they seem to understand without my having to say it, how sacred that place is to me. They send me pictures of Mom's wild roses and good morning messages as if they sense what's important to me, namely that the things Mom loved live on. Like her garden. Thelma also loves gnomes, so she's added to the collection, and has given them all names.

Right now Gigi can't seem to get the words out, so I answer for her. 'And you and Enzo plan to move in together?'

She bites her lip. 'We do.'

'Aw, Gigi, that's great news. Are you staying in Venice long term?'

'We are. I'll move into Enzo's flat above the *osteria*.'

'I'm so happy for you both! And, Enzo, I hope you're ready. Your flat is going to get the makeover of its life.' Gigi already told me he's a neat freak too, so they should live in relative harmony in that respect. Still, I don't understand why Gigi is struggling so hard with this. Sure, I'll miss her at the hostel, but it's not like she's moving continents. There's more to it. But what?

Enzo grins. 'I'm ready! I'm just going to say yes to everything because she is my queen and I'm her loyal servant. At least, that's what she told me.'

That's more like the Gigi I know and love! 'It's the best way to be. So what's the second part to this announcement? I know there's more.'

Gigi grins. 'The girl with the gift of clairvoyance who continues to deny it.'

'It's not that! I asked the magic eight ball.'

We burst out laughing and it takes the pressure off. I realise what she's about to tell me a moment before she does. So, I am little prescient – what can I say? Or I'm just using common sense, when I realise Gigi hasn't touched the champagne on the table and also didn't partake in any of the oysters, and she loves oysters.

'There's a little Gigi and Enzo on the way?' I ask.

'YES!' she screams so loud other diners turn to us. 'Oh God, Luna, it has been so hard to hold this in! We didn't exactly plan it, but it happened and we're so happy! Turn away for a minute and don't listen, Enzo, because I don't want this to go to your head.' He listens to his queen and complies but he'll hear every word anyway. They're so cute together, it's a perfect match.

'Remember when I said there was no point being with a guy until he set my world on fire? Well Enzo set it on fire and then poured gasoline all over it. I've found my place here with them, in the family *osteria*. His mom loves me, his dad is so protective of me because of the baby, and Enzo loves me the way a man should. He does what he's told. I don't ever want to leave and thank God I found Mr Right in a country with the best food ever.'

I laugh and stand to hug them. Gigi always did want to settle down and start a family, but she would never settle for second best. I know she's in the right place, at the right time. And when I do move on, and I know I will, I'll have her, Enzo, the baby and Giancarlo to visit. And maybe a sister. Who knows what fate has in store.

'Let's make a toast!' I say and fill Gigi's water glass. 'To Venice, to true love and to finding that missing piece!'

'*Salute!*' they say in unison.

It's a downright scorching day in the shop as we prepare to host the book concierge service. I'm training a new staff member, Mario, because the bookshop has been so busy of late. Giancarlo says it'll settle down once summer is over, but I don't want him left in the lurch if one of us decides to leave. Namely me. Every now and then I have that prickling sensation that means it's time to wander again, time to move on. If not now, then soon.

'Giancarlo, why the farce about hiring only one of us when Oscar and I first started?' I ask, as it's been bugging me.

He gives me an impish grin. 'Staff never stay long, so I figured if I made it sound a little more difficult to get hired then you'd both work harder at the after-winter clean-up before one of you gave up and left.'

'You crafty so-and-so!'

'It worked though, didn't it? Like fiends, you were. Although, you did gang on up on me, and I wasn't quite sure what to do about that. All these changes, ViewTube posts. Urgh, can't a man be left alone to read in peace?'

'You're quite the sensation on ViewTube, these days.' I grin. Who'd have thought that filming Giancarlo being stony and gruff would take off like it has. People are fascinated by this reluctant bookseller as much as Giancarlo is reluctant to let us film him. We annoy him until he gives in, and I'm sure he's enjoying the notoriety. Somehow Oscar even managed to convince him to do one of those TikTok dance challenges with Dostoevsky in his arms, which I now can't unsee.

Mario hefts a box of second-hand books to the floor and unpacks them. He's a studious and serious worker, who gets along just fine with Giancarlo. They use as few words as possible to communicate, which suits them both. I go through how the book concierge service works and he takes copious notes, which bodes well. Mario's taking this very seriously indeed.

We get the call that our guests are on the way, so I yell out for Oscar to come and help. Giancarlo surprises me by tapping me on the shoulder and announcing, 'Why don't you let me and Mario handle this one? See if we're capable? You and Oscar can step out for lunch.'

Ah. He knows. 'I'm not leaving Venice just yet.'

'But it's coming soon.'

'Yes.'

'So we better learn the ropes, eh, kid?'

I'm so touched that he's actually going to help out. Does this mean he's fallen in love with his little bookshop once more? 'That would be great, but I can stay and help.'

'They're Italian, right? I can wow some Italians with literature, don't you worry.'

'OK.' I grin. He will probably do a much better job than me, because when Giancarlo wants to be, he's quite the charmer. It's the Italian in him, I guess. Born with that innate fashion sense and way of pleasing a crowd.

'Take Oscar and charge your lunch to me. You've both earned it.'

'Wow, are you going soft in your old age, Giancarlo, or what?'

'Don't think of charging some expensive bottle of wine. I have limits, you know.'

'OK, we'll just charge a moderate one.' I grab my bag and Oscar before he changes his mind.

We had planned on a quick strategy meeting about the bookshop social media accounts, so we can do that over lunch.

'Where should we go?' I ask and link my arm through Oscar's, excited to be sneaking out on a workday.

'Let's go to Giancarlo's favourite place.'

It's the little place right near where we first faux kissed. 'Sure.'

We settle at the little bar. It's more casual than a restaurant and Giancarlo will like that we're not spending too much of his money. 'Look at these numbers.' I take my phone from my bag and go to show Oscar a post on Facebook that has been shared thousands of times. But before I find it, I click a notification and am surprised to see a photo of Oscar and I, heads bent together. I try and place when it was taken and who posted it, but the name is a made-up one, KittyCatsForLife, and the text is in Spanish.

'What's this?' I show him.

He takes my phone and reads the post. A flush creeps up his cheeks. 'It's nothing, just the Spanish people from the book concierge event saying they enjoyed their evening.'

'Oh, Eva and her family?' I take the phone back and look again. There's quite a lot of text so I hit translate and read it.

We found out about the famous bookshop cats so of course we had to visit them in Venice. Cats, books and champagne, the perfect trio for us. What we didn't expect to find was a love affair happening right before our eyes between Oscar and Luna, our hosts. Oscar told us the history of the bookshop and admitted that he found solace in reading and writing his own novel because unrequited love was his cross to bear. We asked who he was in love with, and he gestured to his co-host Luna.

It became clear in that instant that they were a perfect match – it radiated off them. They couldn't seem to admit their feelings or find their way to each other. Why? We couldn't work it out. It became a big topic for our family afterwards. It's been a few months now and we haven't forgotten our visit to that beautiful little bookshop where we met our feline favourites. Today we were going through the photos and found this picture of Oscar and Luna and we wondered, has love blossomed among the books, or are they still hiding their true feelings?

'Oscar, is this true?'

He waves me away. 'No. Yes. Maybe.'

'Where are your words in times of crisis?'

'Vanished in my hour of need.'

'But . . .'

'It's OK, Luna. I know you're not ready for love right now. To be honest, I'm not really sure about where I'm going either with everything. I love it here, but I know you're ready to move on – I heard you talking to Giancarlo about it.' He blushes and averts his gaze.

I go from high to low in an instant. Have Oscar's feelings changed since Eva and her family's visit? Have they softened into more of a friendship? 'It's the wrong time for us, I guess.' I'm about to leave for shores unknown, and who wants to be swept away like that with no plan, no schedule, on a whim wherever the wind blows me? Oscar has plans for his writing and has always maintained that the bookshop is where he's most inspired. I can't ask him to follow me on a whim when I don't know for sure what this even is. Or even if he wants to! We've had so many things to contend with: Sebastiano, saving the bookshop, the book concierge biz, and the whole muddle of my paternity. Part of me wonders if things might have turned out differently if we'd just been two ordinary backpackers with no messes to untangle.

Right guy, bad timing.

I wish I had the magic eight ball. Everything feels up in the air, so I don't push it. Instead I change the subject back to bookshop matters.

A week later, I'm restocking the front display of romance novels. Giancarlo finally agreed that they deserved to be shared, probably because they've been our bestsellers and he's got a glut of them packed away. Everyone wants to be loved, I've learned. And there's so many kinds of love. From family, to friendship, to fiancées.

Oscar has been friendly but distant. I take that as a sign that I'm right not to act on my feelings, but still there's a part of me that pines for what might have been. Each day that passes brings me one step closer to leaving and I can't help feel that things will be left unresolved between us. We need to chat, but how to go about it? He brushed me off fairly easily before, so it feels like he just wants to be left alone.

Will I make a fool of myself if I say I want to explore these feelings? And how, if I'm leaving? I could stay, but I feel it right down in my very soul that it's almost time to go and I always listen to that internal voice that has been so silent of late. Missoula is calling. She hasn't said, but Aunt Loui needs me for a while. And if there's one thing I've learned from all of this, it's that family comes first and it always will.

Once I've neatened the stacks, I dust my hands, grumbling to myself and making a mental note to buy that apron, no matter how silly I look.

'Romance novels, that's new.' I look up at the voice. It's her. Sole.

Now the time has come, I don't quite know what to say. I don't want to scare her off. She still doesn't know about me; I'm not mentioned in any of the letters. Do I say something now and risk it, or see if she's here to make peace with Giancarlo first?

'Umm, yeah. I convinced him. It was a bit of a mission – you know what he's like, headstrong, bullish.'

'Stubborn. Grumpy.'

We share a smile of understanding. 'I take it you were the one who brought the letters back from Ruby?'

How does she know? 'Yes. I found them . . . after.'

'Thank you for bringing them. I know it must have been hard for you too.'

'You know who I am?'

Heartbreak dashes across her face. It's all I can do not to reach out for her, tell her it's all going to be OK. A ghost of a smile appears. 'I wish I could say I was like Ruby in that way, having

236

the gift of knowing, but I don't,' she says. 'I saw you both, that time at Harry's. Although I didn't show my face, I peeked out to see what my mother looked like. Who she was. And I saw you with her. It doesn't take a genius to see the resemblance, although your colouring is different.'

I take a deep breath. 'I'm sorry, about everything. Ruby was a good person, even if she made some bad choices.' I have the instinct to defend Mom. She was a great mom, but I can understand if Sole doesn't feel that way.

Sole gives me a small nod. 'Yeah, maybe. But it's hard for me to think of her like that.'

'I know. I get it. But from what I can see, she never stopped loving you, even if she did it from afar.' It's why Mom chose to settle in Missoula. She wasn't tired of the roaming life; she wanted a base so that Sole could easily find her. That's why she settled right after our trip here. She always hoped that she could make it up to Sole, that they'd have some sort of relationship. If only time hadn't run out.

Sunlight lands in shards on the blonde of Sole's hair, giving her a halo-like quality. Is it a sign? Mom is close. 'That's just the thing. I never told Dad this, but Ruby called me every week for years after that trip she made here. I would always hang up on her. I wanted her to suffer, like I suffered. But she persisted. I grew to love those calls, hearing her voice, but I didn't know how to bridge that gap, or to forgive her. The calls stopped a few months back, and I knew, I just knew something had happened to her. And the regret I felt then . . .' She shakes her head and her eyes pool with tears. 'Now it's too late to tell her I forgive her. That I loved her, even though it hurt to admit it.'

I go to her and pull her tight against me as she cries. 'She knew, Sole. I'm sure of it. If you give me a chance I can tell you all about her, and the times she shut off from the world, which I know now is because she was missing you. And how she hoped you'd find her in Missoula. She settled there hoping that one day you'd come. Even she didn't know it would end the way it did.'

'What's your name?' she asks abruptly.

I smile. 'Luna.'

She laughs. 'The sun and the moon.'

'They belong together.'

She gives me a knowing look. 'One can't exist without the other.'

This time she steps forward and hugs me as I cry. The ground doesn't shimmy or shake. Instead, sunlight settles over the both of us, bathing us in its warm glow.

Chapter 30

I wait for Gigi at St Mark's clocktower on the north side of Piazza San Marco, which has become our regular meeting spot. I love the blue face of the clock and its gold zodiac symbols, proving even Venice has its spiritual side. In the distance I see Gigi's lithe form scurrying along. It's not until she's closer I see the small swell of a burgeoning baby bump. Her face is truly radiant – I guess some clichés are true! Pregnancy suits her well.

'Luna! Sorry, I'm late. This might be TMI but I already need to pee all the time. It's taking me forever to get anywhere.'

I give her a hug and when I do I have a vision of Gigi's future. It's painted so vividly in my mind, it almost takes my breath away. Usually my visions are useless, but this one is clear. When we pull apart, she says, 'What's with the glassy eyes? I thought I was the one who was supposed to be a hormonal mess of tears?'

How can I tell her the truth? Her future with Enzo is going to last a lifetime. Their family will grow and be front and centre of every aspect of their lives. Gigi's love of food and Venetian culture will seep into her bones until she'll forget she ever lived anywhere else. She will be fluent in Italian and her kids will tease her about her pronunciation of certain words forever.

Perhaps, like me, Gigi also had to find her place in the world. Was she also yearning for a place to call home, a place she fit? Her confidence always convinced me that she knew right where she wanted to be, but was it all a bluff? And she too wanted to belong? 'I'm just so happy for you, Gi! It's like you found your very own utopia here. It's all happened so fast, but I get the sense that's the way it was always supposed to be.'

We find a table. 'Right? I've wanted to be a mom ever since I can remember, but I'd started to think it wouldn't happen for me. At almost thirty-five, and no man on the horizon, I'd thought maybe it wouldn't be on the cards for me, after all.'

'Well, you've definitely found a place to call home, right?'

'I have. I really have. And I remember us back in the town of tiny homes, planning this trip and worrying about what we might face. I don't know if it's the hormones, but sometimes I get this sense that your mom had a hand in this. Isn't that crazy?'

I smile. 'It's not crazy. It would be just her way to orchestrate something from the afterlife for the ones who've comforted me, been there for me, like you have.'

'You're purposely trying to make me cry now!'

We laugh. 'How's it going with Enzo?'

'Perfect. He's just as loud as I am. He's so much fun. Sometimes I wish I'd met him sooner, you know?'

'You met him just at the right time.'

She lifts a brow. 'You saw something when you hugged me, didn't you? You KNOW something.' Her voice carries loud and high.

I smother a grin. 'I did but I can't tell you or it won't come true.' OK, that's a lie but I don't want to tempt fate, either.

'Aww, where's the fun in that?'

'Let me just say, you're exactly where you're meant to be at exactly the right time.'

'And what about you, Luna?'

'I'm still working on that.'

'Oscar?'

I shrug. 'Hardly see him these days. He's been busy working on his novel. When he does come into the shop, he has this wild look about him like he hasn't slept. I guess when you're connected to your work like that, real life fades into the background.'

'So you're not going to tell him how you really feel?'

'I don't think so. What would it matter? I'll be going back to Aunt Loui soon.'

'Come on now, Luna. Didn't you promise you were going to face your emotions head on? What if he's feeling the same and neither of you are willing to speak up first?'

Is she right? 'I can't help but think that spark we shared might have fizzled for him, that's all. If not, wouldn't he try and catch up with me? I'm not sure I should be running after him.'

'So instead you're going to run away?'

Ooh, that hits me right in the soft part of my heart. I made a promise to my mom, didn't I?

Chapter 31

As summer leaves for another year, Venice is lashed with rain, but still tourists come and squelch through the streets. The bookshop sales increase day by day and we continue the book concierge service. I also curate books for people who fill out forms on the website and I send those pretties all around the world. I delight when reviews come in about how much those books are welcomed and loved in their new homes, despite being a little worn, a little scarred. Aren't we all? And it's those dings and dents that make our own stories so great, so rich and varied: the tapestry of our own disordered messy lives that got us here, to this very point.

I've barely seen Oscar; he's been so wrapped up writing his novel and probably avoiding me in the process. Mario has picked up the extra shifts when Oscar hasn't been able to help but I know he's on shift later today.

I catch Giancarlo one-finger typing on the boxy computer and it's all I can do not to laugh at the look of fierce concentration on his face. Just what is he doing? He hates technology with a passion so it must be important. I sneak up behind him and look over his shoulder. He's typing an email.

'An online order?' I ask, making him jump in surprise.

'Ah . . . no.'

'Then . . . ?'

Is he blushing? I take a step closer and survey his face. Definitely blushing.

'It's Mary. She emailed me a few days ago. I'm replying, that's all.'

I try to hide my grin but it's impossible. 'Mary from the cruise ship?'

He nods. 'We're just friends, before you go getting any ideas.'

My heart lifts. 'Friends are good.'

His eyes well up and I know it's more than what he's letting on. 'You see, I promised Ruby I'd wait forever for her, and I did. And now . . .'

'And now it's time to follow your heart, Giancarlo.' I hug him tight, blown away by the kind of person he is. He made a promise and he kept it.

'Get back to work.' He pretends to be gruff.

'*And* he's back . . .' I grin and walk away.

The wind whips through the bookshop, like a long lyrical sigh. Like it's calling to me, that same siren song. And I know what that sound means. It's time to move on. There's more for me to explore, to find, to unearth. The newest little bookseller has arrived, a kitten the size of my palm who we found huddled near the door, wet and meowing for food. Giancarlo let me name him, so Supertramp it is. It's the name Christopher McCandless went by in *Into the Wild*, Oscar's book that came to an unfortunate end when we first met.

He's a furry little fuzzball who makes even Dante play with him, albeit reluctantly. Madame Bovary even allows him to paw at her face but will unceremoniously roll over on top of him if he goes too far. Tolkien is already teaching him bad habits, too. I caught Supertramp swatting at a water glass but he is still too small to have enough muscle power to move it. Won't be long though. I'll be sad to miss Supertramp's journey from kitten to cat, but at least I know he has found his home and will be here when I come back – whenever that is.

Leaving Giancarlo and Sole will be like leaving my heart behind, but it's not forever. Just like Aunt Loui. Now I'll have two places to shelter in this big wide world when I need it. When the call for home sounds loud and clear, I'll know where to go; whose wide loving arms I need to fall into.

How to tell them the time has come. That the wild part of me is back. And how to tell my beloved Gigi, whose belly grows big already. The tarot says it's twins, but she doesn't know that yet. Her first ultrasound didn't pick it up but the next one will. And Enzo will be thrilled. His parents too.

I go visit my sister Sole at the ristorante. I don't think I'll ever tire of saying 'my sister'. When she sees the expression on my face, she knows. We've talked about this eventuality many times. 'So soon?'

I nod. 'But I'll be back. Next summer, if not before.' What I've learned is, I might still have the urge to roam but those family connections need more tending, more attention, because tomorrow is not guaranteed. First port of call is Aunt Loui, and then who knows where? I'll have to wait for a whisper on the wind, and then I'll know.

'OK, I can live with that as long as you call me every week.'

'Every day, more like it.'

She wraps me in a hug. It's such a strange and wonderful feeling having a sibling. We're inextricably linked and our relationship grows stronger every day. Old hurts heal, slowly, slowly. They won't fade to nothing, but they'll be stronger where the scar is.

'Will you come for dinner, and I'll tell Giancarlo then?' I've been living in his little apartment the last few weeks; he insisted on it. We get along just great and he's become the very definition of a father to me. Sometimes you don't get to choose who your family is, they choose you. And the love I feel for him is as big as the world – as my mom would say.

244

Somehow, our little ragtag family of three have become a solid unit. And that's everything I wished for. It's obvious to me that I'll never know who my biological dad is, and it doesn't matter as much anymore, because what I found in Venice is even more special. I haven't given up hope, but it doesn't occupy my thoughts as much as it did before.

'Yes, I'll come. He's going to cry, you know.'

What I love most about Giancarlo, this big hulking bear of a man, is that he shows his emotions quite freely these days. 'We're all going to cry!'

'We're hopeless.'

And hopeful. For the bright shiny future.

We hug and I head back to work. There's another thing I need to resolve.

Oscar and I have been sidestepping our feelings for too long now. He took it to heart when I said I wasn't ready for love again. But what I really meant was I wasn't ready for love with the wrong guy.

He's behind the counter, sorting the orders that are awaiting shipping, when I arrive. There's only one other thing this story needs. The love interest.

'Luna, there you are,' he says, as if he's been waiting his whole life for me. I'll take that as a sign. Plus I asked the magic eight ball if today was the day I should tell Oscar how I really feel and it said: *Without a doubt*. And the tarot showed the lover's card, so it's an auspicious start.

'Oscar, I'm leaving soon, but I wanted to tell you . . .'

His face falls. 'You're leaving?'

'Soon.' I decide to tell Oscar that my feelings for him have developed and even if he doesn't feel the same, I owe it to myself, to speak up. One thing I've learned from this experience, and my mom's before me, is speaking my truth is its own form of freedom. And one I must do much more loudly so I'm heard over the din. 'The thing is . . .'

'Wait!' He dashes to the office and comes back with a stack of papers bound together. It's his novel.

'You finished it?' Does he not know I'm about to declare my feelings for him? Yeah, sure a finished novel is something to rave about, but still!

He nods. 'I want you to read it before you go. I got so swept away in this novel, Luna, I had to get it finished. I thought it would show you . . . Maybe it will change things.'

'Change what things exactly?'

'You love the written word; the sound, the shape of it, the way the words click into place to make the perfect sentence and the perfect story. Metaphors give you life and you also don't mind a misunderstanding or two. You love every romance trope but particularly second-chance love. I tried to do all that and more between these pages, Luna. For you. I might be able to bore customers to tears with my book recommendations but it turns out when it comes to speaking aloud matters of the heart, my confidence vanishes. So instead of fumbling and bumbling how I feel about you, I wrote you a novel: a romance novel.'

'You wrote this for me?'

'And on a deadline too. I didn't want you to leave without knowing how I feel. And it's in there, if only you have time to read 77,000 words or so.'

I can't help but laugh but I'm touched right down to my very soul. *He wrote a book for me!* He's listened to me wax lyrical about my love of the written word and he went to all this effort to show me the way he knew I'd appreciate.

'What happens in the book?'

'Lots of up and downs. Spoiler alert: they fall madly in love with each other and admit their feelings on the very last page. In a bookshop on the canal.'

'Wow.' I grin and feel swoony all over a sudden. 'I can't wait to read it.'

'Do you want to know how it ends?' He doesn't wait for a response; he takes a great leap towards me and pulls me into his arms. When we kiss, fireworks explode and my legs feel like jelly. *The stars align*. My aura, my chakras, everything tingles. A small laugh escapes as I look down and see we're surrounded by the bookshop cats, as if they're giving us their blessing.

'Will you come with me, Oscar, on my travels?'

'I'm already packed.'

And soul recognises soul as the gauzy winter sun of Venice fades and the moon ascends.

And our tale is born, once upon a time in the little Venice bookshop.

A Letter from Rebecca Raisin

Thank you so much for choosing to read *The Little Venice Bookshop*. If you would like to be the first to know about my new releases, click to sign up to my mailing list: https://signup.harpercollins.co.uk/join/signup-hq-rebeccaraisin

I hope you loved *The Little Venice Bookshop* and if you did, I would be so grateful if you would leave a review. I always love to hear what readers thought, and it helps new readers discover my books too.

I'm active on social media and would love to connect with you there. I mainly chat about my writing process and keep you in the loop of what's coming next. I also love talking about books I'm enjoying and am slightly obsessed with sharing my TBR pile and asking for other book recommendations too! I'm still trying to learn TikTok so bear with me as I fumble my way around that site!

Thanks,

Rebecca

http://www.rebeccaraisin.com/
https://twitter.com/jaxandwillsmum
https://www.facebook.com/RebeccaRaisinAuthor
https://wwwtiktok.com/@rebeccaraisinwrites

Elodie's Library of Second Chances

Everyone has a story. You just have to read between the lines . . .
When Elodie applies for the job of librarian in peaceful Willow
Grove, she's looking forward to a new start. As the daughter of
a media empire, her every move has been watched for years,
and she longs to work with the thing she loves most: books.
It's a chance to make a real difference too, because she soon
realises that there are other people in Willow Grove who might
need a fresh start – like the homeless man everyone walks past
without seeing, or the divorcée who can't seem to escape her
former husband's misdeeds.
Together with local journalist Finn, Elodie decides these people
have stories that need sharing. What if instead of borrowing
books readers could 'borrow' a person, and hear the life stories
of those they've overlooked?
But Elodie isn't quite sharing her whole story either. As the story
of the library's new success grows, will her own secret be revealed?
**An uplifting story about fresh starts, new beginnings
and the power of stories, from the bestselling author
of *Rosie's Travelling Tea Shop*!**

Elodie's Library of Second Chances

Rosie's Travelling Tea Shop

The trip of a lifetime!
Rosie Lewis has her life together.
A swanky job as a Michelin-starred sous chef, a loving
husband and future children scheduled for an exact date.
That's until she comes home one day to find her husband's
pre-packed bag and a confession that he's had an affair.
Heartbroken and devastated, Rosie drowns her sorrows in
a glass (or three) of wine, only to discover the following
morning that she has spontaneously invested in a bright pink
campervan to facilitate her grand plans to travel the country.
Now, Rosie is about to embark on the trip of a lifetime, and
the chance to change her life! With Poppy, her new-found travelling tea shop in tow, nothing could go wrong, could it . . . ?
A laugh-out-loud novel of love, friendship and adventure!
Perfect for fans of Debbie Johnson and Holly Martin.

Aria's Travelling Book Shop

This summer will change everything!
Aria Summers knows what she wants.
A life on the road with best friend Rosie and her beloved camper-
van-cum-book-shop, and definitely, definitely, no romance.
But when Aria finds herself falling – after one too many glasses
of wine, from a karaoke stage – into the arms of Jonathan, a
part of her comes back to life for the first time in years.
Since her beloved husband died Aria has sworn off love, unless
it's the kind you can find in the pages of a book. One love of
her life is quite enough.
And so Aria tries to forget Jonathan and sets off
for a summer to remember in France. But could this trip
change Aria's life forever . . . ?
**A heartwarming, uplifting and hilarious novel
of friendship, love and adventure! Perfect for fans
of Debbie Johnson and Holly Martin.**

Aria's Travelling Book Shop

This summer will change everything,

Acknowledgements

A huge thanks to my family, as always, for cheering me on when those deadlines creep up so quickly. You're the best!

To readers new and old, I hope you enjoyed the journey to Venice as much as I enjoyed writing it. Luna has a special place in my heart and I hope she will take up residence in yours too.

To book bloggers, bookstagrammers, booktokkers and booksellers, thanks for all you do to champion my work. Without you, I'd be shouting out into the void. You're amazing and I appreciate you.

To Hilary Steel, thanks for being on this journey! The wine and cheese were fabulous and so was the encouragement day and night! Let's do this, is now our catchphrase! You're a ball of energy and you inspire me!

Thanks Abi Fenton, for everything! I love how I can chat about a murky idea with you until it takes shape and becomes a book with characters who become so real, I feel like I'm losing my friends when we finish it!

And thank you Helena Newton for your eagle-eyed copy-editing skills, which help make the story shine even brighter.

And likewise to Helen Williams for your super sharp proof reading! I always love getting the book back once you've worked your magic!

Belinda and Frankie, London calls and I can't wait to see you soon. Thanks for the support and friendship.

Dear Reader,

We hope you enjoyed reading this book. If you did, we'd be so appreciative if you left a review. It really helps us and the author to bring more books like this to you.

Here at HQ Digital we are dedicated to publishing fiction that will keep you turning the pages into the early hours. Don't want to miss a thing? To find out more about our books, promotions, discover exclusive content and enter competitions you can keep in touch in the following ways:

JOIN OUR COMMUNITY:

Sign up to our new email newsletter:
http://smarturl.it/SignUpHQ

Read our new blog www.hqstories.co.uk

https://twitter.com/HQStories

www.facebook.com/HQStories

BUDDING WRITER?

We're also looking for authors to join the HQ Digital family!
Find out more here:

https://www.hqstories.co.uk/want-to-write-for-us/

Thanks for reading, from the HQ Digital team